IVAN VLADISLAVIĆ

The Distance

archipelago books

Archipelago Books
232 3rd Street #A111
Brooklyn, NY 11215
www.archipelagobooks.org

Library of Congress Cataloging-in-Publication Data
Names: Vladislavić, Ivan, 1957- author.
Title: The distance / Ivan Vladislavić.
Description: First Archipelago Books edition. | Brooklyn, NY : Archipelago Books,
2020. Identifiers: LCCN 2020014546 | ISBN 9781939810762 (paperback) | ISBN
9781939810779 (ebook)
Classification: LCC PR9369.3.V57 D57 2020 | DDC 823/.914--dc23
LC record available at https://lccn.loc.gov/2020014546

Distributed by Penguin Random House
www.penguinrandomhouse.com

Cover art source: 1974 Zaire Ali vs Foreman "Rumble in the Jungle" Fight Poster
Design: Zoe Guttenplan

This book was made possible by the New York State Council on the Arts with the
support of Governor Andrew M. Cuomo and the New York State Legislature.

This publication was made possible with support from Lannan Foundation, the Carl
Lesnor Family Foundation, and the New York City Department of Cultural Affairs.

For Dave Edwards

The Distance

1

The Fight of
the Century

The commander of South Vietnamese forces in Laos said today that his troop had seized three main junctions on the Ho Chi Minh trail and were achieving the two objectives of their drive – destroying North Vietnamese bases and cutting the supply network.

– *Pretoria News*, March 1971

Joe

In the spring of 1970, I fell in love with Muhammad Ali. This love, the intense, unconditional kind of love we call hero worship, was tested in the new year when Ali fought Joe Frazier at Madison Square Garden. I was at high school in Verwoerdburg, which felt as far from the ringside as you could get, but I read every scrap of news about the big event and never for a moment doubted that Ali would win. As it happened, he was beaten for the first time in his professional career.

It must have been the unprecedented fuss around the Ali vs Frazier fight that turned me, like so many others who'd taken no interest in boxing before then, into a fan. 'The Fight of the Century' was one of the first global sporting spectacles, a Hollywood-style bout that captured the public imagination like no sports event before it. In the words of reporter Solly Jasven, it was as significant to the Wall Street Journal as it was to Ring magazine, and it generated what he called the big money excitement.

I don't know what I thought of Ali before the Fight of the Century, but I came from a newspaper-reading family and had started reading a daily when I was still at primary school, so I must have come across him in the press, and not just on the sports pages. In March 1967, after he'd refused to serve in the US army, the World Boxing Association and the New York State Athletic Commission had stripped him of his world heavyweight title. This was big news in South Africa, but I cannot say what impression it made on my nine-year-old self.

Although Ali was absent from the ring for more than three years, he was not idle: he was on the lecture and talk-show circuit, he appeared in commercials, he even had a stint in a short-lived Broadway musical called *Buck White*. In short, he was doing the things celebrities of all kinds now do as a matter of course to keep their names and faces in the spotlight and build their 'brands'. He went from the boxing ring to the three-ring circus of endorsements and appearances. He was also speaking in mosques and supporting the black Muslim cause. But very little of this activity, whether meant in jest or in earnest, was visible from South Africa.

In 1970, when I was twelve, a Federal court restored Ali's boxing licence. His first comeback fight was against Jerry Quarry in Atlanta and he won on a TKO in the third round. Six weeks later he beat Oscar Bonavena and that set up the title fight against Frazier in March the following year. It was a match Frazier had promised him if his boxing licence was ever returned.

We had no television in South Africa then and our news came from the radio and the newspapers. The Fight of the Century produced an avalanche of coverage in the press. My Dad read the daily *Pretoria News* and two weeklies, the *Sunday Times* and the *Sunday Express*, and so these were my main sources of information. In the buildup to the fight I started to collect cuttings and for the next five years I kept everything about Ali that I could lay my hands on, trimming hundreds of articles out of the broadsheets and pasting them into scrapbooks. Forty years later, these books are spread out on a trestle table beside my desk as I'm writing this. Let me also confess: I'm writing this because the scrapbooks exist.

The heart of my archive is three Eclipse drawing books with tracing-paper sheets between the leaves. These books have buff cardboard covers printed with the Eclipse trademarks and the obligatory bilingual 'drawing book' and 'tekenboek'. In the middle of each cover is a hand-drawn title: ALI I, ALI II and ALi III. The newsprint is tobacco-leaf brown and crackly. When I rub it between my fingers, I fancy that the boy who first read these reports and I are one and the same person.

Branko

I am the sportsman in the family. My brother Joe doesn't mind kicking a soccer ball around in the yard, but when I need him to keep goal while I practise my penalties he's got his nose in a book. Now all of a sudden he's a boxing fan. Not that I've seen a lot of boxing myself. I've been to a couple of Golden Gloves tournaments at Berea Park with my cousin Kelvin, where they put up a ring on the cricket pitch in front of the grandstand. But we prefer the rofstoei in the Pretoria City Hall.

The thing about wrestling is the rules are easy to understand. If Jan Wilkens is on the bill, you know he's going to win. He's a huge Afrikaner and he's the South African champion. Kelvin always shouts for Wilkens. My guy is Rio Rivers. He doesn't often win but he puts up a good fight. The last time my cousin and I went to the wrestling, Dad insisted we take along Joe and Rollie – that's Kelvin's little brother. It was a fiasco. Joe started rooting for Sammy Cohen. Sammy's a pile of blubber in a black leotard. He looks like he hasn't slept for three days and he always loses. That's his part to play. Joe doesn't get the principle: you're not supposed to support the bums.

And now this thing with Ali. It comes over him like the measles. The boxing bug is going around because of the upcoming fight between

Ali and Frazier. Naturally I support Smokin' Joe. I would support him in any case, but the fact that my little brother has picked the other corner is a bonus. Another chance to get under his skin.

Joe Frazier's going to give Cassius Clay a boxing lesson, Dad says. He's going to knock seven kinds of crap out of that loudmouth.

Eight kinds, I say.

And Mom says, Watch your mouth. Even though eight is just a number.

Dad won't say Muhammad Ali. Over my dead body. It's always Cassius Clay. It drives my brother to tears of frustration. Sometimes he goes out in the yard behind the servants' quarters and smashes tomato boxes with a lead pipe.

Sport is my thing and I wish he'd leave it alone. My plan is to win the Tour de France one day. I prefer road racing but I join the track season to keep fit. Cycling is not a popular sport. If we're lucky fifty or sixty riders turn up at the Pilditch track in Pretoria West on a Friday evening, most of them seniors, and a handful of us in the schoolboy ranks. Juveniles, they call us, a stupid term you would never apply to yourself. The stands are nearly empty: the wives and girlfriends and mothers cluster together in a few rows with crocheted blankets over their knees. Ten rows back Joe is sitting alone under the icy corrugated-iron roof, wearing a knitted cap with an enormous pompom. He'd rather be at home but Dad says: You boys have got to stick up for one another. When the starter's pistol goes or the timekeeper rings the bell for the last lap, he pretends to watch. He's half interested in the Devil-Take-the-Hindmost because of the name, but mainly he's reading a book in his lap, struggling in his black leather gloves to turn the pages of *The Canterbury Tales* or *David Copperfield*. The explosive pompom, the biggest one Mom ever made, hovers over his head like an unhappy fate.

When I go to bed, I find him shadow-boxing. He's supposed to be sleeping, but he's got the desk lamp swivelled to cast a shadow on the wall next to the window. Bobbing and weaving, he says.

Ja, I say, float like a bumblebee.

Joe

On the cover of the first scrapbook – a book of scraps, about scraps – I spelt out the word ALI in upright capitals using red double-sided tape from my father's garage. When this tape dried out and fell off like an old scab, leaving a tender trace of the name on the board, I outlined each letter in black Koki pen to restore its definition. The numeral after the name must have been added when the growing volume of cuttings demanded a second scrapbook.

The first cutting in ALI I is headlined in red 'The Fight of the Century'. It was published the day before the fight. Like most of the cuttings this one is unattributed, but judging by the typeface and layout it was taken from the *Sunday Times*.

It's a busy page. There are drawings of Frazier and Ali side by side and between them, under the headline 'How the Fighters Compare', the stats on weight, height and reach, the dimensions of waist, thigh, chest (normal and expanded), fist and biceps, and finally age. Boxing writers call this the Tale of the Tape. Unfurled below are 'Fight Histories' with the highlights of each boxer's career accompanied by a photograph. The picture of Joe Frazier knocking out Bob Foster, his most recent challenger, is not familiar. But the other is one of the most recognizable images in sporting history: Cassius Clay standing over a prone Sonny Liston after knocking him out in the first round of their return match in May 1965. Clay's right forearm is angled across his chest, as if he's still following through, and he's looking down at Liston with a snarl on his lips. It's a stance that makes perfectly clear what a boxing match is about. Ali later told a reporter he was saying: Get up and fight, you bum!

The rest of the page is devoted to Frazier, and his comments reveal why the interest in the fight was so intense. Clay lost his licence because he refused to be drafted into the United States Army. That's something I can't have sympathy about. Frazier goes on to tell David Wright how he himself tried to join the Marines when he was just fifteen and was turned down because he couldn't cope with the IQ tests.

Further on he describes his childhood as the son of a one-armed sharecropper in South Carolina, his working life on the killing floor of a slaughterhouse in Philadelphia, where he began boxing to keep his weight down, and the importance of the Bible in his life. Recently I've been kinda stuck on the seventh chapter of Judges – where Gideon is fighting those tribes and everybody. Gideon only had a few men against thousands, but he won the war because he had the Lord on his side. That's just how I feel about this fight with Cassius Clay.

Judges 7 is one of those cheerfully brutal Biblical episodes in which the righteous smite their enemies. In this case, the Lord delivers the

Midianites into the hands of Israel. He instructs Gideon to choose a conspicuously small army of men, no more than three hundred from among the thousands. So Gideon leads a crowd of men to the water, dismisses those who kneel down to drink and recruits only those who lap the water up with their tongues 'as a dog lappeth'. These men are sent out against the enemy camp armed with trumpets and lamps inside pitchers, and in due course the Midianites are well and truly smitten. Their princes Oreb and Zeeb are slain and their heads cut off and brought to Gideon on the banks of the Jordan.

The Book of Judges is a cloudy lens, but if you squint through it what comes into focus is Frazier's aversion to a man who had renounced Christianity for a 'foreign religion' and refused to fight in the Vietnam War.

The week before the fight, Frazier and Ali were on the cover of *Time* magazine under the headline 'The $5,000,000 Fighters'. The story, based on hours of interviews with both boxers, summed up the simple symbolism of the fight: Shrewd prefight publicity has turned the billing into Frazier the good citizen v. Ali the draft dodger, Frazier the white man's champ v. Ali the great black hope, Frazier the quiet loner v. Ali the irrepressible loudmouth, Frazier the simple Bible-reading Baptist v. Ali the slogan-spouting Black Muslim.

On 8 March 1971, 20 000 people packed into Madison Square Garden to watch what turned out to be one of the most memorable heavyweight boxing matches in history. The fight went the distance and all three judges scored it in favour of Frazier.

It's the happiest day of my life, my father said. Except for the day I married your mother, the day she gave birth to your sister, and the day I bought my first car, a '38 Chevy with a dickey seat. Jissie that was a beautiful car.

Branko

I'm a glorified taxi driver, Dad says. I should put a sign on the roof.

It's Saturday night and we're fetching Sylvie from a session in the Skilpadsaal. Usually the hall is used for roller skating, but tonight there's a band. When we dropped her earlier a boy in a pink shirt was leaning against a pillar smoking a cigarette and she said, He's the bass guitarist. And Dad said, Ag any mampara can play the bass guitar.

The streets around the showgrounds are full of cars but Dad finds a parking close to the hall. It's just the two of us in the car. Mom's at home with Joe.

Dad's idea of being on time is to be half an hour early, so he's always waiting, ready to be impatient when the time comes. Sylvie is always late, especially at the sessions. She'll push her luck by fifteen or twenty minutes. So help me, Dad says, if you keep me waiting again I'll come in there and drag you off the dance floor. She would *die* of embarrassment. But he'll never do it. For one thing he's wearing his pyjamas under the old houndstooth overcoat he bought with his first pay cheque. That was round about the time Moses fell off the bus. For another, Sylvie always gets her way.

Dad opens his window an inch so the glass won't mist over and the music from the hall drifts in on the cold air. 'Whiter Shade of Pale.' They've started with the slow dances and that's a bad sign in Dad's book. He's left the ignition key turned so his parking lights will show and some joker won't ride into us. There's a dim green light coming off the dash. We're parked under a plane tree and the streetlight throws a lace of leaf-shadow over the bonnet. When cars come up behind us, long slow shadows creep over the cab. I shouldn't fall asleep like a kid, but after a while my head gets heavy, and I breathe in the animal scent of the leather seat, which creaks every time Dad jogs his foot.

I must have dozed off because Sylvie is at the window. She's ten minutes early and she's got her friend Glenda in tow. Never mind the weather, they're both wearing bolero tops. It's an old trick: she wants to stay a bit longer and the friend is there to make it harder for Dad to say no. Dad man, she says, everybody's still dancing. Who is this everybody? he says. I'd like to meet him. But he always says yes in the end. She's his princess.

There are goosebumps on Glenda's arms. Perhaps we'll drop her at her house in Valhalla afterwards.

Dad complains about driving, but there's nothing he'd rather do. On a Sunday, when we get back from church, he'll say: I think it's time to see if the fish are biting. This means we're going to drive out to Hartebeespoort Dam or Bon Accord or maybe even all the way to Pienaars River or Loskop. Dad was a fisherman in his young days and the dams are his landmarks. The rest of us are bored with these places, we want to go to Bapsfontein or the Fountains, but Dad never tires of them. He likes to be near water, but not in it, watching people potter around in motorboats or cast a line. Mom doesn't mind the drive because it gives her time to knit. On a round trip to Pienaars she can finish the whole front of a cardigan.

Bon Accord sounds grand but it's just a sump of muddy water in a tangle of rutted roads and scrub. There's no caravan park but campers carve out sites under the thorn trees to rig their tents. The whole place smells of mud and unhappy fish. We bump around on the tracks from one fishing spot to another. We're looking for the bank where Dad and Uncle Arthur used to pitch a tent for the weekend before either of them was married.

Mom and Sylvie wait in the car while we go exploring. Dad walks off in one direction with his hands behind his back. There's an angler sitting on a camping chair down there and he'll strike up a conversation with him about rods and reels. Joe and I go the other way. We pick up old bait, stinking lumps of carp and mieliepap packed around rusty hooks, and we get our feet caught in tangles of blue-green line that look like the balls of hair Sylvie combs out of her brush and leaves on the edge of the bath.

When we get back there's a commotion. Some clot in a Studebaker has got stuck in the mud reversing his boat trailer down to the water's edge.

Dad insists we go to the rescue. I'm in my new running shoes with the red and blue stripes on the side and I want to take them off before I wade into the shallows, but Dad won't let me. You'll stand on a hook or something, he says. You'll get lockjaw like Uncle Franjo. Now get in there and push.

They're just a pair of tackies, Joe says. Everyone knows there's a difference between tackies and running shoes. He's wearing his old slip-slops.

The driver of the Studebaker revs the engine, the wheels spin and the car sinks deeper into the mud. Dad talks to him through the window. Then the man gets out, high-stepping to dry ground, and Dad gets behind the wheel, and he knows how to do something with the clutch, and with all of us pushing, the car and trailer come free. The driver applauds.

My shoes are covered with thick black mud. Joe rinses his slops off in the water, but there's not much I can do.

We'll touch them up with shoe white, Mom says. They'll be good as new.

But they're never the same again. Dad makes me put them in the boot so they don't spoil the mats, even though he has extra mats on top of the standard ones to keep them clean. One day when he sells the Zephyr, one day soon, the mats will be in perfect nick.

Brainless bloody monkey, he says when we're driving home, meaning the man who got stuck in the mud.

Why did we have to help him then? I ask.

He says nothing. So Mom says: That's what you do. You help your neighbours and when you're in trouble they help you back. You hope.

On the way we stop off in Sunnyside. Normally the rest of us go window-shopping for a block or two while Joe hunts around in the book exchanges, but I won't get out of the car. I'm not going to walk around kaalvoet in town like a rock.

Joe

The Fight of the Century was promoted by a theatrical agent called Jerry Perenchio, who blithely told the world: I really don't know the first thing about boxing.

Perenchio was an innovator. Even before the fight he had the idea of auctioning off the fighters' shoes and gloves. If a movie studio can auction off Judy Garland's red slippers ... these things ought to be worth something. You've got to throw away the book on this fight. This one transcends boxing – it's a show business spectacular.

The purists were not pleased with the turn boxing had taken. They railed against the playacting, the vaudeville routines and costume changes, and their resentment just fuelled the fire. The circus was in town and there was no turning back. At the head of the parade, fitting the new style like a fist in a glove, was Muhammad Ali. He had been annoying the authorities for years: his showboating at the weigh-in for the first Liston fight had seen him removed from the venue and fined. But this seemed innocuous by comparison with the carnival atmosphere before the Frazier fight. *Time* magazine's description of Ali's retinue, published on the eve of the fight, captures it vividly: There is Bundini, the cornerman and personal mystic who calls him 'the Blessing of the Planet'; a handler whose sole job is to comb Ali's hair; assorted grim-faced Muslim operatives; imperturbable Angelo Dundee, his trainer since 1960; Norman Mailer; Actor Burt Lancaster; Cash Clay Sr. in red velvet bell-bottoms, red satin shirt and a plantation straw hat; the Major, a high roller from Philly who tools around in a Duesenberg; and Brother Rahaman Ali (formerly known as Rudolph Valentino Clay), his yeah-man. Ali had said before that white America was unsettled by the spectacle of black people with money to burn, by the men in mink coats and hats, the women in spangled gowns, the customized Cadillacs.

The sight of two men pummelling one another senseless for prize money must always have attracted the merely or morbidly curious, those with no understanding of the finer points and a taste for blood. But as the era of the mass media dawned and boxing became less like sport and more like entertainment, it found a new audience among people like me, the know-nothing fans who could hardly tell a hook from a jab.

While boxing in general did not appeal to me, my interest in Muhammad Ali was all-consuming. I might have forgotten the full extent of it, as we forget so much of what we thought and did in the past, had it not been for the archive of cuttings.

When my obsession faded away, I put the scrapbooks and loose cuttings in a cardboard box. In time, I moved out of my parents' house and went to university, and I left the box behind in a cupboard. But the past is not so easily disposed of. I wanted to be a writer and the box came to seem like a key to my past. It was a journal written in code, the most complete record of my teenage life to which I had access, despite the fact that I was not mentioned in it once. I retrieved it from my parents' house and carried it with me to a dozen homes of my own.

Over twenty years, I went through the scrapbooks so many times I lost track, intending to write something about them, intrigued anew by what they might reveal of the world I grew up in. A book eluded me. Why? I wasn't sure what I was looking for: I didn't know what questions to ask of these yellowed pages. Each pass through the archive produced some sketchy drafts of this chapter and that passage. It also produced pages and pages of notes and outlines, scattered associations and half-formed structures, summaries and quotations, all added to a lever-arch file, and then revised and annotated at each revisiting. Finally, this file stuffed with contradictory notes became as intractable an obstacle as the scrapbooks themselves, a shadow of obscure intent over the blank page on which a book might actually start.

Branko

We've been living in Clubview for five years. Before that we were renting in Pretoria West, but this house belongs to us. It's in the ranch style, which means the bedrooms are all in a row and the garage is joined on next to the lounge. The plate-glass windows are nearly as big as a garage door. It's like we've moved to America.

One wall of each bedroom in the house is covered in wallpaper. If it's just one wall it makes the place look modern, don't ask me why. Sylvie's room has scenes from the Ming dynasty. You can see pilgrims making their way through the landscape, which is the colour of tea, or resting under frilly trees and pagodas. In the room I share with Joe the paper is a sky-blue backdrop for hot-air balloons, paddle steamers and Bugattis. It's like a page out of Jules Verne. The wall behind the fireplace in the lounge is papered to look like knotty pine. The mantelpiece is made of real slate.

An oil heater stands on the hearth like a lunar module. Dad doesn't believe in open fires: apart from being a fire hazard, he hates the smell of coal smoke and soot. He likes things to have more than one purpose.

That's why he brought home the side-table-cum-lamp (as he calls it) with a green Formica tabletop and two pendant lights with orange plastic shades.

The homework has been done and the dishes have been washed. Dad is relaxing in the armchair next to the radiogram, with his legs stretched out and his head cocked towards the speaker. No one else ever sits in Dad's chair. We're as attached to our chairs as the chairs are to their places in the lounge: their legs have made little hollows in the pile of the carpet and so they must occupy that spot for ever. Dad is reading the *Pretoria News*. Before supper he read as far as the editorial; now he's busy with the sports pages and the classifieds.

Some joker in Villieria is selling a Sprite 400, he says.

Mom ignores him. She's supposed to ask what he wants for it.

Only wants seven hundred rand for it, he says regardless.

Nothing escapes him. If some joker in Villieria has a caravan for sale, if Harlequins beat CBC Old Boys 2-1 in the Sunday hockey league, if the Russians are threatening to put a man on the moon – bloody Russkis, that'll be the day – he knows about it.

The devil finds work for idle hands and so Mom's are always busy. Every summer she knits each of us a jersey for the coming winter. She crochets baby clothes, bootees, matinée jackets, bedspreads, runners, doilies. She knits cardigans and pullovers for the rest of the family on order and presents them to the buyers wrapped in cellophane as if they came from Garlicks.

This evening she's cutting out a top for Sylvie. She kneels on the carpet with the material and the tracing-paper pattern that's pinned to it spread flat. It's always better to do your cutting on the floor, she says. She makes a lot of my sister's clothes, so she can keep up with the latest fashions without breaking the bank (as Dad puts it). We've had tent dresses and granny-print pinafores. Now it's bolero tops. Joe's been saying the word all evening as if he's learning another language. *Bolero, bolero, bolero.* When he gets like this I want to hit him.

Dad puts down the *News* and picks up the *Reader's Digest*. There's a red silk poppy sticking out of it like a tongue. The *Digest* comes every month and the volume of *Condensed Books* every second month. It's a racket, he says. They send them whether you want them or not and then you have to pay for them. He piles the books on the floor next to his bed, and the pile never grows because whenever he puts a volume on top, Joe takes one from the bottom.

For your edification and your delight / our headline's the deadline on Thursday night.

Turn that up, Dad says, the news is about to start, but Joe pretends that he can't hear. He's at the dining-room table, squeezed into the narrow space between the wall and the tabletop, with a big drawing book and a pile of Koki pens. He's making the first Ali scrapbook. I go and turn up the radio.

Mom picks three pins from between her lips like fishbones and stabs them into the pincushion. What's happened to my scissors? She starts unpacking her knitting bag. That green thing is the front of my winter jersey. I wish she'd ask. They'll have to kill me first. That fat stack of cuttings in a bulldog clip is crossword puzzles. And that black notebook is where she writes down the LM Hit Parade every Sunday so we can see which songs are on the way up or down and take bets on what will be number one. And those things are rabbits. She's knitting them for the school fête and each one has a different jersey.

Jissimpie, Pats, Dad says. Are they multiplying in there?

That's not funny Bo. Anyone seen my scissors?

Joe is using the sewing scissors to cut an article out of the paper. That won't be funny either when Mom finds out. The sewing scissors are meant for nothing but silk and satin. They're supposed to fall through chiffon like a hot knife through butter. We're strictly forbidden to use them on our school projects. But Joe always gets away with murder.

It's half past nine – way past your bedtime, Dad says – before Sylvie tries on the *bolero* and then it's just a waistcoat.

2

Lessons

By attaching a few hooks to a
plumb line and testing the depth
and bottom for signs of grass
or mud one can soon find the
mud banks. Eric Willsden got
a 5k mirror carp at Meerhof on
Sunday.

— *Pretoria News*, June 1971

Branko

On 7 November 2011, Joe Frazier dies of liver cancer. It's on the news, it's in the papers, it's all over the Internet.

A few days later Joe calls me and he sounds upset. Maybe he's been mugged again, I think, he's a magnet for trouble, terrible things are always happening to him. But no, it's some problem with his work, and by *work* he means writing, as if everything else is leisure. We need to talk, he says. I'm not usually the person he turns to for *feedback* and anyway it's not a good time. My last-minute son Jordan – we thought Louis, people assume Michael – is making a film on his laptop, a mash-up (his word) of *Pulp Fiction* and something else, presumably, and I've promised to give him some help with the sound this afternoon. I'm curious to know what you get when you pulp pulp: a purée? But I'm more curious about my brother's latest crisis.

He arrives with a cardboard box that has Pres Les printed on it. While I'm trying to remember where I've seen it before, he unpacks it on the dining-room table. The Ali scrapbooks! It's thirty years since I saw them. We start paging through the first one, or rather, he pages and I look. Many of the cuttings have come loose and he's careful to keep them in order, slipping a palm in under the tracing-paper sheets and turning them tenderly as if he's an archivist with a set of rare prints. All that's missing is the white cotton gloves. He's marked the loose cuttings in pencil to show where they belong: the numbers and keywords in the corners of the cuttings match those between the brown sticky-tape scars. Why bother to keep order in this mess?

I start asking a question but he shushes me like a stern librarian. *Look.* Just keep looking. The archive will clarify everything.

The archive! I see. Here's an incredulous little report under the headline 'Taken as red' that says the Soviet news agency TASS devoted no more than a couple of lines to the Fight of the Century, simply noting that Negro sportsman Cassius Clay, also known as Muhammad Ali, had lost a fight to Joe Frazier on points. Here's a picture of Ali punching Jimmy Ellis over the headline 'Ali says he showed mercy'. And another taken after the fight, headlined 'Cassius Snarls'. In the article below: Cassius Clay says he has received a visa to visit South Africa. But Government spokesmen in Pretoria contend they have had no application from the boxer. I don't remember this. Did he come to South Africa? Before I can ask, Joe starts paging again. Now it's 'Buster broken'. Poor Buster Mathis on all fours after taking one of Ali's linger-on punches. A headline calls it 'Clay's new weapon'. Paging again. Pausing here and there so I can get a good look or scan a paragraph, pointing to a headline with his pen, unfolding a concertina of newsprint to show me a photo of Ali swallowing flies. The loudmouth pose.

Here's a fact: Joe was a terrible archivist. He should have kept full pages from the newspapers and magazines, he could have put them in box files, conveniently numbered and indexed, or sorted them into cardboard folders, fight by fight. Instead he cut them and folded them into ludicrously complicated origami, and attached part of the cutting to the paper with sticky tape, fitting as many items as possible on a single page. Some of these assemblages are ingenious, with five or six articles unfolding from a single surface like a clever layout in a pop-up book for children. But the sticky tape was inexcusable. Any archivist will tell you it's the last thing you want near a news cutting or photograph you intend to preserve. The glue discolours and spoils the paper, the tape dries out and curls up. The cuttings are a dirty yellow-brown, the colour you'd see on the fingers of a Texan Plain smoker, a pack-a-day man. That's one thing we can't blame Joe for: this was long before acid-free paper, or wood-free paper, not to mention paper-free news. Or the fact-free stuff. But the sticky-tape scar tissue is his fault. No question.

Then again, the thought that he was creating an *archive* never entered his head. It's amusing to hear him talk about it this way. They're a bunch of scrapbooks. Sylvie also had a couple devoted to Cliff Richard. Or was it the Fab Four? The notion that he was doing something for posterity is ridiculous. A thirteen-year-old with bum fluff on his cheeks? His horizons stretched as far as the school bell on Friday afternoon. If he imagined the future at all it was to fantasize about driving an E-Type Jag like Mark Condor, a red one with spoked wheels, and having a girlfriend who was very beautiful but didn't know it because she'd been struck blind by a mysterious illness at the age of six. Obviously not something I would make up.

Years later, when Joe was living in California, I was getting my balsak out of the built-in cupboard in Clubview for an army camp when I came across this box and opened it out of curiosity. On the first page of the first scrapbook, the one we're leafing through now, was a handwritten header in Koki, ALI VS FRAZIER – BEFORE, the chubby cartoon letters surrounded by coloured lines like shock waves, the faintest echo of psychedelia in suburbia. I could see him hunched over the dining-room table to ink this Henry-Mooreish script, with his hand bent in the peculiar way it was when he held a pen, as if his wrist had been broken. He was maniacal about school projects, going to endless trouble to copy line drawings out of encyclopedias and cut photographs out of pamphlets. Not just doing enough, like a normal lightie, doing too much, always. Desperate to please, I suppose. Making everyone else feel lazy and ashamed of their hand-eye coordination. Terrified of being wrong, of not knowing the right answer, of looking a fool. I should have thrown his precious scrapbooks away when I had the chance.

What does he want from me?

We come to the end of ALI I. There's a page of cuttings about Ali's visit to South Africa. Wilbur, the cartoon commentator, asks: Is the Government shadow boxing with Clay? Another page on the fight against Al 'Blue' Lewis in Dublin in 1972. Lewis got his nickname because he liked blue suits and blue cars. It reminds me of the joke about the South African champ Mike Schutte. What kind of car do you drive, Mike? Mike (scratching his head): A blue one. Neil Allen, who watched the Ellis fight for the *Times*, said it provided evidence that Clay did not have a power punch. Then again the *Pretoria News* said that Clay had calmly and brutally despatched another opponent. Chuck Nary, the loser's manager: It was more exhaustion than anything else that beat Lewis.

I'm tired too of these faded images of men throwing punches. How many different ways are there to hit someone? Jab, straight, hook, cross … The photographs of Ali clowning for the camera, mouth stretched to swallow the lens and the viewer, take me back, but there's no warmth in the recognition. He's had a hard time, I know, with the Parkinson's and everything, but my old antipathy for him stirs. I study the faces of the men he beat, Jimmy Ellis with his Elvis sideburns like two tabs of Velcro, Broken Buster with his spitty gumshield jutting, all the men who made a living out of being knocked silly. Christ. Whatever became of George Chuvalo?

Any second now he's going to start on ALI II.

Why are you showing me this?

His fingers drum on the cover of the second scrapbook, where I see a picture of Goofy in boxing gloves. Irritable or just unsure of the answer. Then he says: I need your help. I'm trying to write something about this time of my life.

Fucking hell, this is a new one. My brother, the novelist, asking for my help. I'm no good at making things up, I say. That's your department.

That's the whole point. Making things up won't do any good. I need to remember things as they actually were.

And what makes you think I can help with this?

You were there.

He takes a blue lever-arch file out of the box, flings it open, cuffs angrily through some dense handwritten pages, in pencil nogal. I've been trying to write something about this stuff for ten years, no, more like twenty. I just can't get anywhere. My memory's not what it used to be. I can't tell if I'm remembering something or imagining it.

I turn the file to face me. He's always been fanatical about one thing: no one can read a line of the book he's working on until it's published – or publishable at least. But he does nothing to stop me now.

I read the page that happens to be facing me. I remember a prissy, upright script, but this is drunk and disorderly. There's a column of untidy cursive in pencil with arrows sticking out of it and bubbles full of second thoughts, and I wind my way through three paragraphs. Notes about the Rumble in the Jungle.

You're writing a book about Muhammad Ali? I want to add: You can't be serious, but I restrain myself. What he knows about boxing has always been dangerous, especially to himself.

No, no, he says, exasperated. It's not about him, it's about *us*. Our lives together.

I don't know what's worse. Especially because I can't place the tone. His voice is trembling a little and there are tears in his eyes. Maybe he's hitting the bottle? I scan the page for names and there's nothing about me there. It's all Ali.

Just then Jordan comes in with his Mac dangling from his hand like a paperback. In the doorway the atmosphere sticks to him like a wet shower curtain and he shuts the laptop with a flick of the wrist. What's this old stuff?

Joe scrambles the scrapbooks and files into the box. It's like he's been caught reading *Playboy* under his desk.

We'll speak, he says.

Joe

Paul Skinner gave me a boxing lesson I never forgot. On a summer afternoon, under a Highveld sky that was nearly the blue of my school blazer, he punched me in the mouth and started to like me.

The lesson began in Mrs Worsnop's Arts and Crafts class when Skinner pulled the chair out from under me as I sat down. I'd risen to answer some question, correctly no doubt, and he decided to bring me down to earth. He couldn't help himself. He reached for my stool, which had a slot in the middle of the seat made for a child's hand, and moved it aside, so that I fell on my arse.

I couldn't help it Miss. That's what he told Mrs Worsnop when the laughter had subsided. She was a sluggish, ginger-fuzzed toad of a woman with a fondness for popping green grapes between her teeth and spitting the pips at whatever boy was within range. The floor around her desk was slimed with this spawn. She never stood up if she could help it and even the commotion caused by the prank did not rouse her. I thought she would send Skinner to the office to explain himself to Mr Hobbs or make him stand in the corner with the wastepaper basket over his head, familiar punishments, but apparently not being able to help yourself was an acceptable excuse.

The fall hurt no more than my feelings, but it enraged and humiliated me. I'd been taught at home that pulling the chair out from under someone was *not funny*. It was close to the top of the list of things that a certain class of person thinks are funny but are actually dangerous, like stirring Brooklax into someone's coffee or jumping out from behind a door and shouting Boo! The victim might die of dehydration or heart failure. A person who has a chair pulled out from under them might break their back and be paralysed for life. I knew a girl this happened to, Mom said, and she spent the rest of her life in a wheelchair. A wheelchair! When Donny Drummond had surgery on his fallen arches he was in a wheelchair for months and we had to carry him up and down the stairs at school. What if this happened to me? Perilous possibilities were at the heart of our family philosophy, such as it was, which consisted in keeping your head down and making the best of a bad job.

Unfortunately, another somewhat contradictory family principle required one to stand up for what is right. So I found myself challenging Paul Skinner. I couldn't help myself. I wasn't sure where my indignation would lead, I hadn't thought as far as the consequences, and I wasn't exactly planning to duke it out, but that was the language he spoke, and before I knew it I had challenged him to a fight.

I'll meet you at the taps after school, he said.

Ja, I'll be there Skinner. Don't worry.

As soon as my challenge had been accepted, I wished to retract it. But how to do so without losing face? This question throbbed in my head all through Arts and Crafts. We were making objects out of papier mâché. We'd brought clay for modelling, newspaper to tear into strips and flour to mix the glue. Terrence Jones and Melanie Fuller arrived with modelling clay bought at the art supplies shop in Barclay Square, the new shopping centre in town. But Dad said he wasn't going to waste good money on something you could sommer dig out of the ground. So one afternoon Branko and I rode our bikes down to the Sesmyl-spruit and left them leaning against the railings of the bridge while we scrambled down to the river and dug some clay out of the bank. Melanie Fuller's clay looked like fudge and smelt like the inside of a Mercedes. But this stuff of mine, wrapped in newspaper and taken home on the carrier, was mud, thick brown mud spiked with willow leaves and insect wings, and reeking of the spruit's stagnant shallows. A pile of it, moulded into a grimacing face, lay on the Arts and Crafts workbench as I tried to figure out how to avoid meeting Skinner at the taps. The glue made of flour and water had cloves in it, for reasons known only to Mrs Worsnop, and the spicy aroma of Irish stew barely masked the smell of river mud – three times worse than Bon Accord Dam – as I dredged my strips of newsprint and laid them over the face-mould like mucus-laden bandages. It was a clown's face, actually, with astonished eyebrows and a bulbous nose. When I took it home at the end of term, glossily made up with model aeroplane paint, Branko said: Really, Joe. Tickey the Clown. Is that the best you can do?

After break we had Hygiene and then English, where Miss Drysdale read to us from *The Adventures of Huckleberry Finn*. These closing lessons often dragged, but not today. Skinner caught my eye a few times and gave me a sly smile. When the bell rang, he was first through the door.

I hung around in the classroom, hoping he'd forgotten about me and gone home. Miss Drysdale was at her desk leafing through exercise books and making notes. When she began to pack up her papers, I looked around the door, willing the coast to be clear. And there he was, waiting at the taps, as promised, with his hands in his pockets. His fists.

He was a wiry, red-headed boy whose fair skin was sprinkled with rust-coloured freckles. He had broad hips and turned-out feet, and his shoes were flattened and gaping, as if his elder brothers, who were at high school with Branko, had walked in them first.

I might yet have escaped: all I had to do was go in the opposite direction and loop around the school hall to the bicycle sheds. Instead I put my schoolbag over my shoulder and sauntered down to the taps with my heart pounding. He looked surprised to see me. Even then I expected that showing up might be enough to prove my courage and that we'd talk it out. I was turning my first words over in my mind as I came up to him. Now listen here ... But before I could get them out, he punched me in the mouth. It was a straight right, I think, with his shoulder behind it.

For the second time that day I fell on my arse thanks to Paul Skinner. As hard as the blow was, there was something speculative in it. He wanted to see whether I would fight back. He might have gone on punching me until both of us were blue in the face, but he did not. He was admirably restrained. Somewhere behind me a classroom door closed and Miss Drysdale's heels clicked along the verandah. For an instant, in my fogged-over mind, I thought of calling out to her. Then Skinner reached out a hand and helped me to my feet. He was smiling. I didn't know it yet but the punch, or rather taking the punch without complaint, was a kind of deposit, an expression of good will.

My lip was split and I was bleeding down the front of my shirt. I rinsed my mouth under a tap while Skinner scuffed his boat-like shoes in the dry grass of the playground. So that's why he wanted to meet me at the *taps*, I thought.

We walked together to the bicycle sheds and he waited while I unlocked my bike, and then he came with me as far as the school gate and stood there at the kerb as I rode away down Monument Road.

By the time I got home, my lip was throbbing and jutting like the spout of a kettle. Mom called Auntie Jilly from over the road and they put me in the Volksie and drove me to the doctor in Kloofsig, who put three stitches in the cut. For the next week I looked like I had a skinny fly sitting on my bottom lip.

I stuck to my story: I'd been hit in the mouth by a cricket ball during fielding practice, but Branko soon winkled the truth out of me.

Paul Skinner! he said. You got in a rort with Paul Skinner! Are you mad? I wouldn't fight with Clyde or Henry if you paid me. Their dad's a sergeant at the Tiffie School in Voortrekkerhoogte and he bliksems them all the time, to toughen them up. Nobody looks for grief with the Skinners, you moron.

Branko

Going to the rofstoei on a Saturday night is a big thing for two teenage boys, especially when we don't have to take care of the lighties. Dad drops me off at Kelvin's in the afternoon and the two of us head out early. Charlie's Caffie in Paul Kruger Street is close to the City Hall and we stop there for a steak and kidney pie. Charlie's an old mate of my dad's, he always says they went to different schools together, and when Dad drops in for a chat he'll go in behind the counter and help himself to a cabanossi stick from the jar. It's strange to see my own Dad behind the till. It doesn't seem right. But it's a good thing Charlie knows me because he gives Kelvin and me free strawberry milks with the pies.

The City Hall is a strange venue for wrestling matches. The ball-room has plaster mouldings and flowery carpets as if it's in Vienna. They have official functions here, wedding receptions and chamber-music recitals. It's no place for all this grunting and sweating in the name of sport.

The ring sits in the middle of the room surrounded by rows of fold-up chairs. An immense chandelier hovers high above. At each corner are flower arrangements on meranti pedestals left over from some function hosted by the Transvaalse Landbou-Unie, tall vases of proteas and sprays of baby's breath like clouds of flies. The grand double doors opening into the foyer are policed by bouncers in leather jackets. It's easy for a rort to start and they keep an eye on the troublemakers. Alcoves in the foyer hold the busts of statesmen with sagging bronze jowls and verdigrised moustaches. Some boys from the railway reserve are leaning there. I recognize that breker Billy Darling who was cased to Sylvie. When I wave he just tips his ash into a statue's ear.

The crowd is restless and noisy, everyone is talking and smoking, shouting the odds. Kelvin and I join the okes standing behind the last row of seats. We call this part of the hall the peanut gallery even though it's on the ground floor. You can see better from back here. Anyway we're too excited to sit down. No one can keep still, we're all moving, easing from one foot to the other like boxers before a fight. The lighties are bouncing on their seats, twisting and turning, writhing with anticipation.

Then the room goes dim and four spotlights directed by operators in the balconies bore down through the haze of cigarette smoke. Circus music blares from speakers and the crowd roars, drowning out the voice of the announcer who's introducing the wrestlers. The main doors swing open and the Masked Marvel comes in. He's dressed all in black with a leather mask laced over his skull. He dances down to the ring and swings up over the ropes. While he's taking his bows to the four sides of the room, his opponent comes in and another roar goes up. It's my guy Rio Rivers in a satin robe, hopping and feinting down the aisle. He's an old streetfighter, a skate from Danville with Comanche eyes and a yellow brushcut. He swirls up into the glare and stalks around the Marvel, who's standing like a statue centre-stage, pulsing out energy. Now here's the referee, a slick, darting little dancing master with Brylcreem in his hair. He needs to be quick, he needs to fling himself onto the canvas to get up close to a pinned wrestler and beat out the count with his hand. At some point tonight he'll be struck by a stray haymaker or pinned beneath a crashing body. It has to happen. He must be able to roll with the punches, squeeze out from under the deadweight.

Tonight's wrestlers aren't professionals, they're policemen, small-holders, fitters and turners, panelbeaters who make a bit of bread on the side by pretending to fight one another. Of course the fights are rehearsed and the results are predetermined. You can't have Sammy Cohen knocking the crap out of Jan Wilkens in the Pretoria City Hall. But the contest is still brutal and sometimes the wrestlers get the hell in. No one likes to be hurled to the floor or fallen on by a fat man, even when they're being paid for it.

The fight begins. Rio Rivers and the Masked Marvel go through the motions. They grapple and throw, spin and kick, slap and stagger. Rio ties the Marvel up in the ropes. The Marvel gouges Rio's eyes when the ref is unsighted. It's all routine. Then in the middle of the second round Rio starts to lose his temper and the mechanism falters. There's a flat spot, like when an engine burns a valve, and the machine goes out of kilter. The wrestlers begin to make up their own moves and these are more convincing than the choreographed ones. Rio gets a finger in under the Marvel's mask and jabs him in the nose. The Marvel punches Rio in the belly. It makes a less satisfying smack than the heel of the hand but it hurts more. It knocks him halfway through the ropes. The wrestlers throw away the script. A new mood comes into the room like an ill wind and the skylights darken. We go berserk. Even the lighties are screaming blue murder. The wrestlers pummel one another from one side of the ring to the other. Rio Rivers has a dodgy eye – everyone says he's held together by scar tissue – and it starts to bleed. Soon his pale chest and sky-blue trunks are drenched in real blood. Every time he takes a blow to the head, bloody sweat sprays out like water from a lawn sprinkler and the punters in the front rows reel back in delight and disgust. The news photographer who's been stalking around the ring has to borrow a hanky to wipe his camera lens. When it's over the ref awards the victory to the Marvel even though he's been pinned twice. We bay for the ref's blood but it's too late.

We're supposed to go straight home after the fight, but since Uncle Arthur died my cousins do what they like. There's start left over from Charlie's because we didn't pay for the strawberry milk, so we head for the Mikado near the Square, where they've got a soft-serve machine and they're open late on a Saturday night. As we cut through the gardens, we surprise a couple smooching under the statue of Andries Pretorius on his horse, and she pulls down her skirt while he shouts over his shoulder: Fokkof! Julle draadtrekkers! We run down Paul Kruger Street, exhilarated and shit-scared. The whale skeleton outside the museum sways in its hawsers. In the window of a laundry an automaton bows over his washboard. We go along the arcades, bouncing on our toes, chasing our shadows across the shopfronts.

Joe

In March 2011, the fortieth anniversary of the Fight of the Century rolled around. The newspapers and sports shows were full of reminiscences.

Forty years! Who would believe it? The passage of time sent me back to the cuttings with new urgency. I read through all the scrapbooks, made more notes towards a book and slotted them into yet another outline.

Just eight months later Joe Frazier died. None of the obituarists could separate the man and his boxing career from his legendary rivalry with Muhammad Ali. In the early years, before their first match, Frazier had told reporters that Ali, regarded by many fans as the legitimate champion who'd been unfairly stripped of his title, was a shadow hanging around him. This shadow never lifted. In his obituary in *The Star*, Dan Gelston said that Frazier had spent his life trying to 'fight his way out of Ali's shadow'.

In the months before he died, Frazier had been on the 'autograph circuit', signing photographs for fans at boxing matches. Gelston wrote about his polite generosity and how he would always introduce himself with the line: 'Joe Frazier, sharp as a razor.' The rhyme, imagined in a punchy slur, made me sad.

There were striking differences between the historical reporting on the Fight of the Century and the reporting on the anniversary forty years later. Some aspects of the fighters' background and character had come to the fore and others had faded away. The story of a life is always evolving. The early reports made much of Frazier's humble beginnings as the son of a one-armed sharecropper, the second-youngest of thirteen children, a tough little boy who spent his childhood in the fields or tending hogs, acting as his father's left hand, even steering the car while his father changed the gears. Some of the boxing writers noticed early on that Frazier was essentially a one-armed boxer, relying heavily on his left hook. Only later was it revealed that he'd injured this arm as a boy and could not straighten it fully. This potential weakness was a closely guarded secret while he was active in the ring.

Frazier's openness about his weight problems and his rejection by the military was either naïve or disarmingly frank. The reports from the 1970s made no bones about the fact that he was not the sharpest blade in the barber shop and liked to tell the story of how he flunked the IQ test when he tried to join the Marines. Then again, a similar story was told about Ali: this was the reason he'd first been classified as unfit for military service. It was often reported that he could not read. *Time* magazine's article published just before the Fight of the Century made a point of mentioning that Clay had graduated 376th in a high-school class of 391. I never said I was the smartest, he told their reporters, I said I was the greatest. At the same time, Ali frequently ridiculed Frazier's intellect, and these slights rankled with him all his life. By 2011, sensitivities about such judgements, and the nature of the judgements themselves, were very different, and the news reports on the famous rivalry offered no comment on the intelligence of either boxer.

On 17 January 2012, just months after Frazier died, Ali turned seventy. The newspapers looked back on his extraordinary life and presented potted accounts of his best fights, usually including all three against Frazier. They also compiled lists of his wittiest adages and best-known rhymes. For the first time I saw both lines of the famous couplet: 'Float like a butterfly, sting like a bee, / his hands can't hit what his eyes can't see.'

Mainly though the press focused on Ali's frailty, on how sad it was to see an athlete once renowned for his speed and grace reduced to a doddery puppet by Parkinson's, but also how bravely he had fought the disease. Lesser men, they said, would have been in the grave long ago. Oh God, I thought, he's on his last legs. The rare public appearance Ali made was not reassuring. When he attended a birthday party thrown for him in Louisville at the Center that bears his name, Jeff Powell wrote in the *Daily Mail* that it would not surprise him if this were 'the last hurray'. At the end of the evening, which passed without Ali saying a single word, he was trundled away in a wheelchair. Also there in a wheelchair was his old trainer Angelo Dundee, still full of lip at the age of ninety.

The pictures were heart-wrenching: Ali with his head hanging, lips sealed in an unsmiling line, eyes narrowed, wincing slightly as if someone had raised a hand to strike him. He was not long for this world, as they say, and when he departed it, I knew, there would be an outpouring of commentary second to none. The obituaries were already written. They would only need tweaking. Anything I wrote about him then would be swept away like a twig on the flood.

If I wanted to write about Ali, I had to do it *now*. I was working to deadline.

Branko

Joe doesn't make a good start at high school. I'm in Standard 8 when he arrives and it's my duty to keep an eye on him. There's some boisterous initiation of the new Standard 6 boys: the matrics chase them around on the rugby field and smear them with shaving cream. Strictly, initiation has been banned at the school, but this is good clean fun and no one pays it much attention, until some little tattletale goes crying to his mommy and she phones the headmaster. The matrics are in deep trouble. Porky Laing gets expelled but his dad sees a lawyer and next thing he's back. Who was the snitch? Suspicion settles on Joe. I know it's not him – I would hear all about it at home – but nothing I say can turn the tide of animosity. Maybe some of the boys who were at primary school with him are getting their own back? There he was an officious little monitor. He once told Donny Drummond to close his eyes during the Lord's Prayer, to which Donny Drummond replied: Why don't *you* close *your* eyes, you tit, then you won't know mine are open. Donny's brother Morris told me this story as if I had something to do with it. Joe's know-it-all ways mean nothing at high school. Now he's just another pipsqueak with no say in anything. Telling tales is an unforgivable sin and he gets sent to Coventry. His friends stop talking to him, even that miserable little shit with the gammy leg and the green hair who befriended him at the municipal baths. At break I see him mooching around on the pavilion with a book under his arm.

Ditch the book, for fuck's sake, I tell him at home. You've got to start looking after yourself. You're in the A stream with the eggheads, which makes you a doos by definition, and you've got to do stuff to make yourself popular. Find yourself a girlfriend before everyone says you're a rabbit. Come second in the cross-country like Derek Gibbs, who also won a medal at the Maths Olympiad. Get caught smoking behind the bicycle sheds. Stop worrying so much about what people think. Look at Kevin Fowler, I say. He's a kid in my class, smart as anything but completely out of control. He can't stand being cooped up in a classroom. When he's had enough for one day, he splits. After second break, we see him ambling up the gravel drive next to the hockey field and out the back gate, lighting a Chesterfield as he goes. Harry Casual. Actually Fowler is a bad example: soon after this he steals a box of Simba chips off the back of a delivery van outside the tuck shop and distributes all 144 packets on the playground. Robin Hood himself. He's expelled and he doesn't come back. Presumably his dad can't afford a lawyer.

Anyway Joe doesn't take advice from me. He keeps doing what he's doing, head down, running on his own track. His eyes are open wide, as if he's just been punched by Paul Skinner, but he doesn't see how anything works.

Things brighten up when he gets six of the best for messing around in Industrial Arts. It's the first time he's been hit by anyone other than Dad, who bats our backsides half-heartedly with the palm of his hand. Visser, who runs the school workshop, canes juvenile delinquents for the police in his spare time (we've heard) and he brings his professional equipment to school with him. The boys who've been jacked with this cane have different ideas about it. Louis Ferreira says it's the end of a *deep-sea* fishing rod. Dave Pratt swears it was specially made for Visser by The Blind in the workshop where they make the wickerwork baskets. Joe has no idea what he's been hit with, it was all too shocking, but whatever it was it draws blood. I help him wash his underrods so Mom won't find out. And I show him how to notch the cuts up on the inside of his school belt like a prisoner counting days. We wear our tallies like a badge of honour. But he doesn't take to it and he doesn't get jacked often enough to impress anyone. He just goes on making enemies left, right and centre, real and imagined.

He's no longer scared of Paul Skinner. They're in different classes now, thanks to the streaming system, but Skinner takes a big-brotherly interest in him (he assures me). He says it's almost affectionate, which I find hard to believe. No, Skinner is no threat at all. But Gavin Cochrane has it in for him, he says. He wants to bliksem him. Cochrane is in Standard 7 but he looks like a matric boy. After school he brawls with bigger boys in the bluegum stand on the other side of Clifton Avenue and sends them home with their shirts ripped and their noses bloodied. Cochrane fancies himself as a skinhead. Most of us want to grow our hair long, but he shaves his short and goes around in blue-denim dungarees and thick-soled boots. He's got a bad case of acne, and his velvety scalp, showing pinkly under the fuzz like the belly-skin of a puppy, makes his cratered red cheeks look more livid. If you say anything about these chorbs, you're dead. Joe goes to the ice rink at Sterland on Saturday nights and one evening Cochrane pitches up there. Now he's sure the skinhead is looking for him.

The following weekend, after Dad's dropped Joe at the rink, he takes me there too and I sneak in and watch from the back of the stands. Cochrane is there, showing off for his inexplicably pretty, alabaster-skinned girlfriend, swerving in and out of the slower skaters, getting his dungarees wet to the knee, behaving like a tit. But as far as I can see, he has no idea Joe even exists. On the other hand, there's a girl with black curls, looks like a Greek, who's trying to attract his attention. She keeps drifting into his path on the ice. Why doesn't he notice her? Skinny but pretty enough. An hour before Dad's supposed to pick him up, he takes off his skates and leaves. I'm glad to get out of the rink, which smells like a freezer that needs defrosting, and I'm curious too. Where's he going? Apparently nowhere. He wanders around Arcadia in his army-surplus greatcoat with his skates over his shoulder. My poor lost brother. When some Dutchman comes up to him and demands, Maak 'n las?, he gives him the last few coins in his pocket.

Joe

Mr Palliser the gym master was destined for better things. After languishing in our backwoods school for a year or two, he went off to teach tennis to private-school boys and their mothers. In the interim he did his best to prepare us for adult life. Jumping over the vaulting horse and chucking medicine balls around was all well and good, but if you wanted to produce upright young men who were at ease with the world, you needed to teach them the gentlemanly arts.

The school budget did not stretch far, so Mr Palliser borrowed a few pairs of boxing gloves from a club in town and got us sparring against one another in the gym. He found some fencing épées and masks and we each had a turn. Then it was shooting with .22 rifles at the range behind the rugby pavilion. And then the basic throws and holds in Graeco-Roman wrestling, as he called it.

It was a sensible strategy. We couldn't sit still. The sight of a girl, the thought of her body under her school uniform, a glimpse of *vagina* and *breast* in the dictionary made us squirm with erotic imaginings. We were always hitting one another. Barry Davenport kept flapping his mates' balls and no one put their hands in their pockets when he was around. The best way to get rid of all this energy was hand-to-hand combat, strictly regulated, and Mr Palliser obliged.

The gym class presented me with an opportunity. It allowed a book-ish boy with normal hand-eye coordination to set himself apart from a Snoopy Siebert, who spent his breaks cracking open the new acquisitions in the library, one crisp page at a time so their spines didn't break, or a Colin Deary-Me Favish, whose throat closed up if he touched the fuzz on a tennis ball. In this delicate company, I was a fine figure of a boy. Living with Branko had made me tough. He had absorbed the family creed of standing up for yourself more completely than I. The Blahavić clan doesn't get into a barney for the hell of it, he said, we aren't the Skinners, but we don't let anyone push us around either.

In one of our Graeco-Roman sessions, Mr Palliser paired me up with Charl de Ridder. The mismatch made my classmates snigger. De Ridder was a large-boned, heavy-thighed boy with a disreputable air. He always looked as if he'd slept in his clothes: even his gym shorts and vest were crumpled. The first time he wrestled me to the mat, I felt the stubble on his chin and it reminded me of rough-housing with my father on a Sunday morning when he was trying to read the *Express*. De Ridder's schooldays had not gone smoothly and he was two years older than the rest of us.

I was agile and stubborn. More to the point, I'd been to the rofstoei in the Pretoria City Hall with my brother Branko and my cousin Rollie, and I'd picked up a few tips. Not the stupid stuff, like flying kicks and headbutts that obviously required the cooperation of your opponent, but the basics like keeping a low centre of gravity and twisting out of a hold. De Ridder expected to make short work of me, and when he couldn't pin me, he started to get angry. Rio Rivers had taught me that this was to my advantage. Mr Palliser must have been curious about the outcome because he let the match run on for ten minutes. De Ridder always had the upper hand, grinding his wiry head into my mouth, raking my calves with his horny heels, but he couldn't keep me down on the mat. Finally, after he'd pushed me onto the wooden floor and taken the skin off my elbows, Mr Palliser called time and punched me on the shoulder to signal his approval. I wished Branko was there to see me give De Ridder a run for his money. He was always telling me to do this kind of thing, to stand up for myself.

In the changeroom afterwards, as I was lacing my shoes, De Ridder sat down on the bench next to me and began to tie an elaborate knot in his tiny necktie. In a small, petulant act of resistance to conformity, he had cut this tie into a six-inch stub and frayed out the silky edge. I thought he was looking for grief, but he wanted to pay me a compliment.

Ja Brainbox, he said, you're pretty tough.

Thanks.

Another minute and I'd have had you. But well done hey.

Thank you, I said again.

You can moer Wilson.

Wilson. I glanced across at Wilson who was towelling himself down on the other side of the room. What's his problem?

No man, he doesn't have a problem. I'm just saying, you could moer him, if you want to.

Wilson was one of the bruisers of the school. He'd got into scraps with De Ridder a few times and always come second. I wouldn't dream of picking a fight with him. Now here was De Ridder with the tale of the tape. He'd done the measurements, using himself as a yardstick, and on paper, he wanted me to know, I was the better man. The idea was flattering and disconcerting.

Just like Paul Skinner when he punched me in the mouth, De Ridder developed a soft spot for me after this. A few years into high school, the streaming system that had borne Skinner away into the backwaters of Industrial Arts and Business Economics carried him away too. We still saw one another in French, though, where he always came top of the class. This anomaly could be explained: he'd spent four years of his life in France, where his father worked in an aircraft factory. People travelled less in those days and his overseas sojourn gave him a unique status among his classmates. Even more impressive was the fact – could we believe him? – that he'd fucked a married woman, a Frenchwoman of course, slept with her actually, we still used that expression. Sex was completely normal in France, he assured us, even the schoolkids fucked like fish. We were still figuring out how to talk to girls, how to lay our hands on FLs, effies as we called them with counterproductive familiarity, and what we'd do with them if we ever succeeded. De Ridder had been through all that. When he slouched at the back of the class, with his feet hooked under the frame of the desk so that he could bounce it up and down on his knees, up and down, you knew he was thinking about the next married woman who would sit on his lap.

3

Doubles

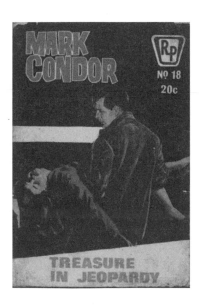

Two miners killed
Krugersdorp – Two African mine workers died after an accident in the West Rand Consolidated Mine near here yesterday. – Sapa

– Pretoria News, July 1971

Branko

Around the time Grandpa Blahavić came to South Africa, his brothers went to South America. If he'd joined them there, Joe says, we'd all be in Chile.

Bull, I say, we wouldn't be anywhere. Grandpa might have had a son, but he wouldn't be Dad. And that guy might have had children too, but they wouldn't be *us*.

He knows I'm right, but he won't shut up. We'd be beetling around in Antofagasta, he says, wearing leather pants and speaking Spanish.

Dad says Grandpa Blahavić wasn't even planning to come to South Africa, he was on his way to Australia, but when the ship docked in Cape Town, it looked so beautiful he decided to get off.

Why didn't he stay in the Cape then? Joe asks.

He knew people in Pretoria. That's what immigrants do. They find some connection to help them out until they're on their feet.

I'd have stayed by the sea, Joe says. Why come and live in the Transvaal where there's no water?

There's Bon Accord Dam, I say.

That's not *water*.

Dad tells us that when he got his first car, he took his mother and father down to Durban. They hadn't seen the sea since they left their island in the Adriatic twenty years before. His mother just sat down on the sand and cried.

In the late thirties, when Dad was a teenager, Grandpa decided it was time to join his brothers in Chile. They'd built up thriving businesses while he was still battling, and they encouraged him to come. It was beautiful, they said, almost as beautiful as Dalmatia. So the arrangements were made; they even applied for passports.

And then?

And then Hitler invaded Poland. Suddenly it wasn't safe to go anywhere. There isn't much to thank the man for, Dad says, but it's a fact that if he hadn't invaded Poland, we wouldn't be here in God's own country.

Joe

Hardly a day passed without someone at the gate looking for work. The women wanted to clean or do the washing and ironing, the men wanted to tidy up the yard. When they rattled the latch on the back gate or the door of the letter box, Mom went out and spoke to them from the end of the stoep. No, we don't need anybody, I do everything myself. We already have someone to mow the lawn. Sorry.

Then one day a man who was not afraid of the dog came to the door. This was in the morning while I was at school and when I got home that afternoon Mom was still trembling. He came right in and went round to the back door, she said, and Cassie sniffed his ankles and trotted behind him down the driveway.

Usually when someone passed in the street, my dog would follow him along the fence, snarling and snapping at the wire, and shaking long gouts of spit from his jowls.

I was sitting at the kitchen table eating a sandwich. Sylvie was there too, so it must have been a Wednesday, because she had Wednesday afternoons off when she worked at the Perm. Mom stood at the kitchen sink with her arms folded, pulling the housecoat tight around her and glancing out into the yard from time to time.

What did he want?

He's very tall, she said, and he has a strange way of walking. His arms are like this – she stretched out her own as if holding a tray – and his head keeps very still. He's been in prison. And you can see by his eyes he's been smoking dagga. They're yellow and wild. Your father should put a lock on that gate, you kids are my witness, how many times have I asked him.

What did you do, Mom? Sylvie said over a Marmite-smeared Provita cracker that was stalled halfway to her mouth.

I saw him coming in, thank God, so I ran to check that the doors were locked. And then I just waited in the passage while he knocked. Tok tok tok. My heart was beating so loud I thought he might hear it. If he'd tried to get in, I would have run out the front and gone across to Auntie Jilly's. No point phoning your father. What could he do? But after a while the knocking stopped. I crept down to the lounge and there he was just closing the gate behind him, so Cassie couldn't get out. Useless mutt. He wouldn't harm a flea.

A few months later the convict came again. I was in bed with the flu and I recognized the man at the gate at once. Very tall, as Mom had said, and upright. A big block of a head, shaven clean like a prisoner's, and his hands held out in front of him as if he was scared of falling. His straw-coloured canvas suit seemed to be ingrained with coal dust and he had white boots like the pair in the bottom of Dad's wardrobe from his cricketing days. I watched through the net curtain as he turned stiffly around to close the latch. Cassie jumped up against him without barking and he put one hand on my dog's head and pushed him gently down.

Mom came into my room with her finger on her lips. She'd seen him from her own window. She stood against the wall and I lay in bed with the blanket drawn up to my chin. After a while the knock came on the door, three evenly spaced taps, repeated three times with a long pause in between. Then he left. Cassie followed him to the gate, bouncing up against the backs of his thighs.

That winter, Granny Reilly came to live with us for three months. She'd moved out of the boarding house in Sunnyside and was going to live with her cousin in Durban. She and Annie had always been as close as sisters and now that they were both widows they'd decided to set up house together. Granny had a few things to tie up before she moved to the coast and so she boarded with us.

Granny and Dad never saw eye to eye. The only thing that made her stay tolerable was that everyone knew it would be over soon. She felt trapped in the house. She complained about the built-in cupboards and the wall-to-wall carpets. Fixed property: things you can't get rid of. The picture windows, letting in so much light and colour, drew her outside on the coldest days. I wasn't made for city life, she said. As soon as the sun had burnt the frost off the lawn, she went out onto the stoep and stayed there all day. Mom was busy at her knitting machine and this arrangement suited her. At eleven she'd take out a pot of tea and a sandwich, and when we came in from school a few hours later the tray would still be on the table.

Granny was a lull in the passage of the day, spilling out of the wire garden chair that cupped her like a big soft-boiled egg. Her legs were crossed at the ankles and her slippered feet rested on their sides. She had a tin of snuff and a packet of humbugs within reach on the tabletop. She wanted for nothing except company. And so when people passed by in the street, she would hail them and begin a conversation. Sometimes these chats were over in a few minutes. More often they went on for half an hour, an hour.

The word got around that there was a white woman in Cambridge Road who spoke Zulu. Granny had grown up in the countryside near Volksrust before the Great War and she'd spoken Zulu before she spoke English. Domestic workers and gardeners from the neighbourhood came to speak to her. They leant on the fence and talked in loud, rolling tones. We didn't know whether to feel proud of her or ashamed.

Dad didn't like it one bit. You don't know these people, he said. You be careful what you say to them. Do they ask questions about us? Do they want to know when we're going on holiday?

One day when I came in from school the man in the canvas suit was sitting on the front steps talking to Granny. He had a slice of bread and jam in his hand and a mug of tea standing on the bricks between his big white boots. The convict! I was astonished to see him sitting there in our yard. When he saw me at the gate, he stood up with his hands outstretched and backed into the driveway. For a moment it looked just as if he were surrendering.

Mom was in the kitchen punching a lump of dough on a floured board. Is he gone? she asked.

No, he's still there.

That grandmother of yours. She asked him in without so much as a by your leave. She'll be the death of me.

Pale flour rose in a haze from the board.

Over supper that evening Dad told Granny this talking to strangers had to stop. You're as simple as a child, he said. Imagine inviting a skelm like that into our yard.

Skelm my foot! she said. He comes from Nongoma. He's a very fine man who's down on his luck. He worked in the trading store at Memel until he hurt his back. He knows the Collingwoods! Where did you get this story that he's a thief?

Branko

The Jag is sitting outside the Sabre Caffie like a shiny red apple. Dad and I have been to the municipal offices in Lyttelton to pay the lights and water and we're on our way home when we spot it. An E-Type with triple carbs and bucket seats in real leather is not something you see every day. Dad makes a U-turn and we go back for a closer look. For him the streets and parking lots of the city are one big showroom. He thinks nothing of asking a stranger to pop the bonnet of his car so he can look in the engine or let him sit behind the wheel and tap the accelerator to gauge the results on the rev counter. Mom says it's a cheek, and Dad says nonsense, they can only say no.

It's a beaut, says Dad. But it could do with a wash.

It's true. There's a thick coat of dust on the duco.

We get out of the Zephyr.

Just then a man comes out of the shop with a grease-spotted brown-paper packet. It's the driver of the Jag. And fuck me if it isn't Mark Condor!

I've got a stack of Mark Condor comics at home and here he is standing in front of me. Dad has never read a photocomic in his life and so this unbelievable fact escapes him. Pardon me, he says to the stranger, have you got a minute?

I grab him by the arm. I want to tell him it's Mark Condor but the words don't come out.

Pardon me, he says again. But Mark Condor gets in behind the wheel and slams the door.

Crikey, says Dad. Excuse me for asking. And then the sound of the engine blows away his irritation. Listen to that. There's 250 horses under that hood.

The Jag accelerates out of the lot and goes up Cantonments Road. The spoked wheels look as if they're turning backwards the way they do in Dad's Super 8 films of the races at Zwartkops.

What's wrong with you? Dad says.

I get my voice back and tell Dad who we just saw.

Mark who?

When Joe and I were young enough to play with the boys from the neighbouring yards, we were the secret agents and mercenaries of the photocomics. I was the Saboteur. All I needed was a vest and an old scarf of my gran's to knot around my head. This guy is a sort of commando, although his hair is much too long for the army. Maybe he's a mercenary? He looks like Sylvie's old boyfriend Flip van Jaarsveld.

Joe was always Mark Condor. He's a James Bond of the Highveld, boyishly good-looking and debonair. He drives an E-Type Jag and packs a pistol with a silencer that he took off a dead KGB man. Some desperate father is always calling on him to save his daughter from kidnappers. Or he's got to stop the terrs from laying their hands on the uranium. Or get back the nuclear warhead while resisting the charms of a beautiful cosmonaut who looks like she comes from Boksburg.

We don't have television but we've got photocomics. The black-and-white panels, with captions and speech bubbles, are like storyboards for films. Some of our heroes are home grown, like Sister Louise and the Grensvegter. You can see by the houses and the veld that they were made in South Africa. Others come from overseas. Everyone looks Italian but they're speaking Afrikaans, like in a badly dubbed film. Appearing in a photocomic is not the most glamorous job in showbiz. It's hardly acting: it's more like *posing*. If I thought for a minute, I'd realize that the people in the comics must have other jobs, like wrestlers, this must be a sideline. But still, I no more expect to bump into one of them than I expect to see Our Man Flint – I mean James Coburn – walking down Schoeman Street.

When we get home I tell Joe we just saw Mark Condor. Of course, he doesn't believe me. So I get out the comics.

Dad confirms it. That's the bloke. He looks like one of The Beatles.

George, says Mom. Or maybe Paul. Paul's unmusical cousin.

And that's the car, says Dad.

The E-Type's actually red, I say to Joe.

Fancy that, says Mom.

I hope they wash it first, says Dad, before they take its picture.

It's weird, I say. It looks red to me now even though it's black and white.

What's black and white and red all over? says Joe.

It turns out that our meeting with Mark Condor – or rather the man who plays him – is not such a coincidence: he lives down the road from us. He has a chicken farm in Rabie Street where the suburbs bump up against the smallholdings. I cycle past there on my way to school every morning. There are a couple of low-slung sheds with dirty white walls and corrugated roofs, a house half hidden by a hedge, a moth-eaten horse browsing on the plot. I've never paid the place much attention, until I see the Jag turning in there one day. Now I can't go past without wondering what Mark Condor is up to. Collecting eggs, sweeping out the hoks, wringing necks. Or does he dispatch them silently with the pistol? I know when he's home, because the sleek nose of the Jag sticks out from behind a drinking trough. You can smell the place from a mile away, chicken shit and damp feathers, and when you drive past you have to wind up the windows. Mom always makes a performance of pressing a hankie to her nose. I don't know how the neighbours put up with it, she says, it makes me sick to my stomach.

Dad has a special way of laughing when something incredible has happened, a head-shaking, conspiratorial chuckle that dares you to disbelieve. Jissimpie, he says, wait till you hear this.

He's sitting at the robot in Botha Avenue when the Jag pulls up next to him. It's Mark Condor at the wheel – Dad knows him now – looking straight ahead through his dark glasses. Dad taps the accelerator as if he wants to dice, just a little joke, and glances over.

And what do you think he's got in the back?

A dead body rolled up in a Persian carpet? A ballistic missile? A beautiful heiress wanted by Interpol? No, it's none of these things.

Chicken feed, says Dad, as God is my witness. Two fat streepsakke full of chicken feed. There's a surprising amount of space under that fastback – but kiepiemielies. In an E-Type. He should be shot!

I don't like having Mark Condor around. Now when we buy chicken pies at the farm stall on the Old Joburg Road I wonder if it's Mark Condor chicken. How many people who read the comics know that he's a chicken farmer? Or that the Jag is red and he drives it around in the full-colour world? Maybe that was part of the deal: he could play Mark Condor if he brought his own sports car.

Joe laughs it off. The gap between how things are and how they appear to be doesn't seem to bother him.

Joe

Cassius Marcellus Clay was named for the plantation owner who had emancipated one of his slave ancestors. He was the sixth man in his family to bear the name. In 1964, after he won the WBA and WBC heavyweight titles from Sonny Liston, he took the name 'Cassius X', identifying himself with the Black Power movement, but he soon discarded this in favour of the name bestowed on him by Elijah Muhammad of the Nation of Islam: 'Muhammad Ali.'

Seven years later, when I started following Ali, most of the boxing writers were still calling him 'Cassius Clay'. You would think the headline writers especially would have embraced the new name, happily trading the alliterative potential of 'Cassius' (as in 'Cocky Cassius') or 'Clay' (as in 'Clowning Clay') for the brevity of 'Ali', but they avoided it so routinely that it could only have been an editorial directive.

There were exceptions. The pin-up magazine *Scope* always used 'Ali'. And the mainstream press sometimes made concessions to his new identity. In the *Sunday Times*'s front-page spread on the Fight of the Century, 'Muhammad Ali' appears in brackets after the article's first mention of 'Cassius Clay'. Everywhere else he is 'Clay'.

The tussle over his name reflected the contradictions in his identity and became part of its elusiveness. In the articles that date from the time of his comeback, some writers seem to be grappling with the shift and trying to muster a response, either determined to pin him down or content to let him float. Others just want to keep Cassius Clay in his place. Malcolm Balfour, the *Sunday Express*'s 'Man in Miami', disliked Ali intensely. He calls him the champ and the Great Himself in inverted commas. Railing against Ali's theatrics before the Fight of the Century, he describes a scene at Dundee's gym in Miami where Ali produced an envelope from the pocket of his robe with The Secret of Muhammad Ali printed on it and then took from it a sheet of paper that simply read Flash! Ali said he would fill in the rest of the prediction in his dressing room just before the fight, which he duly did in the company of another great actor, Burt Lancaster. The prediction was that Frazier would fall in six – not one of his best calls. Balfour mocks this flimflam designed to juice up the theatre gate and ends on a sarcastic note: I was one of the 'privileged few' to get a chance to speak to Clay privately, and was immediately reminded, 'Hey man, the name's Ali.'

By contrast, Alan Hubbard, who was well disposed towards Ali, accepted the name change genially. This went along with a different attitude towards the theatricalization and commercialization of boxing (and sport more generally). In an article published by the *Pretoria News* on the day of the fight, in which Hubbard said he was backing Ali because I like my sport with style and flair or even with arrogance, he also referred to the magnificent enigma that is Cassius Clay, or, if you prefer it, Muhammad Ali.

The cuttings in my archive chart the gradual disappearance of 'Clay' from common use. But the two incarnations persist in the rhetorical armoury of reporters, allowing them to express their ambivalent feelings about the man.

In October 1971, between the bouts against Jimmy Ellis and Buster Mathis, a 'Special Correspondent' in London who saw Ali during his 'Drink Ovaltine' advertising campaign felt that he had no real interest in boxing any more. He used the double name to express his disillusionment: I've finally accepted the sad truth – the great Cassius Clay will never box again. Sure enough a podgy businessman called Muhammad Ali will continue to perform against the talent-starved heavyweight hopefuls, but a meeting in London last week convinced me that the magnificent Cass we all knew has faded away.

Joe Frazier shared these sentiments. I almost always refer to Ali as Cassius Clay. He is a has-been. I don't think he can get back in shape.

Sometimes 'Cassius Clay' evoked the early years of his career more happily. Before the Norton rematch in 1973, many writers commented that Ali had not been in better shape for years. One local sportswriter [probably Alan Hubbard] said of him: 'He looks so young I almost called him Cassius Clay.'

For David Wright, the two names reflect two personas, the private and the public. He wonders about the perceptions of the fans who flock to the gyms to watch their idol. Who do they see? Not the sullen Muhammad of the dressing room. Nor the militant Muhammad. They see the Ali they know, the man who is intoxicated by the crowds that bring out the Cassius Clay in him. Perhaps it's even the real Ali. So 'Ali' is a sullen mask and the authentic, attention-seeking persona is 'Cassius Clay'.

To me he was always 'Ali': it's there on the first page of ALI I. But I liked the sound of 'Cassius Clay'. It had a ring to it. My Standard 6 setwork was Shakespeare's *Julius Caesar* and so I'd come across the Roman general Cassius. The alliterative combination with Clay made it seem slightly artificial, like something a writer would make up, and it tripped more musically from my tongue. I didn't much like 'Muhammad' – which is why 'Ali' on its own was always a good option.

As for my father, there were no two ways about it. It's Cassius Clay, he said. That's the name his mother gave him and it's good enough for me.

Branko

The Bakers are a big family. They should start a bakery, we always joke. Taffy who's the eldest left school in Standard 8 and went to work at Iscor, and his youngest sister is still in the grades at primary school. Georgie is in Standard 7, right between Joe and me. He was at primary school with Joe and he sticks to him like chewing gum. As hard as Joe tries to keep out of his way, lurking at the far end of the playground under the cypresses or avoiding the taps, at some point nearly every day he finds Georgie planted in front of him. He has a pudding-bowl haircut, like all his brothers, and black-rimmed glasses.

What's your name, little boy? he asks.

You know my name. I told you yesterday.

No, you have to say it for me today. What's your name?

Joe.

Joe who?

It's not your business.

But it *is* my business, Georgie says.

He clamps one hand around Joe's wrist and leans in close. His breath smells of the condensed milk he had for lunch, squirted down his throat out of a little pyramid-shaped carton. Behind the lenses of his glasses, which are covered with greasy fingerprints, his eyes are boiled sweets sucked down to different sizes. When Joe speaks, as he has to sooner or later, Georgie watches his mouth as if beetles are clambering out of his throat.

Again, he says, again, blinking his gobby eyes and turning up the corners of his pink mouth. Say it again, little boy.

Joe stands there shivering in the spangled robe of his name.

It must be said.

Joe

In the space of a few decades we've come to take access to video records for granted. We expect to see everything that happens happen again, almost instantaneously, repeatedly if necessary. News is global: it flows everywhere like, with, as money. In South Africa in the 1970s, before the advent of television, sports events happened once only, in real time (a term we didn't need). Sport was essentially territorial and expressed the local. To be there you had to be there. Sometimes, but not always, there was radio commentary on an important match. Occasionally you might see a clip or two from an international sports event on a newsreel in the cinema. After a Test series, a commemorative booklet would appear and the vivid images seemed miraculous. But the main record was in the press, in print columns and grainy images.

After major boxing matches, and nearly always after heavyweight title bouts, the newspapers carried a blow-by-blow account of the action. There are half a dozen in my archive. These detailed descriptions of every round allowed a reader who'd missed the radio broadcast to imagine the fight for themselves. Even someone who'd seen the action was able, in the absence of instant replays, highlights packages, podcasts, PVR recordings, websites and camera-phone images, to revisit the fight and refresh their memory or analyse the action. We're unused to this kind of reporting now. After a few paragraphs the account begins to read like the choreography of an obsessive performance artist. How many lefts or rights can be *dug, driven, sent, shot over, steamed in, pumped over, peppered, landed* in a single boxing match? The text engine could be shuffling them at random with the targets: head and body.

On the day after the Fight of the Century, the *Pretoria News* carried a round-by-round reconstruction. Each of the fifteen rounds is described in a paragraph of 150 words or so. Frazier is mentioned 94 times; on one of these occasions he is called 'Joe'. His opponent is mentioned 107 times; he is called 'Ali' 80 times and 'Clay' 27 times. To put it another way, he is 'Ali' three quarters of the time and 'Clay' the remaining quarter.

The effect of this 'elegant variation' is dazzling: as the fight unfolds, one of the boxers magically doubles into two persons, Clay and Ali, while the other, Frazier, is stuck with being himself.

This is from round 4: Ali shot over two more lefts to the head followed by a good left hook and two left jabs to the head. Frazier manoeuvred Clay to the ropes once more but it was Ali who landed at long range. If you didn't know the Queensberry Rules, you would think there were two men in the ring with Frazier, one called 'Clay' who could be cornered and one called 'Ali' who was getting in the telling blows.

And here's round 14, in which Frazier, smelling blood, goes after Clay, but Ali steps in to defend him: Frazier was puffy above both eyes. He walked into two light lefts and rights from Ali. It didn't stop Frazier from going after Clay who again cuffed Frazier with a left and right to the head but took a hard left hook to the body in exchange. Ali shot over a series of lefts and rights to the head landed at long range.

In the end there was no strength in numbers. Frazier won the fight on points.

4

Americans

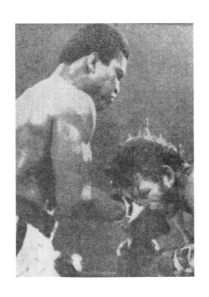

Knitting machines. Many well-known makes. Demonstration models as new. Guaranteed perfect condition. Very low price. Free lessons. Terms arranged. Knitter's Friend, 25 Harvard Building (Cor. Joubert and Pritchard Street) JHB.

– *The World*, September 1972

Branko

A single year brings two big changes: I become a man and my brother becomes an American. My new status is announced by Mrs Mitchell from over the road when she hears that my voice is breaking. My brother's change of nationality is promoted by Jolyon Barlow, a new kid in the neighbourhood who has some experience in the matter. His father is a missionary, a Methodist, and the family has spent a few years in Illinois. When they come back to Pretoria they move into a house in the next block, a place that always looks strange to me because the facebrick walls have been painted white. (Dad agrees: Why would you *paint* a facebrick?) Kids are territorial – we become friends with the neighbours mainly, the kids we share fences with – and the next block is another country. On top of this, Jolyon goes to a private school in the city rather than the local government primary like most of the boys in Clubview. In time, though, he and Joe cross paths at Funchal Caffie and they become friends.

Two lame ducks, you could say. Jolyon is a sad boy with a cheerful name. We call him 'Jolly' although he asks us not to. Some childhood illness kept him in a hospital bed for a year and a half, and although he and my brother are in the same standard, he's older. Also smaller, with blue-black hair and wet sea-green eyes, and an impressive scar all the way down his breastbone. He was opened up, he says, unbuttoning his shirt to show us. When he touches the pale skin on his chest you can almost see through it. I think he's a clot, but Joe needs friends.

In the summer holidays, Jolly starts coming over to our place. Sometimes they ride their bikes through the veld to the old quarry or the fence around the airfield, although Jolly isn't supposed to, he should always be near a telephone in case he collapses and someone has to call an ambulance. Mainly they wage war in the yard with machine guns made from tomato-box pine and spark plugs. Although it seals his fate, Joe agrees to be the Germans so he can use the lines he's picked up in war comics and Alistair MacLean books. Maybe he feels sorry for Jolly too. Our yard makes a good battlefield because of the fruit trees and the crumbly bricks and rusty scaffolding piled up behind the servants' quarters. Jolly's yard is too neatly suburban for warfare, full of delicately flowered ground covers in wavy beds. In any case, it's quiet as a hospital over there. His mother gets migraines and lies on her bed all afternoon with a damp cloth over her face. The rumour is that she's stark naked: her head hurts so much she can't bear to keep her clothes on. Peter Hendricks, who sits next to me in Biology, claims to have had a good look at her through a crack in the shutters. That's another odd thing about the Barlows' house: it has shutters instead of curtains. Something Mr Barlow picked up in America. In this climate? says Dad. He needs his head read.

Now and then I go with my brother to visit Jolly, who's nearly my age and could actually be my friend if he wasn't such a tit. We never set foot in the yard and I never go near the shutters. We sit in his room listening to Elvis Presley records, no rock and roll, just hymns and Christmas carols, and reading comics. Some people think comics are bad for you because they stop you from reading books. Nonsense, Mom says, just look at Joe. We have as many comics as we like, so many we pack them in boxes and keep them under our beds. Jolly's parents think comics are the work of the devil and he's forbidden to read them. Naturally he has a huge collection, which he hides in jigsaw-puzzle boxes and under cricket pads. When we're reading comics in his room, with the Monopoly board open on the rug just in case, it feels like we're doing something daring. You'd think it was *Scope* instead of *Little Lotta*. Sometimes, after I've gone for a slash, I hang around in the darkened passage near the door to the master bedroom hoping to catch a glimpse of Mrs Barlow, imagining I can hear her stretching her naked limbs and smell the fruity perfume on her skin. In her birthday suit, Peter Hendricks said. The phrase gives me a hard-on.

Now Joe comes back from the Barlows with a stack of Archie comics in a tartan togbag and an announcement. He and Jolly have decided to become Americans. They've made a pact. Eventually they plan to go and live in Chicago, which Mr Barlow says is the most American of cities, and they've made a start by changing their names. From now on Jolly will be known as Little Louis Carnovale and Joe as Nate Simms.

At the kitchen table that evening, he tells us the plan and asks us to start using the new name. Nate Simms! Now I see that it smacks of *simulation*: it's the half-real sort of name he would give a character in one of his novels. But then it could only sound preposterous.

Carnovale, says Mom. Isn't he that chap you played football with at the Italian Club, Bo? The one who went out with Dottie Fisher and broke her heart?

What about the rest of us? says Dad. We'll all have to change our names or people won't know we're related. The Simmses have to stick together.

Joe is silent. He hasn't thought this through.

Let's start with Branko, Dad goes on. Suggestions?

Branko Simms, Mom says.

No, no, that won't do. It's un-American. How about Harvey?

Harvey Simms?

Harv for short.

Over my dead body, I say. And we all laugh like crazy.

The idea of becoming an American grows on me, if I'm honest. I'll never be a Harvey, forget it, but I'm happy to play along, using my American vocab and speaking with a twang. Nate and I egg one another on. Howdy pardner. So long bub. At the supper table, Dad joins in. Pass me the ketchup, Harvey Wallbanger. When Mom asks how we're doing, we say, Just swell. Nate tries to carry his library books strapped up in his school belt. It's a stretchy elastic belt and the books keep falling out. Why do American kids do this? Don't they have bags? Mom puts up with all this malarkey. It's not the first time Joe has found a language between the covers of a book and it won't be the last. There was a time when he'd always jis clumb a tree or half drownded hisself. That was the Huck Finn phase. You's the orneriest, block-headedest boy I ever did meet! It was even worse after Philip Marlowe. Dad loses patience quickly, although he's always been a bit of a Yank himself with his Buicks and Chevs and his toolboxes full of spanners made in Detroit.

My brother's game gets to me because I understand his longing. I also want to do American things and own American stuff. Eat hotdogs and drink root beer, hang out at the soda fountain and go to the ball game, live in a suburb where there are no fences between the yards and the kids blaze their own trails across the blocks like frontiersmen. I want a pogo stick, a baseball cap, a fishbowl full of sea-monkeys with little crowns, just add water. Most of all I want a television set. I want to watch TV so badly it hurts.

This surfaces in my mind now: two little boys, two naughty little bastards, one black and one white, climb into a washing machine and are whirled around in the suds.

Where does it come from? Maybe it's Our Gang, a black-and-white flicker on the screen before the main attraction. What else is left in my memory? A boy tilting a slat in a wooden fence, passing through the gap, ghosting across the neighbour's yard like a cat. Huck Finn? No, that would be Joe's story. Let's say Dennis the Menace. It's a fantasy of knowing the territory expressed in a borrowed register. We belong exactly where we find ourselves. We swing over fences as if they're hurdles for our amusement, play kleilat down at Sesmylspruit, come home with pine resin stuck to our shirts, blackjacks in our socks and the new hairs on our calves, we are smeared with the brown dust of our own world. And still we wish we were somewhere else.

America doesn't last. In the new year, the accent fades away, as Mom knew it would, and Nate Simms is forgotten. But I'm reminded of this American boy a few years later when my brother starts with Muhammad Ali. Falls in love? I prefer not to think of it that way.

Then again, my brother's need to be someone else never goes away. He becomes a writer. You can see the catastrophe coming down the pike.

Joe

Without the boxing writers, my love for Muhammad Ali would not have bloomed. You could say I fell in love with the writing rather than the boxing. After all, I never saw Ali box. Everything I knew about him came down the wire; it was all at second hand, on the page.

I loved the boxing writers for their bluster, their bombast, their purple patches as livid as bruises. They were full of rhetoric and hyperbole, grandiose circumlocutions and cock-eyed similes. There was something grand, I decided, about saying 'the busted-beak fraternity' or 'the fistic arts' when you could just have said 'boxing'. Or saying 'a fight-minded individual' when you meant a fan of the sport. Or referring to your fellow hacks as 'the scribes of the fistic kingdom'.

Perhaps the brutality of the 'sport', which some people were putting in quotes even then, encouraged the scribes to reach for figures of speech. Or did the crude repetitions of the fights, the rounds as repetitious as chewing gum, drive the search for new turns of phrase? Every boxing match, every sporting contest, is an original arrangement of the same basic moves. The boxer throws lefts, rights, hooks, straights, jabs in an endless improvisation, trying to impose his own plan on proceedings, but also responding to his opponent's. He bobs and weaves and ducks. The evasive actions are orchestrated with the offensive combinations in a unique sequence and rhythm. The real artists of the ring imbue these moves with their own style. But in the end, two men are hitting one another and avoiding being hit, trying to land their own punches and ride the other man's. How many ways are there to say this? The writer wants to find out. His great tool is metaphor.

Whenever I page through the Ali scrapbooks, in search of a book that always eludes me, I remember reading these reports for the first time and the thrill comes back to me. There must be something in the spectacle of boxing that brings out this ornate yet loose-jointed lingo, where rhetoric is like ringcraft, where you work your sentences like well-oiled combinations and try to land a punchy metaphor on the reader's jaw like a straight left.

For the boxing writers, Ali was a godsend. His extravagance and theatricality fuelled their own, just as his antics in the ring brought out the clown in his opponents. You can see them trying to beat him at his own game. Here is Alan Hubbard describing how Joe Frazier knocked Ali down in the fifteenth round of the Fight of the Century: Clay collapsed in a corner, his legs flying first into the air and then falling grotesquely, like a splintered twin mast of a sinking ship. It's that last-gasp tweak – *twin* mast – that holes the sentence and saves the day.

Branko

My brother has a screw loose. When we first move to Clubview, he sinks into the deep end of the new house. For a while he's nowhere to be found, until we remember that he's underfoot. Like a mechanic on a creeper in the workshop, he's taken to scooting around on his back, propelling himself head first along the shiny wooden floors. He'll go all the way down the passage, in and out of rooms, passing under the beds, butting aside Dad's cardboard suitcase full of receipts and expired licence papers, Mom's slippers, Uncle Eddie's bugle from when he was in the Transvaal Scottish. He barges through the bicycle parts under my bed like an icebreaker. Only the barricade of shoes under Sylvie's bed repels him. Elsewhere it's a free run. He can make an entire circuit of the lounge, sliding beneath one armchair and then the sofa and then another chair on the narrow channel of gleaming parquet between the rug and the skirting boards. What's he doing down there? Examining the undersides of things, discovering what holds the furniture together, finding a new perspective from the bottom of the world.

The lounge suite is ball-and-claw with cushions that are red on one side and green on the other. Dad must have chosen this robotic colour scheme (we say) because Mom never learnt to drive. Something to do with her nerves. Now Joe surfaces to reveal the signs we can't see: the carpenter's code of numbers and arrows on the unvarnished struts of the chairs.

Mom tries to break the backsliding habit because he gets polish on the back of his shirt and the seat of his pants. Dad just thinks it's wrong to be hanging around in the shallows like a sea creature. One of those sand sharks with eyes in the top of its head. He's helping Mom with the housework, I say. It's a joke, but he does lend her a hand during the school holidays, running the chrome-plated polisher with its hammer-head and wheezing canvas lung over the floors. Would a normal boy enjoy such a thing?

After a few years, Dad has wall-to-wall laid over the parquet and that puts an end to the polishing. The wooden suite goes too, replaced by a softer one covered in old-gold velveteen with buttons and fringes, better suited to our modern life in the suburbs.

When Mom acquires a knitting machine, Joe can make himself

useful again. The machine is set up in the dining room, which is seldom used for dining or anything else, because the dresser beside the table makes it impossible to pull out a chair. The machine has a long bed of needles and two wire feelers that the wool's threaded through to keep the tension. There's a sliding carriage with a handle that must be swept up and down over the needles. That's how the knitting happens. We're used to Mom's knitting needles and crochet hooks, but she looks odd at the machine, hunched over like the driver of a front-end loader. There's craft in this machine work too, she's figured out how to thread the needles and set the buttons and dials that make the pattern, but mainly it's a way of eking out the household income. Dad went in over his head moving us out to the suburbs, but it had to be done. The economy is booming and we'd damn well better boom with it. White people have never had it so good. Mom sits at the machine for eight hours a day. When we leave for school in the morning she's headed to the knitting room with the transistor radio and a mug of coffee, and when we get back in the afternoon she's still there, with an empty mug and an ashtray full of stompies, and the front or back of a jersey hanging down from the needles. The machine can be set up to make pictures, so there might be a snowman or a Model T Ford inching out of it, row by row.

She knits until she rubs the skin off her fingertips and drips blood on a new cardigan. Then she makes thimbles of Elastoplast for her fingers. When Sylvie wants a pair of boots from Foschini, when I want a saddle for my bike, Dad says: Can't you see your mother is working her fingers to the bone?

The machine is supposed to be perfect but it's not. There isn't enough play in the tension arms and the wool snares on the needles.

Stitches are dropped and rows unravel. One mistake spoils an hour's work. Dad keeps tinkering with the mechanism, adding loops of insulation tape like Band-Aids and guy lines of copper wire and gut threaded with lead sinkers from his tackle box, until Joe solves the problem. In the afternoons, after he's done his homework, he perches on a bar stool between the spools and the feelers, with the yarn looped around his forefingers. His fingers waggle as if he's an insect, letting out some yarn here, taking up the slack there, holding the balance. Now there's scarcely a stoppage. Mother's little worker ant, annoyingly busy and obliging.

One afternoon when Tim Knowles from over the road is nowhere to be found and I'm bouncing a soccer ball on the garden path alone, trying to outplay myself, I hear the machine at work. Each pass of the carriage across the bed is a long ragged gasp. It's the sound Grandpa Reilly made in the ward at the HF Verwoerd before he died. I look through the net curtain into the dining room. Mom has her back to me, leaning forward with her feet planted in the wall-to-wall, her shoulders spread, hands floating. Joe is facing me but his eyes are turned inward. He waggles his fingers like a conductor or (it comes to me now) a two-finger typist who can do sixty words a minute.

Joe

I did not fall out of love with Ali when he lost to Frazier. To my credit, I became a bigger fan than ever. All through 1971 and 1972, I stuck with him as he fought his way back into contention for the major titles. In this period he held the NABF title but not the WBA or WBC.

Ali's first comeback fight was against his former sparring partner Jimmy Ellis at the Astrodome in Houston on 26 July 1971. Before the fight, Ali entertained an audience of fight fans, mothers and children by miming his way through the final round of the Fight of the Century, exaggerating the details to the point of parody, bobbing, weaving, shuffling and shooting out his famed left jab. This variety-hall act included the left hook from Frazier that knocked him down. (Ali opened up with two fast lefts and a right to the head. Frazier dropped Clay with a left hook to the jaw, but he was up at four and was given the mandatory eight count.)

A reporter asked him how he would feel if by some miracle Ellis were to win.

I wouldn't feel bad, he replied quietly, because it would be a miracle.

A miracle was not forthcoming. Ali won the fight on a TKO in the final round.

Four months later, he fought Buster Mathis at the same venue. The fight went the full twelve rounds and Ali won a unanimous points decision, but it was obvious to reporters that he had held back from knocking Mathis out. Questioned about this, Ali said: I'm a religious man ... I don't believe in killing a man just to satisfy a few people. He also pointed out that Mathis was a family man with a nice son and that his wife was at the ringside. Should I kill a man, a Black brother, in front of them? But it wasn't just about Mathis, as this comment made clear: I just can't get mad at anyone anymore ... The more I fight, the more I realize how silly it is, two men beating each other up.

The Mathis reports mention Ali's forthcoming fight with Jürgen Blin in Zürich, but the archive doesn't contain a single cutting about the event itself. Of the 22 fights Ali had between October 1970 and October 1975, this is the only one that left no trace.

In the course of 1972, Ali fought six times, and half of these fights took place in foreign cities. Professional boxing was becoming a global business.

The first of the fights was against Mac Foster in Tokyo on 1 April. It took place in the Martial Arts Hall and it was the first professional heavyweight boxing match ever held in Japan. Apparently Ali was still finding boxing silly. In the seventh round, according to one report, he appeared to be deliberately allowing Foster to hit him. Ali had predicted that he would knock Foster out in round 5, but the fight went the distance and he won on points.

On May Day 1972 he fought George Chuvalo in Vancouver. Again he predicted a knockout, but went on to win on points over twelve rounds. The fight could easily have ended earlier: sometimes Ali appeared to be toying with his opponent. Afterwards Ali's hands were badly bruised. He explained it to a reporter: Chuvalo's head is the hardest thing I have ever punched.

Next up was Jerry Quarry. Quarry had been Ali's first opponent after his licence was restored and the rematch at the Las Vegas Convention Center was charged with exceptional animosity. At the medical check-up in the Tropicana Casino, Ali shouted at Quarry: I'm told you don't like Coloured people. And he told reporters: This isn't going to be just a race war, it's going to be a riot. He called me a nigger. Quarry denied the accusation. In any event, what rioting there was occurred in the venue after the fight, which Ali won on a TKO in round 7. Two brawls broke out in the crowd, one of them involving the entire Quarry family, including his mother Awanda, his sister Diane and his son-in-law Robert Coobaugh, who was arrested.

Afterwards Ali shouted, Bring on Joe Frazier. I'm ready for him now. But it would be more than eighteen months before he got his wish.

On the immediate horizon was a fight with Al 'Blue' Lewis at Croke Park in Dublin. Lewis, who was from Detroit, had spent eleven of his 29 years in prison, including a stretch for second-degree murder. The *Pretoria News* ran a four-part series by Alan Hubbard in which he described Ali's reception in Dublin. The visit had been vigorously endorsed by the Irish Tourist Board and the Irish public were thrilled to see him, especially when it was revealed that one of his great-grandfathers was an O'Grady. With this Irish ancestry, Ali might want to kiss the Blarney Stone, Hubbard wrote, and warned: They had better be careful that he doesn't swallow it.

The O'Grady story delighted me. I had Irish blood in my veins too. My grandfather Tommy Reilly arrived in Pretoria via Birmingham before the Great War. When he was asked about his name, he always said: I left the O in Ireland.

Crowds turned up to watch Ali spar and he kept them entertained with his call-and-response routines:

Who is the greatest?
You are!
Are you for bad old Blue Lewis?
No.
Are you for Muhammad Ali?
Yes.
Said Hubbard: The pantomime season has arrived five months

early in Dublin. On stage every day at Croke Park, Muhammad Ali is giving a matinée performance as a big, black Buttons. (Hubbard was referring to the servant in the Cinderella panto who always insults the ugly sisters.) Blue Lewis, kept waiting in the wings for an hour and a half, was not amused: Listen to that crap. He's not a fighter, he's an actor.

Ali told reporters he was the only man alive who could stop under a lamppost in any city on earth and the kids would know who he was. That may not sound humble. But it's hard to be humble when you're as good as I am. The story echoed an earlier one from his childhood. His father had shown him a telephone pole where Joe Louis once leant for five whole minutes talking to the people. The great champion of the 1940s was always a marker. Ali joked that he looked just like Joe Louis in his cradle.

The Irish were not quite ready for a global boxing extravaganza. The timekeeper, a bespectacled old man with an ancient stopwatch, kept allowing the rounds to run on past the three minutes. Whether he needed the extra time or not, Ali toyed with Lewis and in the eleventh round the referee stepped in. Gracious, or grateful, in defeat, Lewis followed Ali to his corner and lifted him up into the air.

Hubbard's series fills the last pages of my first scrapbook. In these articles, Ali talks about being ready to fight Frazier. He also mentions South Africa. See how everybody wants to meet me. Black, White, Jewish, Muslim, Protestant or Catholic. They want me in Peking. They want me in Estonia, Russia. They want me in South Africa. I'm just blessed to draw crowds.

Branko

Goofy attaches himself to us on the road to East London, easing in through the car window along with Mickey, Minnie and other furry animals. Every year when white families head for the coast on their Christmas holidays, the petrol stations hand out cheap collectables to the kids to attract business. Last year when we went to Margate it was pictures of Formula 1 cars and drivers. The year before – Margate again – tinny medallions showing the high points in the history of aviation, from the Wright Brothers to Apollo 11. This summer, with the Munich Olympics coming up, it's stickers of Disney characters representing the sporting codes. I was half interested in the medallions, but I'm too old for ducks in tracksuits. Sylvie, as Mom keeps saying, has only one interest and that's boys. So we leave Goofy and the gang to Joe.

East London is Dad's idea. The rest of us want to go back to Margate, to the same old caravan park and the same old beach. We're quite happy with the shows at the Palm Grove, where Tony Feeb and the Forbidden Fruit play all the stuff on the hit parade and a comedian does 'I'm My Own Grandpa' and 'Jake the Peg' just like Rolf Harris. Last year Sylvie entered Miss Lucky Legs and came second. We were proud of her even though it's a bit scaly checking out your own sister. The main beach has a grass terrace where Dad can sit on a camping chair and not get sand between his toes. When Joe and I go to the beach on our own we put our towels by the wall so I can sit up and watch the girls in bikinis and also keep an eye on my brother in the water with his hired bellyboard. He's got to be watched every second because he can't swim properly, but half the time I'm lying on my stomach to hide my boner and I don't have eyes in the back of my head (like Mom). Once he vanishes completely and I think he's gone and drownded hisself, but then I spot him way out beyond the breakers, not waving for help or anything because that would be embarrassing, just stuck to the bellyboard like a leech. I'm no banana boy and the thought of going so far out to save him is scary. Just when I'm about to call a lifesaver, a long-haired surfer takes him in tow and paddles him back towards the shore. He comes out of the surf shivering like a half-drowned puppy, but he says nothing and I can't even shit on him in case he tells the folks.

We always go to the South Coast with the rest of the Vaalies: the Cape is another country and we don't want to discover it. But we need to learn more about our beautiful land, Dad says. This year it's East London or nothing. It's very nearly nothing. Dad has bought a new caravan, a new second-hand Gypsey at a good price, voetstoots. The bargain becomes clearer when we put up the side tent in the back yard and discover that it has a canopy but no walls. Now what? The van only has four berths and I'm supposed to sleep on a stretcher in the tent. No problem. Dad goes off to a factory in Pretoria North and buys thirty yards of striped green canvas.

Pats, can you run something up for us? he says. It can't be all that different to making a dress.

For two days and two nights Mom sits at her sewing machine. The canvas is too thick to fit under the foot of the machine and she breaks a dozen needles. Most of it has to be done by hand. In the end her fingers are bleeding from forcing a darning needle through the fabric. We all pitch in with Dad supervising. He's found a gadget for punching holes through canvas and attaching brass eyelets.

I challenge anyone to find fault with this tent, he says. Five gets you ten they'll say *this* one was made in a factory.

The tent looks a bit weird because the walls don't match the roof, but it doesn't really matter in the municipal caravan park at Orient Beach because there are half a dozen home-made caravans around us, including one that used to be a horsebox. Some of the makeshift tents make ours look very professional, as Dad promised.

What the hell is that? It must have been made by a drunken Bedouin.

Who needs a Winnebago when you've got a tent like this?

It rains. The canopy leaks and I wake up soaked. After a couple of miserable nights, I move into the van and sleep on a lilo in the space between the wardrobe and the galley. It's so cramped no one can get out to pee in the ablution block. It also ruins my plan to sneak out when everyone is asleep and screw some suntanned girl in the dunes. I have a beach towel rolled up and ready to go: Porky Laing says if you get a single grain of sand on your cock it feels like a boulder, so you have to take precautions. In the middle of the night, with the rain drumming on the skylight and the wind rocking the van on its landing legs, the occasional spray of salt water blasting in through the air vents, it's like we're on a boat somewhere, tossing about in a storm.

It's not beach weather. The wind whips sand against your legs and into your eyes. Dad uses the ploegskaar braai in the side tent even though Mom says he's going to splash fat all over everything. Sometimes we get pies for supper from the beach caffie and sometimes we eat at the Wimpy. The same waiter helps us every time.

He's adopted us, Mom says. We're like a family to him.

Ja, he's giving us extra ice cream in the banana splits.

It's a lovely gesture, especially because he's a deaf mute.

When Dad tips him a ten-cent piece, he claps his hands and sticks the coin in the middle of his forehead, where it stays while he's clearing off the table. We all laugh like crazy. How does he do it? Mom won't let us try it in the restaurant, we're not a bunch of gommies from Gezina, but when we get back to the caravan she gives us each a coin from her purse and we try sticking it on our forehead. After a few seconds it falls off.

It's a special skill, Mom says.

East London is a terrible place. The only people who go on holiday there are poor whites from Stutterheim and King William's Town who can't afford to go to Durban. We've never had such a pathetic time. We drive around to the sights. There aren't that many: after we've been to the lighthouse and the lagoon, and twice to the harbour to see the ships, Dad takes us out to the industrial areas to look at the factories. South Africa is making great progress in manufacturing. Especially in the border areas, although there's not really a border there.

Then we come back to the caravan and sit around. Sometimes we play rummy and general knowledge and sometimes we listen to the radio. If the sun comes out for an hour we go to the beach and by the time we get there it's clouded over. The caravan park is a flat field of kikuyu with some stunted trees growing sideways into the interior. There's a recreation room with a ping-pong table and one day I meet a girl there from the horsebox caravan. Her name is Estelle and her brother doesn't like me talking to her. She's got beautiful legs, as far as I can see, she could easily be in the Miss Lucky Legs competition if there was such a thing at Orient Beach, it's just a pity she broke one of them playing netball. She can't go anywhere, so I sit there talking to her. She's got her plaster cast up on a chair and I see her panties with Mickey Mouse on them. On the second day of keeping her company she lets me kiss her and puts her tongue in my mouth. I've practised French kissing on the back of my hand but I didn't imagine it would be like a small wet animal over your lips. I put my hand on her thigh, on the smooth skin above the plaster cast, which has a peace sign on it and messages in Afrikaans, and she doesn't seem to mind. But just as I touch the soft warm cloth where the Mouse must be, her brother comes in and challenges me to ping-pong. He beats me hollow and calls me a useless rooinek. I'd like to punch him one, but I just slink back to the caravan. At least we're not living in a bloody horsebox.

It's not as bad as it sounds, actually, with the rain on the fibreglass shell of the van and the kettle boiling on the gas ring and the plastic coffee mugs decorated with the stamps of the world. We go on doing the things we do at home, but more carefully because there's so little space, and it all feels more important. Everyone's more considerate. We feel like a happy family: I wish we could live here for ever. Mom spends a lot of time on Sylvie's hair, not rolling it up so that it will curl, which is what we're used to, but stretching it out with tongs to make it straight in the sea air. Curls are out. She's met a boy on the beach, a long-haired hippie who's doing a BCom at Wits, and everything must be perfect. The weather gives Joe an excuse to read even more than usual. He finds three Simon Templars in the book exchange on the beachfront, rare ones he never saw in the Transvaal, and he swears they were left here by sailors on shore leave. It's possible: the corners of the covers are curled up and the pages are covered with rust spots.

Dad lies on the stretcher in the tent with a Lion Lager balanced on the gas bottle beside him. The grass is wet and everything is standing on something else. This is the life, he says, this tent would stand up in a gale. He can live without the beach anyway, he doesn't like getting sand in his shoes. Once he buys the *Daily Dispatch*, but it's full of liberal rubbish and so he reads his *Car* magazine instead, studying the prices of new cars and used ones, plotting his next purchase.

Christmas lunch is not as fancy as when we're at home. Mom can't make a trifle because the fridge is too small, but we have a slap-up braai. We pull crackers and wear paper crowns. Dad says the meal is fit for a king and we laugh like crazy because of the crown. Afterwards he makes a speech about how we should always take care of one another. Things are about to change: Sylvie has finished school and when we get back to Pretoria she's going to work at the Perm. This is the last holiday we'll all be together.

On 26 December 1971, Ali fights Jürgen Blin in the Hallenstadion in Zürich. For a change, Ali is actually boxing instead of clowning around: maybe someone told him it's Boxing Day. He knocks the German out in the seventh round, his first knockout victory since returning to the ring. But we're on holiday and no one is paying attention to the news. The fight comes and goes without a trace. And that's why there's nothing in my brother's archive about Jürgen Blin. If he was here, I could explain it to him.

Joe

ALI II is another Eclipse drawing book with its pages separated by sheets of tracing paper. It's slightly smaller than the first scrapbook and so the cuttings are even more elaborately folded and collocated. The tail ends of stories continued on an inside page are sometimes stapled to the main cutting. Occasionally the chronology has been broken to fill an awkward space and this makes it difficult to trace a story through the yellowed newsprint.

My handiwork on the cover is more ambitious: ALI II is printed in blocky Koki-pen shadow caps. The shadows stretch up and back as if a light is shining on them from the bottom left-hand corner. Beside the title is a laminated sticker showing Goofy in boxing gear. He has his gloves up and is leading with the left. His white trunks have a red stripe down the side and his boots each have three stripes on the instep. You might expect a boxer to show a bare torso, but he's wearing a red T-shirt, as befits a cartoon character. Questions of modesty aside, cartoonists usually obscure the anatomical details of their anthropomorphic critters. What on earth would Minnie Mouse have under her blouse? In place of paws the half-humans have hands with opposable thumbs, so they can answer the telephone and eat with a knife and fork. Under the boxing gloves Goofy must be wearing another pair, white and three-fingered.

The first cutting in ALI II also happens to be a cartoon. It's an advert for Cassius Extra Fine Brandy. A boxer sits on a café chair, legs crossed, holding a glass in one big brawler's mitt. Perhaps he's just finished a sparring session? Unlike Goofy, he is bare to the waist and some wiry hairs are sprinkled on his chest. With his lumpy, busted beak of a nose and cauliflower ears, he looks a bit like Henry Cooper. On the spindly table beside him is a man-sized bottle of Cassius brandy – the only photographic image in a world composed of lines of ink – and he looks at it warily, as if he's met his match. The caption floats above his head: …mmm this Cassius has got punch!

Speculation that Ali would visit South Africa arose in the middle of 1972 and continued into the following year. A handful of cuttings on this subject occur out of chronological order at the start of the second scrapbook. In an article headlined 'Ali: A serious non-political fight', Ali spoke about a forthcoming fight in Johannesburg against Negro boxer Al Jones. Nothing came of it.

Some time later, at the beginning of 1973, Theo Mthembu (one of two black journalists in the archive) reported that Muhammad Ali (Cassius Clay) would definitely hold two exhibition bouts against Jimmy Ellis in Southern Africa. The fights were scheduled for the Somhlolo Stadium, Mbabane (21 April) and the Lesotho National Stadium, Maseru (23 April). The purses and travel arrangements had already been finalized: Ali would touch down at Jan Smuts Airport on 17 April en route to Swaziland, where five new chauffeur-driven cars would be placed at the disposal of his retinue. But these logistical certitudes were not enough to make the visit happen.

In September 1972, Ali fought Floyd Patterson at Madison Square Garden (this is the first actual fight covered in the second scrapbook). They had met once before, in 1965. Despite his professed admiration for Patterson, a boyhood idol who was now 37 years old and past his prime, Ali's comments were laden with sarcasm: He's what you call a White House boy. The bitter wordplay rested on the fact that Patterson and his family had recently met President Nixon. He's a good American, that's all, a real good American Negro. He don't bother nobody, just a nice fella. He's humble, has a real spiritual, righteous attitude. He's a real gentleman. The mockery continued in the ring, with Ali clowning around, at one point adopting such an exaggerated crouch that Patterson had to punch down at him. The ringside doctor stopped the fight at the end of the seventh, judging that Patterson's left eye was too badly cut for him to continue.

Two months later, Ali met Bob Foster at the Sahara Casino on Lake Tahoe, Nevada. The fight took place in the High Sierra nightclub before a crowd of just 1 700, but it was broadcast on closed-circuit and satellite TV in one hundred North American cities and twenty foreign countries. Technology was changing spectator sport fundamentally. As the Madison Square Garden matchmaker Teddy Brenner commented: Ali could box Bozo the Clown and draw a crowd. There is not much in the archive about the Foster fight, which Ali won by a knockout in the seventh. According to a report in the Afrikaans daily the *Hoofstad*, Foster, who was a policeman, had become famous in 1969 when he gave his own wife a traffic ticket.

For nearly two years (as long as I had been following Ali) the boxing press had been focused on the imagined rematch between Ali and Frazier. Ali himself was always talking up this fight, accusing Frazier of hiding from him and urging the press to smoke him out. Call him yellow, call him a coward. But after Foreman beat Frazier in Kingston in January 1973, the focus shifted to an Ali-Foreman title bout, which the press dubbed 'The Fight That Had to Be'. Foreman's demolition of Frazier had been brutal: he knocked him down six times before the fight was stopped in the second round. Several boxing experts declared that the referee's intervention had saved Frazier's life. Despite Ali's showboating – he claimed that Frazier had never recovered from their previous fight – a myth quickly sprang up around the noble and savage new heavyweight champion of the world. Foreman, the devout Christian and patriot, would put an end to Ali's money-making antics and restore the integrity of heavyweight boxing.

Ali laughed it off. Who needs it? It was a question some of his fans must have been asking. I doubt I saw it at the time, but when I read the reports now his heart does not seem to be in boxing.

Ali's next fight was against Joe Bugner at the Las Vegas Convention Center in February 1973. Ali wore a spangled robe given to him by Elvis Presley, and Sammy Davis Jr and Diana Ross were at the ringside. He had predicted that the British fighter would be in heaven, in round seven, but the fight went the full twelve rounds and Ali won on points. Alan Hubbard observed that Ali could have knocked Bugner out but deliberately extended the contest so as not to destroy a young fighter. The same thing had happened during the Mathis fight. Apparently Ali was concerned to give a good account of himself. Afterwards he asked reporters: Was it a good fight? Was there enough action for you?

Now for Ken Norton. The fight, scheduled for the end of March in San Diego, would set up the inevitable title fight with George Foreman. It had to be.

5

Silence

Did Ali nearly have feet of Clay?

Two miners killed

Johannesburg – Two African mine workers were killed in a fall of hanging on 50-level of the Westonaria Gold Mine today, a spokesman for Johannesburg Consolidated Investments announced here. The men's next of kin have not yet been informed. – Sapa

– *Pretoria News*, February 1973

Joe

On 31 March 1973, Ali suffered the second loss of his professional career when he was outpointed by Ken Norton over twelve rounds in San Diego. Norton broke Ali's jaw in the first round and his corner wanted him to retire at the end of the second, when the damage became evident, but he stubbornly fought on. Afterwards he underwent a ninety-minute operation to put his jaw back together and wire it shut.

It's incredible that he carried on, I told my father.

Say goodbye to Gaseous Cassius, he said. That loudmouth finally got what was coming to him.

My father's antipathy for Ali pleased me in some way. I understood that my allegiance had settled on the wrong hero and that this gave me some clout. Dad did not tolerate backchat from his children. Don't give me a thousand words, he would say. Don't give me a lot of lip. Like most white men of his generation, he also did not expect to be questioned by women or black people, and it did not often happen. Now the Louisville Lip was more full of chat, back and front, than any man alive. This mouthing-off riled Dad, and the more riled he got, the more I liked it.

Ali riled the boxing writers too, but they couldn't stop writing about him. When he lost to Norton their schadenfreude was palpable. He can't talk! He's speechless! They devoted reams of newsprint to the defeat. I pored over these articles, returning again and again to the same photographs.

The first shows Ali leaving the ring after the decision, bruised and dazed, passing his tongue over his lips as if he wants to speak but his mouth is dry. He is leaning on Bundini Brown, whose face is crumpling.

Or perhaps he's already burst into tears – that could be the trace of a tear down his cheek. A smaller photograph above this one shows a beaming Ken Norton, handsome as a movie star and aglow with good health. The caption says that San Diego's hometown hero employed the services of a hypnotist before the fight. That's the power of positive thinking for you!

The third photograph, which now seems to echo out of an unknowable future, is more troubling. It shows Norton visiting Ali in the San Diego Hospital. The victor looks at ease in an open-necked shirt, with huge seventies collar and turned-back cuffs, and teardrop shades. His belt has a large flashy buckle. He stands at Ali's bedside with the fingers of his right hand resting lightly on the bed rail. Ali lies on his side, propped up on the pillows amid rumpled sheets. His face is grossly swollen. He looks like an oversized schoolboy who's come down with the mumps.

The scribes were always ready to think the worst: it was in their headline-chasing, deadline-twisted DNA. The papers were full of speculation, some of it sad and some of it gleeful, that Ali's career was over. An article in the *Pretoria News* under the headline 'End of the road for Ali? Bright flame goes out' carried the pronouncements of doom from Fleet Street. Neil Allen in *The Times* said that as Dr Ferdie Pacheco led Ali from the ring at the end of the fight, he uttered these agonized words: *He can't talk, he can't talk.* Desmond Hackett of the *Daily Express* put it bluntly: *This is the end of the Muhammad Ali era.* He worried that Ali would return to the ring as just another has-been. In Hackett's view, Ali did not stand a hope in hell against an explosive man like the world champion, George Foreman. He might even be beaten by Joe Frazier.

Colin Hart, writing in the Johannesburg *Sunday Times*, said the blow that broke Ali's jaw also smashed a legend into fragments and made Ken Norton as famous and feared as the man who shot Liberty Vallance [sic]! In the more emotional parts of the world, he went on, Ali's Black brothers, who often treated him as a Messiah, will be mourning today as if the man – and not the myth – had died. As much as he loved and admired Ali, Hart expressed the hope that the next time he is able to speak it will be to announce his retirement ...

It's hard to say why Hart referred to Liberty Valance. John Ford's Western, in which a principled but hapless senator is credited with killing a ruthless gunslinger when in fact he was shot by a more capable rancher, is about the persistence rather than the demise of myth. A reporter who uncovers the truth about the story decides to conceal it, uttering the well-known line: 'When the legend becomes fact, print the legend.'

Norman Canale, the most vitriolic of the local sportswriters, could not help gloating: Quite obviously the former world heavyweight champion and a fighter whose name was on everybody's lips – never more so than his own – is washed up as a world title contender. Canale sought the support of Chris Lessing, a local boxing fan and collector who had met Ali the previous year and hated him with a passion. Lessing said Ali might yet fight some corpses from the fistic graveyard, but he would never be a drawcard again. Asked who the best boxers of all time were, he said he wouldn't have Ali in his top ten at any price.

The consensus was that Ali had been *silenced* rather than beaten. Every reporter had to make the point that for the first time in his career Ali was unable to talk. Ali, who for 13 years has been wired for sound, lies in a hospital bed wired for silence … Boxing's biggest mouth will be shut for six weeks … So for once Ali … couldn't speak his mind.

Boxing writers like nothing better than a pun. It is almost a punch, after all. While the scribes were throwing puns left, right and centre, the subeditors went reeling, positively pun-drunk, from one headline to another: 'Muhammad Ali speechless' … 'Injury puts muzzle on Ali' … 'Unspeakable defeat – words fail Ali.'

The thought that Ali might not box again dismayed me, not least because I would never hear the end of it from my father and brother. Amid all the sob stories, I was reassured by one dissenting article under the headline 'Broken jaw hasn't crossed Ali's wires'. According to this piece by an unnamed reporter, even a broken jaw and a mouthful of wire hasn't stopped Muhammad Ali talking. People who'd visited him in hospital said his verbal sparring was as sharp as ever: 'The Mouth' is still as quick with a ready quip as a left jab. Asked whether he was still able to speak, a nurse said, Oh heavens yes. He talks through clenched teeth. A photographer who was present during Norton's visit corroborated this: Ali, speaking through an almost closed mouth, lectured his conqueror on saving money and keeping away from fast women.

Ali's loss to Norton scuttled all the plans for a title fight with Foreman, on which a huge amount of money was riding – and not just for the boxers. It put Joe Frazier, who had lost his title to Foreman a few months earlier, back in the picture. Frazier was at the ringside in San Diego and couldn't wipe the smile off his face.

Branko

I'm rifling through Joe's schoolbag when I come across the shoes. He's gone to Funchal Caffie to buy potatoes or bread for Mom and the canvas bag is lying on his bed with books spilling out of it. It has a peace sign and some other stuff written on it in faded Koki – Jimi Hendrix, Monty Python, What, Me Worry? He would have covered the whole thing with crap like this but the Boss – that's the headmaster – made a rule that says you can't write anything on your bag. He wanted us all to get new ones but the folks said no. So it went in a tin bath with a cupful of Jik. Anyway the bag is lying there asking to be examined. He's my little brother and I need to see what he's carrying around. You never know. Last month it was a copy of *Sex Manners for Men* that Frank Burger found in his dad's wardrobe and was renting out to his classmates on overnight loan for twenty cents a shot. All those sticky little fingers. I had to pick the thing up with a tissue. And once I found a photograph of Julianne Swart when she was in the drum majorettes, which is how I know he's got the hots for her, even though she's going steady with a boy at the Tech who has a car. And there's always the usual stuff: balls of wax paper smeared with cheese spread, a Fanta Orange yoyo, a two-day-old Chelsea bun.

But I don't expect this: shoes. Shoes with a history. They're the school shoes that the dog chewed up. Buster was a stray that pitched up one day and moved in with us. We were a one-dog family, and we already had Cassie, but Sylvie made a song and dance about it and so he stayed. Cassie didn't seem to mind. I've never seen such a stupid mutt, Dad said, and I knew a few on the farm, believe me. Buster's main problem was that he had retriever blood in his mongrel veins. That's what we decided anyway. He kept bringing things home. Things like Mrs Mitchell's favourite jersey which she was drying on a table in her own yard. On the way home he dragged it through a rose bush and then through the hole he'd dug under the fence. Mom knitted Mrs Mitchell a replacement, but it wasn't quite the same as the original, which she'd bought at Debenhams in Leicester and brought all the way to Pretoria with her.

Another time he retrieved one of Mr Burt's clivias. Our neighbour kept his prize plants in a little makeshift greenhouse. Buster fetched the pot in his jaws and shook it out on the front lawn. Then he lay there chewing the roots.

That dog is wicked, Mom said. He's got the devil in him.

He just needs to be trained, said Sylvie. She loves dogs and she's read a book on animal behaviour.

I think he's beyond help, Mom said. Something has to be done.

Buster loved chewing things, shoes, chair legs, rose bushes, tyres. He even found the tennis ball Dad put over the tow bar on the car and chewed that to pieces.

When we got in from school one day he was gone. Joe went all over the neighbourhood, as far as Yale Avenue, calling under hedges and over gates, but there was no sign of him.

He's run away, Dad said, buggered off as suddenly as he came. He'll have attached himself to some other suckers by now. Good luck to them.

But then Sylvie, who was in on the lie all along, let slip that Dad had taken Buster to the SPCA. Where he'd been put down, no doubt. Who would want such an ugly dog? Joe was beside himself with rage and grief. I heard him kicking things to pieces behind the servants' quarters, sobbing and cursing, words I didn't think he knew, threatening Mom and Dad with terrible violence.

It couldn't go on, Mom said. I'm sorry for your brother, but really that dog was making our name mud.

As it happens, the last straw was the shoes, which he chewed to pieces a couple of days before he was dispatched. I know for a fact that those shoes were thrown in the rubbish bin and a new pair bought to replace them. But here the old ones are in Joe's schoolbag.

I'm an old hand at this big-brother stuff. I put everything back in the bag just the way I found it and keep the discovery to myself. The next morning, before Joe goes to school – we used to cycle together but he's leaving early these days, he says he's meeting his friends before class – I check out the footwear. He's wearing the new shoes. Cheap ones from Edworks because times are tough. Dad's having trouble paying off the new Zodiac. Later that day, at first break, I go looking for Joe. Usually we avoid one another at school, he's under instructions not to come within a fifty-metre radius, but I've got business with him. I find him on the pavilion behind the tuck shop eating a jam doughnut. Of course, he's wearing the old shoes. Sneaky little bastard.

Nice shoes, I say, sitting down beside him. He nearly jumps out of them, which wouldn't be hard because there's so little left of them. They look like the dog's breakfast. There's a big chunk of leather out of the back of the left one and tooth marks all over the right. Why the hell are you wearing those? You should be ashamed of yourself. What will people think of us?

The story spills out of him. He hates the new shoes. For one thing they're made of plastic – patent leather, I correct him – and the toes are pointed. He looks like a ducktail from Danville in those things. They're an odd sort of brown – it's true – like watered-down Milo. He's polished them with Kiwi military tan but it's only made things worse. Also the shoes are a size too big for him. They were bought that way so he can grow into them. This still isn't the worst. The main problem is that they squeak when he walks. There's nothing he can do about it. Every step produces a squeal. He tries to tread softly, but that just turns the squeal up at the end, as if the shoes are asking questions. It's totally embarrassing. He complained about the shoes in the shop but Mom insisted. So when they got home, he retrieved the old pair from the rubbish bin. He carries them to school every day and changes on the rugby field before the bell goes. And he changes back into the new ones before he goes home.

This is madness! You can't go around in these broken old things. Dad will kill you if he finds out.

He won't find out if you don't say anything.

The next time there's an inspection before assembly one of the prefects will notice. He'll send you to the office.

At second break, we meet again on the pavilion and he brings the new shoes in a brown-paper bag. He puts them on and walks up and down.

I can't hear a thing.

You're not listening properly, he says. And he paces up and down more slowly, heel and toe, heel and toe, trying to squeeze a sound out of the soles. Still nothing.

You're imagining it. They don't look great, you've got a point, but they're not squeaking. It just looks that way.

It's too noisy here. And this grass is muffling the sound. When it's quiet in class you can hear it easily. Last Monday Shillington called me to the board to do an equation and you should have heard it then. People thought there was a mouse somewhere. Shillo nearly bliksemed me for messing around.

Enough. Sit down and eat your sarmies.

It can't last. He keeps swapping shoes for a couple of weeks. Then he gets careless and leaves the old shoes under his bed, where Mom finds them. She hits the roof. This time they go into the rubbish and out to the dump. Now he's got to wear the new shoes, like it or not. Of course, no one thinks there's anything strange about them. But he blames me anyway. He says I ratted him out to Mom. It's my fault he has to go around dressed like a clown. And it's my fault Buster ended up at the SPCA, he says. You never liked that dog.

Joe

The Ali-Norton rematch took place at The Forum in Los Angeles on 10 September 1973, five months after the first fight. For only the second time in his career – the first being the two victories against Sonny Liston – Ali met the same opponent twice in a row. The loss had been a setback and he'd needed time to recover physically and mentally. The wish to cash in on the big money excitement (Solly Jasven) no doubt played a role too: the promoters wanted to get a title fight with Foreman back on track.

In the buildup to the rematch the joking about Ali's jaw redoubled.

'The Lip must keep mouth buttoned' ran one headline in *The Star*. In fact, this was also the medical advice of Dr Ferdie Pacheco. He explained that Ali's healed jaw would be stronger than ever, but Norton had dislodged three of his teeth, which had been replaced. Dr Pacheco offered a cheerful caution: If Ali opens his mouth during the fight and gets caught again these could fly all over the place.

While most of the sportswriters were predicting that a second loss to Norton would be the end of the road, Ali had found a way to turn the logic of the first loss inside out. When I lost to Ken Norton I took a nobody and created a monster. A Frankenstein has broken loose ... Now I'm going to pull out all his nuts and bolts.

There was greater interest in the Ali-Norton rematch than in any fight since the Fight of the Century, with forty countries taking live or closed-circuit television coverage. The fight went the distance and Ali won on a split decision. The aficionados were not impressed with his performance. Alan Hubbard: The butterfly was back, but the bee had lost its sting.

Afterwards Ali's camp was worried that he had broken his hand, while he complained of old age and aches and pains: Every time I fight, something gets hurt lately ... I've punched and been punched at since the age of 12 ... the pain, the blood, and the bones are all real and they take it out of you.

Towards the end of October, after an exhibition match in Malaysia against sparring partner Alonzo Johnson, there was concern that Ali had injured his jaw again and on his return to New York it was examined by a doctor.

Why am I here? Ali asked plaintively. What's so important about my jaw? People are dying in Egypt and Israel. Ninety-six people killed in a plane crash ... You hardly hear about that. But my jaw is going to be on the front pages all over the world. People are dying, people are bleeding ... and all this fuss over a mere boxing match. It shows how messed up the world is. I don't think it's right to get all this attention. People who deserve it don't get any.

Yet he had no intention of leaving the circus. The long-awaited return against Joe Frazier was scheduled for early in the new year and the signing took place in the Hall of Fame at Madison Square Garden. Ali ran amok when Frazier refused to call him by his name: You are still calling me Clay, you are still calling me Clay. I'm going to beat your bones unless you call me Muhammad Ali.

The press dubbed the second Ali-Frazier match 'Superfight II' and they poured a tankerful of ink into it. The last eight pages of my second scrapbook are devoted to the buildup.

Branko

On a melancholy morning, when the leaves are thick in the gutters and the air crackles with frost, my brother is back at my door. He should know better than to pitch up unannounced. People who work in offices always think freelancers are sitting around at home watching television, but he's a freelancer himself. Still, I can't very well send him away.

He comes in with the Pres Les box in his arms and what Dad would have called a hare-brained scheme in his head. He wants us to *collaborate* on his book.

I'll make space for you in the text, he says. As if he's scooting over on the couch or tidying up the spare room for a visitor.

I remember the box and its contents: his so-called archive and its bastard progeny, the lever-arch file full of half-baked drafts that he calls his work. He showed it to me the last time he was here and complained that he was stuck.

Have you made any progress?

A little.

Let me see then.

He hems and haws about internal pressure and staying true to creative principles, but he unpacks the scrapbooks. The first time round they exuded some sort of charm, but now they look pathetic. What is this old stuff? That's what Jordan asked when he saw them. How quaint all this paper must look to a digital native. Joe reaches into the box and takes out a yellow cardboard folder, opens it and removes a stack of A4 pages – he's come prepared, it occurs to me afterwards – fifty feint-ruled and pre-punched sheets, handwritten in pencil. The pages are so densely packed with corrections and additions in bubbles moored to asterisks and arrows that I can scarcely find my way through a paragraph.

I can't read this, I say. You'll have to type it up first.

I don't have time. And anyway it'll disrupt my rhythm. I've got to press on to the end. It's one of the principles: get the thing down on paper first. You can come back to the editing later.

Doesn't look like you've been following your own advice.

With a sinking heart, I take the pages from him – it turns out to be the first few chapters of his book – and over the following days I hack a path through the jungle. I've never been in this position before and it's not comfortable. It reminds me of our schooldays when I snooped through his diary.

I go to the CNA to buy an exercise book for my notes. The soft-cover notebooks on their shelves have pictures of surfers and sunsets on them and so I settle for a black hardcover manuscript book with a red spine of the kind Mom used to use. They haven't changed in fifty years.

We agree to meet at the Mugg & Bean in Killarney to discuss my *feedback*. It's on the route between his place in Troyeville and mine in Parkview. Let's meet one another halfway, I tell him on the phone, and don't get a laugh.

He's already there when I arrive, sitting at the window. Through the glass we can see the late-afternoon traffic thickening on the M1. It's like having a view of the sea. The rush-hour flows are as reliable as the tides and nearly as reassuring.

You weren't entirely honest with me, I say. You insisted that you aren't writing about Muhammad Ali – but you are. Mom and Dad are mentioned a couple of times and you've got a few pages about your pal Jolyon and that little bully Georgie Baker. That's pretty good. But the spotlight is on Ali. Problem is we've heard it all before, the Fight of the Century, the hoopla, the baiting of Frazier. It's just bits and pieces of your scrapbooks – sorry, your archive – it's a cut-and-paste job.

He's getting het up already, waggling his teaspoon between his fingers like a jazz drummer on speed. His handwritten chapters are lying on the table between us. I tap on them with my finger and go on:

All these details about wins and losses, split decisions and TKOs. The tale of the tape! What's the point? There are hundreds of books about Ali, from pop picture books to heavyweight academic studies. You don't even need to buy a book, just type his name into Google, which is what I did last night. It'll take you a fucking year to go through the results. You can watch three versions of the big fights on YouTube. You can download just about every round he fought. If it was put on film, you can find it. If you'd prefer a movie – last time I looked you were going as a novelist – IMDb says the 2001 biopic is the best of the bunch. You have to watch Will Smith pretending to be Cassius Clay pretending to have sex, but otherwise it's not bad.

Thanks very much.

Fine, I know you're not a fan of Mr Smith. I can live without him too.

Never mind that, he says, you've put your finger on something that's been bothering me. Why Ali? My love for him used to feel inevitable, I would almost say predestined. But the more I think about it, the more arbitrary it seems. I could easily have chosen someone else.

Like Eddy Merckx, I say, or Jackie Stewart.

Exactly, he says. Or Evel Knievel.

Evel Knievel!

He was in the news all the time too. He used to jump over things on a motorcycle, over buses and so on.

I remember who he was, Joe. But he was hardly in the same league as Ali. He was a publicity-seeking lunatic. It's pure luck he didn't break his neck in that Las Vegas stunt and wind up in a wheelchair. Do you know the one I mean? You'll find that on YouTube too. And I'm thinking: how did we get here? Is he losing his marbles?

You'd think he wanted to die, says Joe.

Yes! He had a death wish. He broke every bone in his body at some stage – except his stupid neck. It's like he wanted to get in *The Guinness Book of Records* for total number of fractures.

Apparently he was a prick. Have you heard that? He treated the people who worked for him like shit.

He used to dress up as Captain America. Or in a white jumpsuit. Like Elvis.

Another Big Thing in the seventies. You could have chosen Elvis too.

I know, I know. I would have had ten scrapbooks full of stuff about the King. The Great White Hope.

Question is: would you be trying to write a book about him?

I might have more luck.

You went with Ali, I say – someone has to stop this train of thought in its tracks – you did the right thing.

You and Dad hated him.

Times have changed. I take it all back.

It's a little late.

Actually I've been thinking about that. Did I really hate him? Maybe I was just following Dad's lead. He certainly wasn't a fan, as you say in here.

This is great. He calls the waiter to refill our coffees. Talking to you like this, brother to brother. It's just what I need. We haven't been close in the last few years, but I want that to change. Having this discussion with you is really clarifying things. Perhaps we can do some interviews. Would you mind? I could ask you some questions. We can keep it informal like this, we'd just have a tape running, after a while we'll forget it's there.

I don't know, Joe. You've always left me out of this stuff of yours – and for good reason. It's too arty for me, too cerebral. I'm happy to be left out, really, it suits me fine.

But I could get your impressions of how things were in our child-hood, in our youth. Your perspective.

I suppose I could write them down …

Don't ask me why I say this. Maybe the thought of talking to him about the past makes me queasy or maybe I'm just fobbing him off. And it sort of works. He says:

You're not much of a writer.

Neither are you, to judge by this. I pick up his handwritten drafts and shuffle through them. The chaos on the page shocks me anew: it's as if his mind is going to pieces. Look, it's not my place to offer you advice, but you've got to stop stressing. Go ahead and write about what's in the scrapbooks. It's not bad, actually. Leave the family stuff to me. Let me think about it anyway.

Really? You'd do that? That's fantastic! And then he wants to go. It's like he knew I would make the offer. He waves at the waiter, pins a twenty-rand note under the salt cellar and rushes out. He's trying to go off without his manuscript. I follow him out of the shop and the waiter runs after us waving the bill and the banknote. At the top of the escalator I thrust the yellow folder into his hands and he sinks towards the Ocean Basket, exclaiming and gesticulating in an exaggerated way as if he's in a Woody Allen movie. *Scenes from a Mall*.

When I'm back at the table calming my nerves with an espresso, odd thoughts start sparring in my head. First it's Rio Rivers in his powder-blue Speedo and Sammy Cohen with his cellulite. And then the camped-up entertainers in spangled catsuits, Alice Cooper, David Bowie, that character from Roxy Music. What was going on with Joe in those years? Once I left school, I was so busy with my own stuff, I can hardly recall what he was up to. How well do I know him? They say all obsessions are rooted in the erotic. I remember once Alan Fuchs, who used to race with me, asked if Joe was one of those. One of what? It was a moment before I understood. Surely not. I defended him angrily, outraged on his behalf. But it made me wonder. Why couldn't he find a girlfriend? That was when I tried to set him up with Barbie McCann at Pietie Lochner's party. Big mistake.

And now? Is he in some kind of trouble? Perhaps he really needs my help.

Joe

Crying in public has become as commonplace as laughing. Men are expected to cry easily and encouraged to cry often. Politicians, business-men, sportsmen, movie stars, criminals regularly shed tears of sadness, humiliation, remorse and even joy. Feeling *humbled*, which is to say *exalted*, a man praised by his peers or singled out for an honour will shed tears of gratitude.

A generation ago, men did not cry in public and seldom admitted to having done so in private. An exception was made for one unlikely category: boxers. Yes, the thick-skinned and lumpy journeymen of the busted-beak industry were allowed to weep in defeat. Perhaps the privilege was paid for in suffering, in the blood and sweat they spilled in the ring.

Jerry Quarry wept in the dressing room after losing to Ali. So did Buster Mathis. After Ali lost to Norton, Bundini Brown sobbed and Angelo Dundee was white-faced and shaking. But Ali was not a crybaby. There is no inkling in the archive that the Lip ever did so much as quiver.

6

Collectors

FRAZIE
UT
IN

ALI:
Age 32
Height 6' 3"
Weight 215lb
Chest 42"
Biceps 15"
Reach 80"

FRAZIER:
Age 30
Height 5' 11½
Weight 205lb
Chest 42"
Biceps 15"
Reach 73½"

Durban – Last week the Durban North Presbyterian minister the Reverend Charles Gordon told his Durban North congregation: "I'm tired of seeing only shining pink faces. Bring your servants to Church next Sunday." But yesterday Mr. Gordon looked down from his pulpit on the same shiny pink faces – nobody had taken up his challenge.

– The Star, April 1973

Joe

Have I got long fingers?

My mother takes my hand in hers and runs her thumb over my knuckles. The ring finger curves in at the end, just like my Dad's, and my Grandpa Blahavić's. This crookedness is a mark of the Blahavić men.

They don't look very long to me, Mom says.

But are they longer than normal?

I wouldn't say so. And she squeezes my fingers into a taper, turns my hand over and rubs the palm. You've got your father's hands. Then she puts her finger to her lips. Her radio serial is about to start again.

She's sitting on her bed and I'm on the dressing-table stool. The silver transistor radio is propped on a pile of books on the bedside table. We sit in silence while the Reverend Matthew, the troubled young priest who's the main character, wrestles with his conscience, as he does every day. When it's over she turns the volume down.

Who says you've got long fingers?

It was Tim.

Tim Knowles said you have long fingers?

He said that's what Auntie Jilly said.

Is that so.

She gets up and looks through the window. Auntie Jilly's Volksie is parked in the driveway. She stands there for a while, looking out, and then she turns back to me.

Well, she must be mistaken. Her own children have such stubby little hands. I'm sure they'll all grow up to be street sweepers.

Later that afternoon she pulls on her cardigan, stuffs a box of fags in the pocket and a tissue up the sleeve, and goes across the road to have a cup of tea with Auntie Jilly.

When she comes back, she calls me to the lounge, puts her hands on my shoulders and looks into my eyes. Is there anything in this house that belongs to Tim Knowles?

No Mom. Actually there's a pocket knife that he swapped me for a Hillman Minx with one wheel missing, but I'm not supposed to have a knife and it's well hidden in the bottom drawer of my desk, so I don't mention it.

Anything that belongs to his brother?

No Mom.

His sisters?

No Mom.

All right, she says. Now I want you to stop playing with Tim. I don't want you going over there. Do you understand?

But Mom.

But me no buts. You're not to set foot in that boy's yard again. Is that understood?

Yes Mom.

She doesn't realize (or she does) that it's impossible for me to stop playing with Tim Knowles. We're building a tree house in his garden and the plan depends on me. I'm supplying the materials, the borrowed boards and planks from the stash behind the servants' quarters and long nails from the jars in Dad's garage. Tim has the tree.

Branko

Joe is reading the Bible. He started at 'In the beginning …' and he plans to go all the way through to the last 'Amen'. He's been busy for five or six months and he's got as far as the First Book of the Chronicles. Every night, unless we've come in late from the cycle track or he's listening to Malcolm Gooding's music show on the transistor, he kneels down next to his bed and says his prayers. Then he creeps under the blankets, takes the Bible from his bedside table, opens it at the bookmark, which is shaped like a shepherd's crook and has a picture of St Christopher on it, and reads two pages. Neither more nor less. This way he's calculated it will take him eighteen months to get to the end.

Joe is a *great reader*, as they say. In the school holidays, he lies on his bed in the sun all day and reads like a machine. He can devour a book in a day, *five* books, if you count the *Reader's Digest* condensed volumes, which he swallows like an astronaut eating five square meals in tablet form.

Why don't you just read the Bible in one go? I ask. That time you had measles you got through *Riders of the Purple Sage* without stopping to water the horses. You could do one hundred pages of scripture a day and still have time for a couple of chapters of Leslie Charteris. Ten days and it would all be over. Two weeks at a stretch.

I can't do that, he says. The whole point is to read it in stages.

Like the Tour de France?

Ja, exactly. You can't sommer beetle on to the end. You've got to do one stage a day like everybody else.

There's another rule, I discover: no skipping. He has to read every chapter of every book. Not just Exodus and Proverbs, but Nehemiah and Amos and Nahum. Nahum. Who the hell reads him? Every verse of every chapter too and every word of every verse. All the begats and comings to pass, all the instances of this one saying unto that one and that one arising and going forth, all the lists of the sons of the one and the brethren of the other. He says that's the best part, the *lineages*. He's making a list of all the main manne – he waves a blue exercise book – and that's why he's got stuck for two weeks in the First Book of Chronicles.

All of them? I say. You're making a list of all the Sons of Adam?

No, he says, only the good okes.

I can't tell if he's joking or not, so I snatch the exercise book out of his hand and take a look. I expect to find the House of David and the Sons of Aaron and David's Mighty Men, but this is another story. It doesn't look like the good okes to me. He's gathered together Gomer and Heth and Lud, Mibsam and Shephi, and Jobab the son of Zerah of Bozrah. Not to mention Casluhim of whom came the Philistines. And Hadad the son of Bedad, which smote Midian in the field of Moab. The Ithrites, the Puhites and the Netophathites. No sign of the Stalactites and the Stalagmites. But here's the families of the scribes which dwelt at Jabez. On and on for another ten pages. If I had the original to hand now, I would put it in an Appendix. My reconstruction hardly does it justice. Fuck me George, I say, what's going on here?

It's nothing, he says. Just some lists.

What for?

Oh, a couple of names I might use some day.

For what?

It's not easy to explain.

Take a shot, Joe. Tell me what you're going to do with Mibsam and Huppim and Shuppim?

Well, he says, I might call my firstborn Mibsam.

Your *firstborn*? He's making this up, I can see it from a mile away.

Maybe they're aliases, he says, as if the two of us have happened upon a list made by a stranger. Or pen names.

So that's it. I throw the book at him.

My mockery of his bookish ways has little to do with the writing. It's the *reading* that bothers me. He's spent half his life in books. Lost in them. It can't be good for him. All those Louis L'Amours, for one thing, all the places in them, the high mesas and lonesome buttes, and the people there and everything they get up to, the galloping off, the narrowing of the eyes, the declaring and opining. Where does it all go? Maybe it settles in the back of the mind like dust.

Joe

Mom kept the hit parades in the knitting bag she'd bought one year in Umhlanga Rocks. There were three or four notebooks with black covers and red spines and they contained nearly all the LM hit parades from the last five years, listed by artist, song and position on the chart.

In the same bag, which was made of wheat-coloured straw with a girdle of green checks round its waist, was another notebook of the same design in which she'd written out the lyrics of the songs she loved. Some of them we still heard on the radio, like 'Blue Train' and 'The Carnival is Over', but most were the numbers she used to sing with

Ronnie's Rhythm Section at the Berea Park dance hall: 'Smoke Gets in Your Eyes', 'Goody Goody', 'Who's Sorry Now'. Mom had a voice when she was young, it was her Irish blood, everyone knows the Irish have beautiful voices, but we could not get her to sing for us. I don't like the sound of my own voice, she said. It was beautiful once, if you closed your eyes you would swear it was Connie Francis, people said, but now it grates on my nerves.

Forgetting herself, she would sing along with the radio when she was cooking. *Que sera, sera, whatever will be, will be* . . . If there was a new song she liked and she couldn't work out all the words, she'd call Sylvie or me to put an ear to the speaker when it played. There were lines you couldn't understand no matter how many times you heard them.

Sometimes the bag contained another notebook of the same design but bigger, the adult version of which the others were children, and in these pages Mom had written down her dreams. This was long ago, when we children were small, an unhappy time in her life, and she recorded the dreams so that she could read them to Dr K, who told her what they meant and helped her to get well. Dr K saved her sanity, and very likely her life, and he was a hero in our family, although he was seldom spoken of and then only in a quiet, respectful way, the way we spoke about Father Oliver from the Cathedral or Great-Uncle Cedric who died in the flu epidemic of 1918. It was never clear to me how Dr K had helped my mother, how he had cured her, because it was never clear what had ailed her to begin with.

The dream book found its way into the knitting bag when Mom needed to consult it for some reason, but mainly she kept it in a drawer of her wardrobe. This was part of the bedroom suite Mom and Dad had bought when they started their married life together. The wardrobe was a massive arrangement of doors and drawers all faced with curved and pleated surfaces so that it looked like a stage curtain carved out of oak. The brass handles were vine leaves on sinuous tendrils. We pulled open the drawers from time to time when Mom and Dad were out to see what they were keeping in there. It was always disappointing: nothing but our old report cards and obituary notices from the newspapers. The middle drawer, the one in which the dream book lived, was locked and there was no sign of the key. Mom did not drive and never went out on her own, so the key was not on a ring like Dad's and must be hidden somewhere in a handbag or jewellery box, but we could never find it. When we tired of hunting for it, my brother would try on Dad's houndstooth overcoat and walk around with the tails dragging on the floor.

Mom let me leaf through the song book, but she would not let me touch the dream book. She did not even like me to see it.

I found her sitting on her bed one afternoon with her legs folded under her like a teenager and the dream book open on the candlewick bedspread. She was bowed over the pages, reading intently, with the sewing scissors in her hand. A few slips of paper with her precise handwriting on them lay scattered beside her knee. As soon as I entered the room, she shuffled these scraps into the book, closed it quickly and put her fist on it. Paper, scissors, rock. Outside, a thunderstorm was building and the dark wall of the sky was riven by lightning. Before the open windows the net curtains bulged into the room like sails, snagged for an instant on the winged mirror of the dressing table and then collapsed back against the burglar bars. The room appeared to be breathing. I was in the belly of a sea creature sucking the charged air in through its gills.

The dream book rattled under my mother's knuckles. She had shut the storm up between its covers and it was boiling in there like a demon in a box.

I sat on the end of the bed and we spoke about inconsequential things, perhaps my algebra homework or some funny thing Mrs Mitchell had said when she came over for a cuppa, and all this time we both looked out through the window and watched the curtain being sucked in and coughed out, until the storm burst over the roof of the Mitchells' house like a madwoman spitting out curses. It was only when the ragged sheets of rain blocked out the view that I rose to pull the windows shut, while she slipped off the bed and put the dream book away in the middle drawer.

A month or two passed. Then one day when I came in from school, Mom was not at the knitting machine as usual. In the kitchen a gash of pumpkin lay on the chopping board like a dissected smile and a pot of cold water stood on the stove, lid tilted in anticipation. The sandwich she'd made for me lay on a plate, two pale triangles of white bread with something brown between the slices. I peeled one back to see what it was. Through the window above the sink, I caught sight of her in the yard. She was at the drum Dad had cut and welded to use as a braai, with a toasting fork in one hand and a notebook in the other, while a column of smoke rose into the blue air. It was odd to see her standing out there in her apron as if she was cooking something. The simple fact of it held my attention for a while. Then I realized what the black-bound book was. I had always thought the dream book was intended for me, that it was an inheritance of some kind. One day, not when she died but when I grew up perhaps, when I was old enough to understand, the book would be given to me and its meaning would be revealed. But it would not keep. I understood that she had to burn the book and that I could do nothing to stop her. The flames licked up above the lip of the drum, bright and clean as pennants of silk in the sunlight. It would smell of meat in the yard as the fat on the grill began to melt and sizzle. I took the plate from the kitchen dresser and went to my room.

When she came in with charcoal smudges on her knuckles and her hair awry, I was at my desk. She must have known I'd seen her at the fire, but she gave nothing away. She looked relieved and distraught.

Later that afternoon, when I was in the yard bouncing a tennis ball off the wall of the servants' quarters, a good enough excuse to get close to the scene of the crime, the drum was still smoking. In the ash of the pages, which looked like shards of pewter, I saw the bloodied spine trailing a nervous system of cotton thread.

Branko

My brother wants me to tell his story. Or is it mine? Ours? Can a story ever belong equally to two people? Perhaps I need to answer this question before I can ask another. Where do I start?

I'm hunched over my manuscript book at the kitchen counter, pressing down on it as if I'd like to submerge it in the granite. Nothing comes. I should try writing on my laptop like a modern-day author, but I can't get my brother out of my bones: he's occupied my body, he's squatting in my muscles, so I just sit there, wrist cocked, pencil poised, ear turned downward to the page. The manuscript book is the family standby. But what kind of pencil does he prefer? Most of the scribblings he's shown me are in crumbly graphite. A Staedtler 2B? Or could it be a propelling pencil? It's years since I saw him write anything down. He has a phobia about writing in public, thinks it's unseemly and unlucky.

He doesn't have that problem with reading and I can picture him doing it. The posture is easy to mimic: I slump down on the stool with my head hanging. What would the book be? *The Saint Meets His Match*. There isn't a Simon Templar book in the house, I know this for a fact, but I get up and browse along the shelves in the lounge as if there might be. Most of the books are Rita's: her tastes were always better than mine. The blokes on the bottom shelf, Goodis, Chandler, Hammett, that's me. Joe outgrew this crew and never thought much of my reading habits afterwards. Which makes it even weirder that he wants me in his book. Unless he thinks my vulgar tastes will add a layer of authentic detail to a book about his youth. A portrait of the artist as his ill-bred brother.

I drive over to Bookdealers in the Rosebank Mews in search of Simon Templar books. There were long rows of them in the book exchanges, I remember, tatty post-war paperbacks arranged on industrial shelving that looked like giant Meccano, but now there are scarcely half a dozen to choose from. The Saint must have gone out of fashion. The cover illustrations could be movie stills, showing a man with a gun and a prettily distressed woman. The little stickman with his rakish halo lurks near the barcode on the back cover like an undernourished fan behind a police cordon.

I come away with three books. Two of them – *Alias the Saint* and *Featuring the Saint* – were first published within three months of one another in 1931, when Charteris was getting into his stride, and the new editions appeared in 1980 and 1994. The third, *Catch the Saint*, was published for the first time in 1975 and turns out to be an adaptation of a comic strip ghostwritten by someone called Fleming Lee. That evening I read the first chapter of all three books. I don't want Rita to know what I'm doing. I haven't even told her about Joe's offer, because she'll think he's taking advantage as always. He borrowed some money when his geyser burst and I still haven't heard the end of it. So I sit in the lounge and read while the TV mutters in the background. What am I looking for? I'm not sure. The characters come back to me in my brother's voice. Chief Inspector Claud Eustace Teal, the bumbler, always sounding off and pronouncing, and always having the wool pulled over his eyes by his roguish adversary. Templar himself had a smooth tongue. Joe would pick up his catchphrases, call me 'son' all the time, tell me 'Mind your head, old son' and 'Don't go eating your heart out, old fruit' until I felt like hitting him. Until I did. Sometimes it went further than the lingo. I remember when he started going around in disguise, suddenly parting his hair on the other side and walking with a limp. An *unpronounced* limp. That was The Saint's knack: the uncanny ability to put on a new identity with a pair of horn-rimmed spectacles, a German accent, a shabby coat.

Jordan comes in and I hear him talking to Reet in the kitchen. I retreat to the edit room. University wasn't for him. Like father, like son. Now he's moved to a film college in Kensington where they focus on technical skills and he's doing better. He's making a feature, a 'speculative documentary', he calls it. A bit like the one I'm currently working on. It's a three-part series on the history of the ANC and some idiot recorded all the interviews with music in the background. I'm meant to fix it. The films are already six months late – they were supposed to go out when the party celebrated its centenary in January – and the producer is leaning on me. Problem is I can't keep my mind on what the contemporary commentators have to say: all that interests me is the old footage. Perhaps my brother's 'archive' is infecting me. After fifteen minutes in front of the Avid, I fetch The Saint books and read the second chapter of each one. I could read one of them all the way through, but I like this switching from one to the other. Channel-hopping. At the least it demonstrates how interchangeable they are.

I make a few notes on Chief Inspector Teal – it's one way of getting some writing into my manuscript book. He seems ridiculous to me, as florid and affected as a pantomime villain. What did I think when I was fifteen? I read a couple of them then at my brother's insistence but I can't recall my response. Templar has a love interest, a blonde girl called Patricia Holm, sometimes referred to as his 'girl assistant'. And he has an American sidekick called Hoppy Uniatz, a real meathead, loyal unto death. Joe used to talk like him too. *Chees boss, I brung my betsy. I can give him de woiks.* This was long after he and Jolyon Barlow had tried to become Americans and given it up as a bad job.

All week, I worry about Joe. Something's eating him, I'm sure of it. Should I call Em? The two of us have never got along and we've hardly spoken since the dinner-party fiasco. In the end, I decide to go over and see him. I don't let him know I'm coming either.

Film music's about the only thing I can listen to when I'm driving. I've got a dozen CDs in the box on the console and I rotate them. Dramas all of them, *The Godfather*, *The Mission*, you won't find *Working*

Girls in the player. These days every second movie is larded with pop songs. I like the big themes, their dramatic effects: the way the music lifts the shallowest day into drama. I remember going along Loch Avenue at sunset with Morricone's score for *Days of Heaven* playing and the jacarandas in bloom and it felt like all that purple was coming out of the speakers. That's right: like I was in a fucking movie.

Today I go the long way round to my brother's to avoid Yeoville and Bertrams, snaking up Death Bend to Owl Road and then nipping through Observatory. Christopher Gordon's score for *Master and Commander* carries me there. 'The Far Side of the World.' It's not a bad conjunction.

Dusk is falling when I get to Troyeville and the air smells of coal smoke. It's five years since I set foot in this neighbourhood and it's looking worse than ever: the gutters clogged with leaves and acorns, weeds as tall as men sprouting out of the pavements, razor wire uncoiled along the walls. Practically every house needs a coat of paint. It always looks worse in the winter, he'll say if I comment. When the trees are in leaf and the creepers are flowering, the whole place softens. It's like Greece around here.

I have to rattle on the gate five times before he comes to the bedroom window. Then he glares at me through the bars. He thinks I'm a beggar. He kept complaining about that in one of his books. Or maybe he's not wearing his glasses again. Vanity or forgetfulness, I'm not sure which. At last he sees it's me and waves the cellphone: he's busy.

I feel vulnerable out in the street. The last time Rita and I were here for dinner someone broke into our car. When she told Joe off about the crappy suburb he'd chosen to live in, he had the nerve to defend the thieves, as if we drove a decent car just to provoke them. I swore I'd never set foot here again and I've kept my word. Until now.

I'm about to get back in my car when I hear the alarm beep. He's switched off the beams in the garden. Yet another last-ditch defence after the latest burglary. Then he appears with the phone still pressed to his ear by one shoulder, opens the padlock on the inside of the gate, hands me the keys through the bars and leaves me to it.

He's installed a Heath Robinson system of folding mesh panels on the bottom of the gate to prevent thieves from creeping through the gap. It's like a metallic version of the origami in his scrapbooks and it takes me five minutes to figure out how it works. Finally I'm inside with the gate closed behind me.

When I get into the house I find him pacing up and down in the lounge, but he waggles the phone again, points to a bottle of sherry on the mantelpiece, then slopes off into his study and pulls the door shut behind him. The usual drama, no doubt: missed deadline, lost income, passive aggression. There's a fire burning in the grate, coal in the scuttle and logs in a stack against the wall. An immense axe is propped against the fire screen and the carpet is covered with pine splinters. But the place is pretty tidy, almost too tidy for my liking. He was always like this, keeping a grip. Orderly decrepitude. I used to say he was like the custodian of some provincial museum, sweeping the threadbare carpets, dusting the sagging shelves. Some of the furniture looks like it belongs on the woodpile. He's still using a packing case as a footstool! Why does Em put up with it? Unless it bothers her as little as it bothers him.

I wander through to the dining room. In here it's chaos. Columns of books are crumbling to rubble against the walls. The Ali papers are spread out on the table and for a moment it looks like a ravaged landscape in a chief of staff's war room. At least he's telling the truth about this: he's actually working. Scrapbooks, cardboard folders, envelopes, cuttings, foolscap sheets. It would never all fit in the Pres Les box, which is gaping on a chair.

I sit down at the head of the table. Facing me is the big Eclipse scrapbook titled ALI II. There's the sticker of Goofy the Slugger. I remember the scene in Rob Reiner's *Stand by Me* where the boys are talking about Disney characters. 'Mickey's a mouse. Donald's a duck. Pluto's a dog. But what the hell is Goofy?' I turn the pages, lifting the layered newsprint carefully against the tracing paper as I've seen him do, struck again by the obsessive order in this clutter, the carefully folded cuttings, the pencilled numbers and headline quotes to show which dog-eared scrap was stuck to which yellowed page, the stubby columns attached to larger items with paperclips.

A smokescreen, that's what it is. The illusion of order in these papers is meant to mask the absence of order in his mind. That's why he can't make anything of this stuff, why he needs my help after all these years. Any editor will do, even a sound hack. Perhaps a lifetime of boozing has caught up with him: the folders in his memory bank are out of order and he can't remember what goes where. But as long as he can marshal this pathetic jumble of paper, he can pretend that he's in charge.

A story on the back of a cutting catches my eye. It's about two mineworkers who died in a rockfall at the Westonaria Gold Mine. I'm reading that when he appears.

You look like shit, I say. I mean it.

Thanks very much. It's kind of you to notice.

I'm serious. You look like Joe Bugner after Ali got hold of him. I've just caught sight of poor Joe on a cutting. Where's Em?

Neighbourhood Watch meeting.

I should have guessed.

Everyone's in a flap again. They broke in up the road here. One guy was hiding behind a tree outside, that oak over there. Em looked out of the window and the bastard was busy on his cellphone. Keeping cave. He saw her and drew a finger across his throat. Scared the hell out of her, of course. Now she wants to move.

It's not a bad idea, Joe.

Suppose so. I just can't bear the thought of packing up all this crap. I always say they'll carry me out of here in a box.

We laugh about that.

So, he says, pulling a chair up to the table. What have you got for me?

What do you mean?

Haven't you been writing? I thought that's why you came.

No, I was just in the neighbourhood.

Crap man, Branks. You haven't been south of Louis Botha in five years.

That's funny too. We laugh again.

Actually, I have been putting a few things down on paper.

Really?

On disk I should say. I'm not wedded to the ancient technologies like you. He doesn't believe me, I can tell.

What kind of things?

Little stories of ordinary life. Just what you ordered.

Like?

Well, I remembered how we used to drive all over town on a Saturday afternoon to book exchanges so you could buy some paperback or other. The old man was quite good about it, you know. He looks pleased with this so I press on. And how you used to start reading them in the back of the car before we were even home. Should I mention that I've been reading Charteris myself? Better not. He'll think I'm muscling in on his turf.

You've written this down?

Ja.

I'd like to read it.

No, I'm not ready yet. You taught me that: to play things close to my chest.

Giving him a taste of his own medicine. But he looks quite pleased with this too.

That's great, he says. So long as you're getting it down on paper. That's the hardest part, from the blank page to the first draft. Once you've got through that nightmare, anything can happen. Take your time. Just shout when you're ready.

I've heard your advice, I say. Now can I give you some?

Sure.

Do some laundry.

Jesus Branko.

I can smell that T-shirt from here.

This is my fire-building outfit, you self-righteous prick. I chop wood in this and haul coal. Some of us don't have underfloor heating. Let me know the next time you're coming and I'll put on my tux.

Doesn't Em look after you?

You know she does. I'd have been in my grave by now if it wasn't for that woman. But I've been chained to my desk doing battle with this bloody book. I'm going to finish it this time even if it kills me.

The serial-killer laugh. Haven't heard that for a while.

Don't take this the wrong way, I say.

And he interrupts: Then don't start by saying that.

Just listen. If you're battling with all this stuff, the cuttings and everything, maybe you should change your approach. Stop keeping order and start paying attention.

That's good. Really. Where did you get that?

I've been working with other people's stories for a long time and I've learnt a few things. I know you don't think much of the medium I work in, but some things are exactly the same. Forget the story you want to tell: look for the one that's already there. Listen to the material.

That's great, he says, excellent advice. And he really does seem to be taking it in.

You need to eat, I say. Let me buy you a meal. You look like you could do with a plate of prawns from the Troyeville Hotel. Better still, let me buy you a steak at the Grill House. You should get out of this scummy neighbourhood. We'll leave a note for Em and she can join us later.

But he says he has work to finish, a catalogue piece. Deadlines.

They've ruined his life. That was Matty on the phone laying down the law.

Then I'll get going, I say. You'd better let me out. My mind turns to my car in the dark street outside. If it gets broken into again, Rita will never let me live it down.

No no, he says, you've just arrived. Let's have a drink. I've got some sherry you should taste.

He goes to the lounge and then I hear him cursing and banging. The fucking fire's gone out.

He drags one of the broken leather armchairs closer to the fire and makes me sit, pours me a shot of sherry and starts telling me all about the solera process, how they tap the sherry from one barrel to another, high to low. It's like a metaphor, he says, for how culture works. Also, it's not really sherry, it's better than that. It's *amontillado*. In a butt of which the body of Admiral Nelson was preserved. No wait, that was rum. As Mom always said: You can preserve many things in alcohol – even a dead admiral – but your dignity isn't one of them. Quoting Poe. Running off at the mouth: always a sure sign he's in trouble. Meanwhile he's kneeling in front of the fireplace and holding a sheet of newspaper over the opening. Do you know this trick? It makes the chimney draw. While he's looking over his shoulder, a black spot appears through the newsprint, like the burn mark on a strip of film just before it melts in front of the globe, and then the paper catches fire. And it's a big hullaba-loo, he's dancing around on the hearth stamping out the curling paper in his dog-eaten slippers, and we could be boys again, laughing like crazy on the edge of calamity.

Joe

At my cousins' place in town there was a mouldering khaya in the yard for the girl. We Blahavićes, by contrast, lived in the new world, in a ranch-style house in the suburbs, and we called the cold, cobwebby building in our yard the servants' quarters, never the khaya or the girl's room. It was a facebrick room with a cement floor and a gun slot of a window, and it looked a bit like the ablution block in the caravan park at Orient Beach. There was a toilet attached to one end, screened off, along with the door to the room itself, by an L-shaped wall. There was no bathroom. Perhaps the servant was meant to use the concrete trough in the laundry room at the opposite end of the block.

The servants' quarters acted as a screen behind which Dad could store building materials and equipment, things like scaffolding pipes and window frames, trestles and boards. Some of this material was covered by a tarp; most of it was left to warp and rust in the rain and the sun.

The room, in which no maid or gardener ever lived, caught the household's odds and ends: three-legged chairs, stained mattresses, a leaking washing machine with an immense mangle attached to it. Also camping equipment, fishing tackle, gardening tools. And then a mass of bottles and newspapers. We found it difficult to throw out a newspaper. The dailies stayed on a pile next to Dad's chair in the lounge for a week or so, just in case he needed to cross-check something, a story whose details had become clear, or unclear, a price that had gone up, or down, a sports result. Then they went onto a stack next to the dog's bowls by the back door. And when that stack began to teeter, they travelled in cascading armfuls out to the servants' quarters and were piled on top of old appliances or against the walls. Once the room was full, there was always the trailer under the mulberry tree, a battered yellow box on wheels that came from a road camp and was too heavy to be towed by the Zodiac. That filled up too, eventually, and the paper turned to pulp when it rained.

The servants' quarters was a place where stray cats had kittens and wounded swallows came to die. Mice made nests in the damp paper and spiders trampolined on webs in the corners. When things got bad enough, when a rat was spotted sunning itself on the lid of the dustbin, Mom had a cadenza. Then Dad brought a van home from work and Branko and I spent the whole of Saturday clearing everything out and carting it to the municipal dump. Only the good junk stayed behind, the furniture someone with a will might repair, the boards and pipes that might still come in useful.

After one of these clearing-out sessions, Sylvie decided she needed a rumpus room, like Betty Cooper in the Archie comics whom she fancied she resembled (actually she was more like Veronica Lodge). The servants' room was swept clean and a threadbare rug that once belonged to Uncle Eddie was rolled out and vacuumed. Two pod chairs covered in blue nylon were given a new life: they had snapped off their chrome bases but they worked well enough flat on the floor. Everyone wanted to be down low in those years, on cushions and beanbags, in conversation pits.

The next time Sylvie's friend Geraldine came over, the two of them went to the rumpus room with the transistor and mugs of milky coffee. Music and laughter drifted out. Geraldine's broad shoulders and bronzed eyelids always unnerved me and I steered clear of her, but now my curiosity got the better of me. When I climbed up on the bin and looked through the window, hoping to see them getting up to something, they were just lounging there in the Space Age chairs, chewing gum and paging idly through magazines, which is what they always did in the lounge. And actually it was more comfortable to lie on the carpet in the house where there was a kettle and a telephone and a usable toilet than out here in this cold room with its bare lightbulb. The rumpusing soon came to an end and the tide of yesterday's news swept back in.

In the school holidays after the Norton rematch, when the novelty of having no homework wore off, I became restless. I was sure there was an article in the newspapers I'd missed, some scrap of a story about Ali. Mom was in the lounge drinking tea with Mrs Mitchell, so I was free to ferret around in her knitting bag. No sign of the scissors. I turned to the sewing box where they were sometimes kept. There was a mass of stuff in there I wasn't supposed to touch, crochet hooks, bales of ecru cotton, limp hourglasses of embroidery silk. The pinking shears. The scissors themselves. Especially those. Long use had worn their black enamelled handles down to bright Sheffield steel. Cutting paper with them was strictly forbidden.

When we lived in town, a man used to come around once a year to sharpen all the edges in the house; he carried his journeyman's box from the delivery trike to the stoep and Mom took out the knives and scissors. The suburbs were beyond the knife-grinder's range. Now Dad had to take the scissors to a shop in Bosman Street.

Ah, the sewing scissors. They lay on a patch of velvet like a museum exhibit. Handicrafts of the ancients. The compartment alongside held a spill of buttons like unearthed treasure. I took the scissors out to the servants' room, propped a broken chair on a stack of papers at the kitchen table to which it had once belonged, and sat there like the night editor leafing through one old newspaper after another. Some of them had been pissed on by mice or dripped on by rainwater, but under the yellowed and crumpled front pages the sheets were crisply white.

On one such sheet was a single paragraph about Ali's fight against Rudi Lubbers, which had taken place on 20 October 1973 and passed me by. Under the headline 'Too Darned Hot!' it was recorded that Ali had strolled to a points victory over a plodding Lubbers in the steamy heat of Jakarta. The match ended farcically when Ali trapped the hapless Dutchman in a corner and pummelled him without mercy.

Branko

Ferdi Kouters is a Dutchman, an actual Dutchman, whose parents come from Utrecht. In Holland, not Natal. He's a tall boy with buck teeth and knobbly knees and a tuft of blond hair as thick as a paintbrush. He pastes his kuif to his head with Brylcreem but it springs up again in greasy clumps. He always wears khaki shorts and shirts. It looks as if he's wearing his school uniform all the time, but after school he changes into his regular clothes, which happen to be his big brother's old school uniforms. This brother also happens to be dead. He went on a holiday camp with the Seventh-day Adventists where he fell off a foefie slide and broke his neck.

Ferdi is the undisputed marbles king of Clubview and everywhere else. He's mastered all the games and beaten every boy his age, including me. Trouble is, most of us have stopped playing marbles now that we're in high school. Ferdi has no one to play with – until he discovers that the world is full of younger boys and it's easy to beat them. Like taking candy. A boy your age will give you a run for your money and quit when he knows he's beaten. But a pipsqueak is full of pride. He'll go on playing until his last marble is gone.

I'm not home the afternoon Ferdi comes over to play marbles with Joe. The deal was struck down at the shops. Mom sent Joe to Funchal Caffie for Hubbard squash or something, and on the way he had to pass the Kouters' place which is right next door, and that was when Ferdi challenged him. So Ferdi comes over and they start to play ringer in the back yard. Ferdi snaps a twig off the plum tree and draws a circle in the sand. They set up shy after shy and he wins them all. Joe has his marbles in a leather pouch that once held Grandpa Reilly's tobacco (you can still smell the rum and maple). His beauts are in a Mills cigarette tin (also Grandpa's) in his pocket. He has a glass ghoen and a special ironie, a three-quarter-inch ball bearing with a flat spot that fits snugly on the second joint of his forefinger when he gets ready to shoot and stops the ghoen from rolling when it hits the ground. This iron ghoen has never failed him, but the magic goes out of it today. He keeps missing. The ghoen drops down in the dirt like a meteor striking an uninhabited planet. Ferdi never misses. He has an ironie the size of a billiard ball. The story is it's a ball bearing he got from a train driver. With this massive ghoen he can blast five glassies out of the ring at a time. Sometimes glass chips go flying or a marble cracks clean through like a cough sweet, but it doesn't matter because there are so many others for the taking.

Joe's stock dwindles away. It's taken years of birthday presents, hundreds of games and hard-fought swaps to accumulate these marbles, but it only takes an hour and a half to lose them all. Every time he puts his hand in the pouch, lets the marbles roll over his knuckles, he wants to stop. But he can't because Ferdi is setting up the next shy. You can't stop in the middle of a game, he says. It's not fair. As the pouch gets lighter, Joe starts putting in more marbles, like a gambler who can't believe his luck won't turn. But luck has nothing to do with it. Ferdi's eye is perfect. It's less like a game than a procedure. Joe could just hand over the nearly empty pouch, but they have to go through the motions of competition.

When the glassies are gone Joe tries to call it a day. But Ferdi wants the beauts more than anything else. He's heard them rattling in the tin every time Joe bent to make another contribution. He won't let Joe stop, he says it's unsporting, ungentlemanly. They're playing keepsies. You can't say you don't want to play just because you're losing. Joe takes out the Mills tin and plays the Chinese checkers, the fire-red, the jade-green, the ivory, and then the pearlies, one after the other. And he plays the arlies, the white one with blood and squid ink stirred into its eyeball, then the blue-green planet with a silver equator, and then the others. Finally he plays his three glass ghoens. Now he has only the ironie left, the flawed one, the imperfect sphere. It's of no interest to Ferdi. He goes home with his deep pockets bulging. Joe goes inside with the purposeless ghoen.

When Dad comes home from work, Joe is moping. He was crying as he told me the story earlier, now he's just sitting on his bed looking defeated. I tried to cheer him up – You've lost your marbles, like the rest of us – but it did no good. Dad gets the story from Mom and then from Joe himself. His face goes dark: it's like when there's a storm coming and the horizon bruises over. Dad doesn't lose his temper often. It happened when Willie Cuyler hacked his shin with a hockey stick, and when Uncle Eddie threw an acorn at the Chev to be funny and it cracked the windscreen, and when Granny put her dirty two-way down the back of the armchair. Now he comes out of the room with his fist in the empty pouch. That little bastard, he says. I'm going to warm his arse, so help me, he won't sit down for a week. Mom doesn't even tell him don't you use such language in front of the children.

Joe doesn't want to go to the Kouters, he'll have to deal with Ferdi tomorrow, and the day after, but Dad insists. There's a lesson to be learnt. What's right is right. And anyway, who else will know what marbles are yours? I go along for luck. We park in the street outside. There's a short drive without a gate leading to the back door. All three of us troop up there, with Dad in the lead, and he knocks.

Mr Kouters opens the door. He's a big version of his son, who's skulking in the passage behind him, down to the khakis and the blond brushcut. A maid is at the stove cooking supper. As soon as she sees us, she shifts the steaming pot off the plate and disappears into the house.

Mr Kouters tries to defend his son, but Dad tells him how things are. Your son, he says, is nearly a grown man. What pleasure could it give him to take marbles off a child? Joe starts squirming: he doesn't like being called a child. Ferdi hops about from one scurfy foot to another, tugging at his shorts as if he wants to pee. That little craphouse knew what he did was wrong, Dad says afterwards. It was written all over him.

Dad won't compromise. He wants all the marbles back. Waving the pouch like a piece of evidence. Every last one.

Mr Kouters gives his son an earful. We can half understand the Dutch or maybe he's picked up some Afrikaans, like fokken and bliksem. He sends Ferdi to his room to fetch the marbles.

He comes back with a cake tin and opens it on the kitchen table. He's already added his latest winnings to the stockpile. We've never seen so many marbles in one place.

Dad rumbles around in the stock with his fingers. No, it's not these, he says. He's curious, he tells us later, to see what else Ferdi has. He just has a feeling there's more.

Ferdi goes to his room and fetches another tin, and another. When he opens the fourth one, Dad says, Jissimpie man, how many marbles does one boy need? Come Joe. Take your share.

One glassie is pretty much like another. Joe puts five or six handfuls into the pouch. Then he takes another one for good measure and funnels it into his pocket.

Now for the beauts. This is more complicated. Ferdi keeps his beaut collection in old handbags given to him by his mother. He fetches one from his room, a white patent-leather bag with a gilt clasp, and pours the marbles out into a casserole dish. It's like a feast in a sweet shop.

You can buy pearlies and chinas with clear colours, but the best beauts are priceless. They're arlies with colours swirling in them and each one is unique. Some of them may have been in circulation for generations, passed around in the marble economy from father to son. Joe picks through the dish and finds two beauts that belong to him.

Mrs Kouters appears at the shadowy end of the passage and Mr Kouters barks at her in Dutch and she goes away again.

Ferdi's bottom lip begins to quiver. At a word from his father, he fetches another, bigger handbag from his room and empties it into the dish. Nothing.

All of them! Mr Kouters commands.

So he brings out two more bags and empties them into dishes. Joe picks through them until he's found every last beaut that belongs to him and a few he didn't even know he had.

By the time we leave, Mr Kouters is fuming. We can hear him shouting as we go down the drive.

Don't ever let this happen again, Dad says as we're driving home.

I'm waiting for him to ask me where I was when my brother was being picked on, why I didn't stand up for him, as the Blahavić code requires, but he doesn't say anything. From the way he changes gears and taps his thumb on the steering wheel, I know he's pleased with himself.

At the end of Standard 8, Ferdi Kouters leaves school. A few months later I'm down at the shops when a police van careers around the corner. It's the Wierda Bridge cops looking for pass offenders. The black men shooting dice on the pavement outside the butchery scatter in five directions. Ferdi piles out of the passenger seat in a constable's uniform with a peaked cap. One of the men goes up Cornell Street where the Kouters live and Ferdi runs after him waving his baton. Just as they're passing his front gate, Ferdi's cap falls off and he stops to pick it up.

7

Poems

The highlight of today's arena events at the Rand Show will be sabre demonstrations by the SA Gymkhana Union, comprising the country's five best teams. The SA Police Band will start the afternoon's events with a performance at 1.30, followed by the grand parade of cattle at 1.45. At 3.30 the gymkhana groups will give a sabre demonstration. At 8.30 they will appear again and spike flaming pegs in the dark.

– The Star, April 1973

Joe

Like many Ali fans, the know-nothings who couldn't suck out of a sore thumb the name of a single boxer who hadn't been in the ring with their hero, I was at least as interested in the talk as the fight. I came from a family that set great store by having a 'turn of phrase'. We quoted the sayings of our grandparents the way other families quote Churchill or the Apostles. My Grandpa Reilly was a carriage fitter on the railways, and a good one too: he used to say he was so good with his hands, he could fit a cork to a duck's arse.

Ali was shouting the odds and making up rhymes from the start of his amateur career, but it was before his fight against Archie Moore in 1962 that the posturing and the poesy really got going. The pressmen, writes Gilbert Odd, *were anxious to know what fate he [Clay] had in store for the chrdlu cmfwy should they meet.* 'Chrdlu cmfwy' is a scrap of filler text, nonsense produced by a compositor running his finger down the keyboard of a typecasting machine, and there's not much you can rhyme with it. But 'Archie Moore' is a doddle: *It will have to be four, because it rhymes with Moore.* At the training camp before this fight, Ali came up with his first sustained doggerel: *I have left jabs that fire like pistons / and are twice as fast as Sonny Liston's ... Some say the greatest was Sugar Ray, / but they have not yet seen Cassius Clay.*

The third Ali scrapbook is an Eclipse drawing book the same size as the first, with ALi III inscribed on the cover in black ink. It contains two main sets of cuttings from 1974: those about the rematch against Frazier, Superfight II as it was called; and those about the buildup to the fight against George Foreman, the Rumble in the Jungle.

On the covers of the first two scrapbooks, the word 'ALI' was all in capitals; here it's a mixture of capitals and small letters. The 'A' is a definite, wide-footed cap. The 'L' might pass as a cap too, except that the foot of the letter is too short for the vertical stroke and it seems to be caught between upper and lower case. The 'i' is undoubtedly small. From a distance the letters look patterned or textured. From close up it's clear that each of them is made up of many rows of words, some of them sliced off to the left or right, as if the letters were machine-pressed from sheets of densely packed type. The letters are about 20 centimetres tall and contain 50 to 70 lines of neat, hand-lettered print.

The 'A' is made up of Ali's most famous – though not most poetic – catchphrase, a line that was both a conviction and a challenge, repeated about a hundred times: 'I am the Greatest.' After just ten professional fights, and having broken into the rankings at nine, Ali began to tell reporters that he was 'The Greatest' and he repeated the claim obsessively over the following decades, drumming it into every head, especially his own. One hundred iterations of 'I am the Greatest', packed into the letter 'A' like bricks, capture the obsession graphically.

The top-heavy 'L' is made up of another famous catchphrase, 'Float like a butterfly, sting like a bee', repeated dozens of times. Ask someone for a quote from Ali and this is probably what you'll get. It's not Shakespeare, but it has more poetry in it than the version the Ali camp was using at the time of the first Frazier fight: He moves like silk, hits like a ton. The butterfly and the bee first took flight together, according to Gilbert Odd, at the weigh-in for the fight against that Big Ugly Bear Sonny Liston in 1964. Clay (as he then was) turned up twirling a cane, sporting a navy-blue jacket with Bear Huntin' emblazoned on it in red, and proceeded to rave at Liston about the terrible things he was going to do to him. Ed Lassman, the president of the WBA, had him removed from the dressing room and fined $2 500 for disgraceful conduct. A usually sombre occasion, opines Odd, had been turned into a circus.

It is worth asking why the weigh-in should be taken so seriously. Even today, the occasion is often determinedly solemn, as if the boxers were condemned men being weighed for the gallows. The handlers and trainers all have long faces to show how much hard work goes into preparing a fighter so that he comes in close to the weight limit without slipping over it.

The 'i' in ALi III is different. Rather than being made up of the same repeated phrase lopped at either end, it reads continuously from top to bottom. Phrases or short passages drawn from twelve news articles have been strung into a text. These quotable quotes are arranged in a narrow vertical bar with a detached block floating above it. That block, a magnified dot moored above the body of the 'i', looks like this:

I   AM   THE   MOST   FAMOUS   MAN
IN   THE   WORLD   BUT   I   DONT   LOSE
TOUCH   I   AM   LOVED   ALL   OVER   T
HE   EARTH   I   AM   SO   WITTY   I   AM   PRE
TTY   AND   INTELLIGENT   I   COULD   SIT
HERE   AND   HOLD   MY   OWN   WIT
H   THE   MOST   BRILLIANT   TELEVI
SION   DEBATERS   IN   THE   WORLD   NO
OTHER   BOXER   LIKES   TO   SIT   ON

In those days I liked to while away an afternoon making drawings in Indian ink, intricate mazes and patterns of tiny words and emblems that required a patient, delicate touch. Ink is unforgiving. Once you've put it on paper with a nib it's almost impossible to erase. You can wait for it to dry and scratch it off with a razor blade, but the smooth surface of the page is invariably marred in the process. You need a steady hand and an eye for detail. I learnt as a child to dot my i's and cross my t's. I can imagine the pleasure it gave me to print the title of the third scrapbook, allowing the words to run up against the vertical edge and tumble down to the next line like coins in a fairground game. But I cannot truly remember doing it. How did I choose the constituent parts? I suppose I trawled through the scrapbooks, picking out comments and quips that especially pleased me, that I found funny or clever.

Here is the text that makes up the body of the 'i', with its parts separated out according to the twelve source articles:

the stage with me. I am too smart … Mr Nixon is the President, but he doesn't have the people behind him.

But I'm skilful. I know I'm a great fighter.

George Foreman is a sissy fighter. He fights like a girl … Joe Frazier is a good fighter. This was a great event.

If he whips me I will crawl to his corner on my hands and knees. I will look up at him and say, 'Joe, you are the Greatest.'

'No,' said Ali, 'You gotta talk after a defeat. I always talked after a victory. You got to talk.'

But he still had to have his say. I'm not going to cry, he told reporters.

I'm out to whup all the hypocrites in the power structure ... They're all afraid of me because I speak the truth and can set men free.

'Now I want security for my wife and three children,' he said.

All it would have taken was just three more times, bam, bam, bam ... I can't see possibly giving a man a concussion just to please the crowd.

Tax men victimise me ... Hollering about civil rights, all this integrating mess, just give me my money.

I'll say it again, I've said it before, / Archie Moore will fall in four.

My secret is self-confidence, / A champion at birth, / I'm lyrical, I'm fresh, I'm smart, / My fists have proved my

The first three quotes date from 1974, the rest from 1971. I must have selected lines from the cuttings I was about to stick into ALi III and then from the first scrapbook, and transcribed them into a pencilled outline of the 'i' until it was complete. The final quotation breaks off before the concluding *worth*, thus obscuring the fact that it's a rhymed verse. All the quotes are Ali's own words.

This patchwork of comments that struck a chord with my teenage self may be the clearest index of the qualities that led me to hero-worship Ali.

It isn't hard to see why a teenage boy, caught in a rigid, disciplinarian school system, subjected to the short-back-and-sides regime, the cadet platoon and the cane, at the mercy of teachers who wore their army step-outs to cadet parades and headmasters who took pleasure in making a boy bend over a chair-back to be beaten, would respond to Ali's taunting of the authorities, the hypocrites in the power structure, from the greedy taxman to the lying president. Ali was stroppy – bolshie, my father would have said. He could give you a thousand words without breaking a sweat.

He had a sense of honour and dignity. You have to talk even when you're beaten. And his concern for a beaten opponent tempered the brutality of the sport and was surely a sign of true strength. What did my father say? You don't hit a man when he's down. There are other middle-class truisms embedded here, such as the virtue of doing an honest day's work and keeping a roof over your family's head, indeed of having a family, a neat nuclear family with three children (Ali had only just gotten started). This was something I recognized. Also the notion that integration was a *mess*, which I heard often enough on the radio or in the classroom.

What about the boasting? That went against everything I'd learnt about the value of modesty and restraint. Don't blow your own trumpet!

Ali scarcely paused for breath. He would give Dizzy Gillespie a run for his money. *I'm skilful, I'm witty, I'm clever, I'm pretty. Pretty.* Here he needs it for the rhyme, but he always preferred it to 'handsome'. There was a double game going on whose point eluded me. He called himself pretty, but he was always childishly baiting his opponents with comments like this: *George Foreman fights like a girl.* How I would have liked to say that to Paul Skinner – although he could more justifiably have said it to me. *Now listen here ... bam!* There was no clear boundary between the talk and the fight. Ali was, as one of the scribes put it, as quick with a ready quip as a left jab. Boxing was a kind of physical wit; verbal wit was a kind of sparring.

This is the line that thrills me still: *I'm lyrical, I'm fresh, I'm smart.* I was smart too, or so I thought. Being smart was not the quality that got you into the egghead class at school: all that required was the ability to memorize some facts – the parts of the flower or the stages of meiosis, Pythagoras's theorem or the symbol for hydrochloric acid, the date of the Battle of Blood River or the objectives of communist ideology – and the will to do your homework when you could be playing soccer or chasing after a girl. No, *smart* was an American way of being clever, being extra-clever, even clever-clever, and it could be a liability. *Fresh.* Probably he meant that in the American way too – 'Don't you get fresh with me, child' – but my South African ear heard – hears – new, refreshing, *fris.* Which might also mean fit, robust, well built. *Lyrical.* He made up little poems, but this had to mean something completely different. He was a floating poem himself, an animate, explosive piece of pop verse, a sprung rhythm. In my awkward adolescent body, with my spotty chin and my unmanageable desires, I did not feel lyrical. But I had a sneaking, embarrassed suspicion that I could be, given half a chance.

Branko

We're on our way to Bapsfontein for the talent show. It's become our Sunday afternoon entertainment. Usually there's some professional act like Jody Wayne or Gene Rockwell to make it worth sitting through the roster of amateurs with their off-key renditions of 'House of the Rising Sun' and 'Distant Drums'. Last week it was Johnny Collini, who had a song in the Top Twenty not so long ago. Also on the bill was a plaasjapie in a shabby dustcoat and a felt hat with a turned-up brim, an Al Debbo lookalike, doing his version of 'Sousboontjies', stretching the *sooouuus* out into a gelatinous yowl that brought the house down. Well, not the house, exactly. The show takes place under a big, tin-roofed afdak in the grounds of the Bapsfontein Hotel and Pleasure Resort. The spectators lounge about on garden benches drawn up in rows and the tannies bring crocheted blankets to throw over the wooden slats. When a special act appears, let's say Virginia Lee or Dickie Loader and the Blue Jeans, the kids come running from the pool and their mothers pass around Tupperware tubs full of roast chicken. The girls wear ruched swimming costumes scrunched up like the curtains at the Oppies bio-caffie and they change colour as they dry from top to bottom.

It's a long drive from Clubview to Bapsfontein and it feels even longer out in the country, rolling down the bluegum-shaded back roads through the plots. Joe is sitting in front between Mom and Dad: the Impala has a solid seat like a sprung sofa. I'm in the back with Sylvie and her boyfriend. Out of the corner of my eye I see his slim brown fingers on her leg, just touching the hem of her miniskirt. Billy Darling is an appie at Iscor. Despite the name, he's an Afrikaner, like most of Sylvie's boyfriends. No one knows why she goes for the boys with thick accents and ducktail styles, the rough diamonds, as Mom calls them. Billy's wearing white hipster jeans and a black polo neck that causes the shampoo jingle to play in my head: look who's here, the man in black, he never worries about dandruff. Billy's crinkly blond hair makes a sort of gutter over his eyebrows and he tends it every now and then with a comb he keeps in his sock.

Joe turns around on the front seat, with the road spooling behind him, and leans over the backrest. He begins trying out his new Frisian dialect on Billy Darling.

Hy sleep in my room, he says with a nod towards me.

I've been introduced to the rules of this argot, which involves pronouncing certain English words in a weird Dutch accent to make a grammatically correct, semantically dubious almost-Afrikaans. To an Afrikaner *Hy sleep in my room* sounds like 'He drags in my cream', but what Joe actually means is 'He sleeps in my room'. Either way it sounds suggestive.

Billy Darling doesn't get the ins and outs but he knows it's funny, because the rest of us are laughing, so he laughs along. This brother of yours! He comes out with the strangest things. Sylvie is enjoying herself: her brother is amusing her new boyfriend.

Smeek hom in die vaas, Joe says to Sylvie, jerking a thumb towards Billy Darling. It's just possible that Billy hears this nonsense as: 'Beg him in the vase.' But we know he means: 'Smack him in the face.'

We all laugh like crazy, except for the butt of the joke.

Joe's new language is imperfectly simple. It uses only the present tense – the *het ge-* form won't translate – and the simplest nouns and verbs. It can't cope with polysyllables and abstraction, the leafy verbiage of language, but it clings to the Germanic roots like clay. It favours the imperative. The logic of it is unruly and it's always about to fail. Sometimes 'Smack him in the face' comes out as *Smeek hom in die vaas* and sometimes as *Smook hom in die fees*. Problem is a *smook* is also a 'smoke': *Gee my 'n smook en leet hom.* 'Give me a smoke and light it.' If a 'smoke' is a *smook*, then 'spoke' should be *spook*, but just as often it's *speek* or *spuik*. In the end, he's milling a set of Netherlandish diphthongs into his own half-baked kitchen Dutch. He's a one-boy experiment that demonstrates the hazards of making and breaking your own rules.

Leet haar 'n smook, he says to Billy Darling. He wants him to give Sylvie a smoke. The laughter dies in the back seat. Sylvie's been smoking the odd fag on the sly and if Dad finds out he'll hit the roof.

Billy Darling has a pack of Texans in his sock (the other one). The sock is white to match his jeans, and his shoes are white too, soft white moccasins.

Darling Billy as Dad calls him looks glum. He still hasn't picked up the language, but he knows the joke is on him.

Sylvie catches Dad's eye in the rear-view mirror.

That's enough, he says to Joe.

But with Joe it's never enough.

Joe

The first two pages of the ALi III scrapbook are devoted to the Ali-Frazier return, which took place at Madison Square Garden on 28 January 1974. Superfight II went more or less as the scribes foretold. From the bell, Frazier bulldozed Ali relentlessly, and Ali backed away, used the ropes, and peppered Frazier with every counterpunch and combination in the book. The bout went the full twelve rounds and Ali won a unanimous points decision.

This was Ali's first fight after he started training at Deer Lake – Muhammad's Mountain as the press took to calling it – and he attributed his victory to the new camp, saying he was in the best physical shape of his life.

The rest of the scrapbook deals with the buildup to the Rumble in the Jungle. Fully nine months passed between Frazier in January and Foreman in October, and Foreman actually had a fight in between, against Ken Norton in Caracas in March, which was over in two rounds. The amount of coverage on the buildup is extraordinary. Roughly half of it concerns the time just after the announcement of the fight, while the other half deals with the time just before the event, once the boxers had arrived in Africa.

From the start, many of the sportswriters predicted that the fight in Zaire would be Ali's last and few gave him any chance of winning. In August, Archie Moore came to Johannesburg at the invitation of Maurice Toweel to attend the Trek multiracial tournament at Rand Stadium, and stayed on the 16th floor of Joubert Park's Landdrost Hotel, which had 'international status'. Moore told Norman Canale that he had taught Foreman how to beat Ali: George is like a little pink elephant ... he never forgets what you teach him. Later he contrasted Foreman the elephant with Ali the racehorse. Whereas the elephant can pick its way through the jungle, the racehorse keeps banging into trees: Yes, I see Ali panicking in the jungle and the trees he'll be running into are Foreman's left hooks and straight rights.

The prospect of a boxing match in Africa got everyone's blood up. Ali told reporters: When we get out in Africa with all my soul brothers and everyone rooting for me, he won't want to fight. He knows they'll put him in the pot. Foreman begged to differ. Ten years after Ali's conversion to Islam, Foreman goaded him: I'm going to beat your Christian tail. When ticket sales were slow, promoter Don King complained that Ali's talk about voodoo dolls had scared off US fans. But Ali was sure he'd have plenty of company in Zaire. En route to Africa, he told a press conference in Paris: ... I shall be fighting in my homeland. For 400 years I have been separated from my homeland. Me and thousands of other Black Americans are going home.

Under the headline 'It's goodbye to eternal butterfly – Annihilation awaits Ali in Darkest Africa', Alan Hubbard predicted the end: If the setting for the forthcoming 'superfight' is primitive, then this is as it should be. For there will be nothing sophisticated about the way Foreman sets about the final, brutal annihilation of Ali. It is a fight that belongs to the jungle. The Rumble flushed the animal imagery out into the open in Hubbard's piece too: Two men alone drawing others from their kraals in Kinshasa and their semi-detacheds in Kilburn. They'll come out of fascination, tugged along by a legend and the prospect of an exhibition of animalism normally reserved for the dark secrecy of the jungle itself. Ali's predictions of victory, Hubbard joked, were just a case of whistling in Darkest Africa.

In mid-September, Foreman cut his eye during a sparring session and the fight had to be postponed for six weeks. The citizens of Zaire, wrote Hubbard, [r]eared in tribal wars of harrowing intensity, found it hard to believe that such a tiny cut could stop the champion – boxing's chieftain is how he put it – from fighting. In fact, some American commentators said the postponement was a godsend because the television communications facilities for broadcasting the fight were not yet ready.

One *New York Times* reporter quoted in *The Star* thought the problem ran deeper than that. He was struggling to get through when he called. 'Oh, Zaire,' replied the operator. 'You know, they don't pick up the phone in that country.'

Meanwhile, the Zairean censors were cutting perceived criticism of the country from reports by foreign correspondents. Ian Wooldridge of the *London Daily Mail* had his copy ripped from the telex machine in mid-sentence for referring to Mobutu Sese Seko as Joseph Mobutu. Had the arrangements been left to Zaire, ran one joke the censors did not find amusing, Stanley and Livingstone would never have met. When it came to criticism, Hubbard wrote, the government was as sensitive as the skin around Foreman's eye.

The last few cuttings in ALi III date from late September and early October 1974, three weeks before the fight. Foreman was at the airport in a denim shirt and a floppy jockey cap seeing off Miss Viki King and Miss Trina Booker, who had been doing some PR work to promote the fight and were now going home to the US. Meanwhile, Ali was fooling around in the training ring, slumped on the canvas, pretending that singer Philippé Wynne of The Spinners had knocked him out.

A cartoon from late September shows the interior of the Zaire Press Club. Half a dozen scruffy newsmen are propping up the bar or playing snooker. There are posters of Ali and Foreman on the wall, an 'Out of Order' sign dangles from the doors of a telephone booth (perhaps the very one the *New York Times* was trying to reach), a notice behind the counter, where a buxom barmaid is preening, advertises 'Your Ali Lunch'. A man in a dark suit, who looks a bit like Don King, introduces a newcomer to the sceptical scribes: Meet our Mr Mongo – ringside commentator Regional News. Mr Mongo has curly white hair and a goatee and is dressed in a loincloth. He carries the tools of the trade: a talking drum and two sticks.

Branko

Curious idioms wash through our schoolyard conversations. Peculiar ways of saying things, odd intonations and catchphrases come and go. 'It must be Thursday' means you're behaving like a moffie. 'Psssshaw!' means absolutely, go right ahead. We pick up and toss aside crude terms for making every kind of judgement: tit, grand, evil, scaly. But nothing rivals the weird inventiveness of the inverted lingo that arrives with a single phrase – 'Did I feel large?' – and then infects all our talk.

'Did I feel large?' This means: I felt small. I was belittled, embarrassed, made a tit of myself.

The inversion is simple to grasp: you take a statement, replace the key word with an antonym and pose it as a question. You lay an exaggerated stress on the key word, which carries the weight of the line. 'Did I feel *large?*' And you can add a Gallic hand gesture, used in no other circumstance, in which the right hand shoots out, palm open, drops emphatically to the groin, so that the bottom edge of the hand strikes the body just as the key word is uttered, and then rebounds slightly towards the listener. It's a double underline. 'Did I feel *large?*' No, I felt very fucking small.

The Large is a flourish rather than a language and has obvious limitations. It's not the double Dutch the girls speak to conceal their secrets. You can't say much with it, but you can twist the tail of a story, underscore a punchline or turn a spotlight on the moral. When we stand around in circles at break, retelling the best parts of the latest Trinity film or acting out scenes from *The Party*, let's say the one where Bakshi loses his shoe and covers his foot with a piece of paper, the back-to-front interrogative, which always carries an element of mockery, threads through the laughter like a knowing chorus. Jack Barnard, who knows entire scenes by heart, is our most eloquent exponent. Bud Spencer taps the bandito on the shoulder. Excuse me? He turns around. There's the double take, the roundhouse, the duck and counterpunch. Bam! We laughed like crazy. 'Did we *cry?*'

The rhetoric of The Large allows even a compliment to be charged with ridicule. Vince van Lingen hails Derek Gibbs who's just won the cross-country: 'Shot hey Gibbs! Did you come *last?*'

Joe

Ali's schoolboy rhymes still make me laugh. A month before his fight against Foreman, he recited his poem of the day to Joe Durso at Deer Lake: If you think the world went mad because Nixon resigned, / You just wait till I whip Geroge [sic] Foreman's behind. Later, before he left for Zaire, he aired a variation on this theme: If Evel Knievel can make that jump, / I can beat George Foreman's rump. As the anonymous author of the article in which this poem appears points out, Evel Knievel's jump across Snake River Canyon in September 1974 ended in failure.

When Henry Cooper turned 32, Ali sent him a poem: After I've finished whipping you, / you'll think that you are forty-two. Happy Birthday. Your London Bridge will fall down. The couplet is no more than amusing. The afterthought, on the other hand, is superbly silly.

I didn't know then that stylized boasting was an American tradition. This is Ali at the press conference to announce that Madison Square Garden would telecast the Rumble in the Jungle: I'm fearless ... I wrestle with an alligator, I tussle with a whale. The other day I murdered a rock. I injured a stone. It's Davy Crockett. And sometimes, thirty years in advance, it's Chuck Norris: Last night, testing mah speed, I hit the light switch on the bedroom wall and I was in bed before the room was dark. It started raining last week. I handcuffed lightnin' and threw thunder in jail. I'm so mean I make medicine sick.

In a press conference, Ali referred to his first fight with Frazier and the fact that the referee and all three judges were white: I know I have the wrong complexion to get the right connection and the right protection. This is proto-rap.

At the time of the Norton fight, two Oxford dons supported an invitation for Ali to take up a professorship in poetry at the university. One of them said: This is not simply a joke. We should like to see him win. Apparently Ali could picture himself in the role. When Durso asked him what he would do if he won the fight in Zaire, he said: I'll get my briefcase and retire. No more fighting. Lots of speaking at all those colleges, nice-looking guy carrying the briefcase around. I'll be fine. They'll all have to bow and smile.

Angelo Dundee always assured reporters that Ali wrote his own doggerel. Ali himself used to joke about it. He told students at Harvard: I can't read or write very well, but I've got enough money to buy someone who can.

Branko

At the back of Joe's chest of drawers is a secret compartment. Except that it's more of a gap than a compartment and it's not exactly secret. The chest was mine before it was his. Why would I not have discovered the space behind the drawers when a sock or a pair of underrods disappeared into thin air? Before it came to me, the chest belonged to Uncle Eddie, which is why the interior smells of Vitalis hair oil. I reach into the splintery space and feel around with careful fingertips. First out is the blue exercise book full of names from the Bible. Huppim and Shuppim.

Nothing new there. I drop it back into the dark. Next: a diary with Reliable Appliances on the cover. Some rep must have given it to Dad, but he has no use for such things. Promising. And finally: the blue exercise book Joe's always scribbling in with his arm crooked over the page so that no one can see. Why write it down then? If you want to keep your secrets, don't put them on paper. Even then I suspected what I know now: we are a family of secret-keepers, secret-stealers and secret-dealers. We want to be found out.

The diary disappoints. Page after page of useless information, revealing nothing. Rode to school with Bob. Double Maths with Shillo. IDA after break. Worked on paperknife. Burger lent me new Bowie album. Read in the afternoon. Mom made pork chops. Listened to Test the Team after supper. Cool day. Jesus Christ. Pork chops! It's enough to make me puke.

But the exercise book wakes me up. The first five pages are all about Chloe Woodward. Bingo. Sonny Woodward was Dad's boss when he was still at the warehouse in Pretoria North. The Woodwards had money. More than us anyway. They lived in Irene in a house with French doors and a patio (which Lois Woodward called the *pay-she-oh*, as if it was also French) and a pool and a stone wall with a lychgate that was meant to look like England. Mom thought the Woodwards put on airs. When they invited us for supper she said she could do without it, but she came along anyway because you can't say no to the boss. Afterwards Dad said the beer tasted of Brasso: the Woodwards' houseboy must have polished the inside of the beer mugs. And Mom said that wouldn't be surprising, because didn't he once polish the soles of their shoes? Can you imagine. The first time Sonny went out in them he fell on his guava.

One shouldn't laugh, he nearly broke his neck. He could have ended up in a wheelchair. We didn't have a girl at home, never mind a houseboy. Mom did all the housework. That's the difference between us and the Woodwards, she said, we don't have houseboy stories. That's why we'll never be friends really. And also if we fall on our guavas it's no one's fault but our own.

Chloe was Sylvie's age. She had thick brown hair and the walls of her room were covered with posters from *Jackie* magazine. In front of her spindly wooden desk stood a fibreglass chair, the latest thing, a glossy scarlet pod like a wine glass on a slender stem. *Fibreglass.* The word made it seem fragile. Joe went mad, darting around the chair like a tribesman confronted by a pocket watch. Chloe invited him to sit on it, but he cowered behind the door as if it was about to explode. Everyone laughed like crazy. Then she demonstrated how strong the chair was by standing on the seat and twirling around like a fashion model and I couldn't stop looking at her legs. Joe must have been looking too because he made all these notes in the exercise book. He goes on about her alabaster skin and the hollows behind her knees and the rich coils of her hair all bristly with static as if she's just brushed it. Also her kindness and her tinkling laughter and her smell.

Then a blank page.

Then a page about the Afrikaans girl from three houses down. I've seen her slinking past in the street with her low-slung hips and her big nose. I didn't think he'd noticed her, never mind the little graph-paper checks of her skirt. Apparently she's called Lianie, which is a strange sort of name.

Another blank.

Then ten pages of love poems in his blocky print with a fountain pen, the mawkish things you'd expect from a schoolboy. I'm on poem three, which describes a girl with black curls and yellow bell-bottoms, before I realize it's the girl from the ice rink, the one who obviously fancies him, the Greek. But he's so terrified of her, terror being one of the more powerful manifestations of love, that he can't pluck up the courage to speak to her. Whenever their paths threaten to cross, he veers away and watches *from afar*. Usually I would keep the book, that was my plan when I fished it out of the shallows, and use it to blackmail him into mowing the lawn or washing the Zodiac. But the poems have a strange effect on me. He's got a way with words, that's what everyone says, but I've never understood it. Suddenly Chloe Woodward is interesting. I wouldn't have said she was much of a looker, but now I can't get her musk-scented mouth out of my mind. Of course, he didn't get anywhere near her mouth, he just saw the box of Beechies lying on her bed, but knowing this makes no difference. I put the diary and the exercise book back in the hidey-hole and say nothing. Until now, when it no longer matters.

8

Tactics

CAPE TOWN – Tonight's boxing tournament here had to be postponed for a second time when West German Arno Prick, brought in to fight Mike Schutte, had still made no appearance late last night.

– *The Star*, January 1974

Joe

Everyone knows that Muhammad Ali was more than a boxer, that he was an artist of the ring. Alongside the catchphrases and prophetic rhymes that have become part of popular mythology, he invented an idiosyncratic tactical language to describe his artistry. Most boxers are journeymen who learn the trade without expanding its possibilities. Ten thousand hours of sparring will knock the ideas out of your head. Ali was an innovator, in the ring and out of it, and naming his innovations magnified their power.

Like the virtuosic riffs of a musician or the metaphorical embellishments of a writer, Ali's figures were meant to astound. He nearly always spoke of them extravagantly, drawing attention to them as aspects of a show, in the same way a magician pops his cuffs or flourishes his empty top hat. This routine was designed to psych out his opponent, a technique he perfected, but it bore little resemblance to the jaw-thrusting and chest-butting practised by later boxers.

Ali's best known tactics were the rope-a-dope and the shuffle. The rope-a-dope, where he lay back on the ropes and defended, was showy but functional, aimed at keeping out of trouble when his own offensive moves weren't working, and tiring out the other man; the shuffle, which involved shifting from one foot to the other in an eye-crossing blur, was a purely rhetorical demonstration of speed and virtuosity.

In the run-up to his fight against Buster Mathis in 1971, Ali told reporters: I've developed a new punch. I found it during my fight here against Jimmy Ellis four months ago. It's a half-chop right hand and it dazed Ellis. He *found* it, the way a painter might find a new method of applying paint to the canvas or a guitarist a new tuning for his instrument. Demonstrating the short right on an imaginary opponent, he explained the mechanics: It's a chop with a twist ... I call it the linger-on punch. I'll execute it on Buster in the third round ... and he won't know where he is. After the fight, he spoke about the new punch as a means of protracting his opponent's suffering: It doesn't make you critical. It just makes you linger on.

Whether or not the punch was new in Ali's repertoire, Henry Cooper had felt something like it in the ring with him: [Clay] is a long puncher, he said. He flicks with his wrists at the last split second. It is a reflex down-clip with the heel of the glove. He drags the skin, and tears it.

Bout by bout, the tactics multiplied. By the mid-seventies, Ali was expected to unveil a 'secret weapon' before each fight and they rolled straight off his tongue and into the press. Before Chuck Wepner, it was the 'Wepner Whupper', before Foreman, the 'Ghetto Whopper'. The latter was a version of the 'Bolo punch' invented by Kid Gavilan, the former world welterweight champion from Cuba, who was then in Ali's retinue. The Ron Lyle fight prompted a new awkward offence: I'll rush at him and stop short ... People won't recognize me. The idea is to confuse Lyle. After a couple of rounds of him trying to figure out what I'm doing he'll get tired and I'll finish him off. Bamboozled into submission.

In the event, Lyle proved difficult to fool. He would not fall for my rope-a-dope game, Ali said afterwards. So I played the mirage game from the centre of the ring. That's when a man thinks he sees an opening and he don't. No other fighter can do what I'm doing. Lyle didn't even try. When Ali went into the shuffle, he stood back and watched in admiration.

The tactical rhetoric reached a manic climax before the fight against Joe Bugner in Kuala Lumpur. One of the not-so-secret weapons rolled out before the press, the 'Russian Tank', was a parody in itself: it involved wrapping both arms around his head with his elbows jutting forward like the prow of an armoured vehicle. The 'Malaysian Waltz' was designed to knock Bugner off balance.

After one training run, Ali told reporters he would be using both the Malaysian Waltz and the Ghetto Whopper on Bugner. This is in addition to my mirage, rope-a-dope, the Russian tank, the Ali shuffle and double shuffle to outwit, out-hit and outclass Joe Bugner ... My five tactics will throw him off balance, and with two more new styles, I predict now that he will not last the distance with a man of my experience.

Five tactics! Two new styles! It was comically excessive, like the five boxing-themed cocktails they were serving up in the Ringside Bar at the Hilton.

Entering into the spirit of things, Bugner's camp gave as good as it got. Manager Andy Smith said that in addition to his 'Bazooka' tactic – a sensible response to the Tank – Bugner would use the new Kuala Lumpur lumper – a hammer-like punch on which Bugner was practising very hard. 'Ali will be disagreeably surprised when he gets one of these in.'

The press devoted a remarkable amount of space to Ali's inventions and Bugner's ripostes, despite the fact that no one was taking any of it seriously. Ali was a copy-generator and column-filler. Sometimes the demand was so intense that the dynamo faltered. Even as the tactical repertoire grew, the threats became more generalized. I've got a new tactic to surprise him. In the first round I'm going to do something that will put fear into his heart. He'll be so frightened he'll go weak at the knees. There will be a slaughter – they're going to lock me up for what I'm going to do to him. It will be against the law.

Not long before he fought Bugner, he unveiled yet another fighting style, but wasn't bothered to name it. It is defensive and I'll tell you the name later. The new style involved blocking Bugner's punches. The whole point is to manoeuvre your opponent into vulnerable positions, hit him quick and get out, and at the same time stay out of hitting range.

In other words: boxing.

9

Pictures

Charlie Chaplin plans comeback
London – Charlie Chaplin, after nine years of retirement, is planning a return to film-making. During the past weeks at his Swiss home he has been completing a film he has written and hopes to direct. It is called "The Freak." It is the story of a scientist in South America who captures a girl with wings and is exploited. Chaplin has also been writing music.

– *The Star*, March 1974

Joe

Two composite pictures. The first was taken from a magazine, probably *Scope* or *Personality*, and is made up of three images over the headline 'Louisville Loudmouth'. Three full-figure portraits floating on a pale-grey background show Ali the boxer at three different ages. From right to left, counter to convention, they show the boy, the teenager and the man. The three figures are not in proportion: they've been scaled to suggest a progression in a pleasing visual arrangement.

On the right, Ali as a ten-year-old. He has his guard up, bare-knuckled, and wears a pair of satiny shorts with LOU KY in block capitals on a white stripe down the side, and black shoes. He's looking straight out at the camera with a questioning expression on his face. Like so? he could be saying. His right shoulder is dropped and his chest turned away defensively.

In the middle, Ali as a youngster around the time of the Rome Olympics. This time he's gloved up, the guard is a little lower and his muscles are slack. He looks like a gangly, uncertain teenager. His chin is down and his eyes don't meet yours. The high-waisted Everlast shorts and flat-footed stance make his legs look skinny.

There is little in the first photo, and not much more in the second, to suggest that you're looking at The Greatest. But that's him in the third, no doubt about it, the heavyweight champion of the universe. He's around thirty or so and in his prime, perfectly toned, handsome and groomed. His stance is coiled, his gloves dropped almost to his waist, elbows floating out from his sides. He looks straight into the camera, eyebrows raised in a look of supreme assurance. Nothing in the pose is defensive: he's itching to throw a punch. Note the haze around the right glove, a flicker on its glossy curve, as if it's already moving.

The second composite picture, possibly cut from the same magazine and accompanying an article on the documentary *a.k.a. Cassius Clay*, shows Ali in loudmouth mode. Five matchbook-sized portrait photos are stacked down the edge of a page like a strip of film. Two of them are famous images of a young Ali shouting the odds, with his mouth stretched so wide you can count his teeth. His nostrils are flared, the whites of his eyes glaring. You can tell at a glance that he's clowning around, playing the fool. In the third open-mouthed portrait, Ali – caught in the middle of an uncharacteristically modest knockout prediction? – is showing the camera nine fingers. The remaining images, the top and tail of the strip, belong to a later era. In one he has a folded towel draped over his head as if he's just finished fighting or working out, in the other he's bareheaded; in both, his eyes are shut and his mouth is wide open. If you didn't know the context, you would assume it was a scream of terror, pain or rage.

It's striking that a boxer who made so much of his good looks, his *prettiness*, should so often pull faces for the camera. I was surprised then not just at the shape Ali managed to stretch his face into, but that he did it at all. Adults did not usually behave like this. Even children were discouraged from mugging. If someone sneezes, my mother used to say, your face will stay like that.

Some of the loudmouth pictures are like freeze frames in which the camera, seeing so much more than we do, reveals exactly what happens when a fist hits a face, how skin and muscle bulge away from the bone, what purpose is served by the skeleton. These pictures bear some resemblance to the photographic convention of the mock blow – the posed image in which the boxer pretends to punch someone. This accomplice, who could be anyone from a fan to the president of a country, or very occasionally another boxer, and then usually a former opponent or a fighter from an obviously different weight division, contributes to the charade by pulling a face, trying to look like someone who's just been punched. The mock blow with its affectionate assertion of dominance sends a double message: I could punch you, it says on the part of the sender, and break your jaw, but I wouldn't dream of it. And on the part of the recipient: I trust you not to punch me, but here's my jaw anyway, go ahead if you must, my pleasure.

There are mock-blow portraits of Ali scattered through the archive. The edition of *Time* magazine that hit the streets on the morning of the Fight of the Century contains two. The first is on the 'Letter from the Publisher' page and shows Ali with his left fist resting precisely on the chin of *Time* correspondent Joseph Kane. Ali is glaring down at the reporter, who looks back through black-framed spectacles and gives him a goofy grin. The other is in the body of the article and shows Ali mock-punching his beefy handler Salameh Hassan. The two are side by side in the back seat of a car. Ali has his right arm crooked around Hassan's neck to pull him close and his left fist mashing into his nose. Hassan has the mug of an old brawler anyway, but he enhances the effect by screwing shut his eyes and pulling a crooked mouth. Ali is biting on his bottom lip, all concentration.

While Ali was in training for Foreman at Deer Lake, he posed for no fewer than three mock-blow shots with animals (there are three in the archive at least, and there may be others). Perhaps the country atmosphere captured in the name of the camp had something to do with it.

First up was his horse. Ali has the reins in his left hand and his right fist raised as if he's going to use the horse's nose as a speed ball. According to the caption, he and this spirited animal are getting acquainted. In the second photo, Ali is shaking his right fist at a chained cougar. Illusionist Doug Henning used the cat in his magic show, which so impressed Ali that he invited them to visit Deer Lake. The caption reads: Muhammad is doing his share of the snarling in this Ali-cat show. In the final image, Ali is standing at a wire fence, which calls to mind the ropes of a ring, with his fists raised, gazing apprehensively at a cow in a field. The cow turns its long white face towards the camera and looks pensive and bemused, as cows often do. Who knows what it's thinking? In the article overleaf, Ali says of Foreman: He's slow as a cow – got a face like one too.

In the whole of the archive there is not a single photograph of Ali with a bloodied nose or a cut eye. The closest thing to an injury is his swollen jaw after the loss to Norton, and then, lying in his hospital bed, he looks more insulted than injured. He's always going on about his *unmarked* face, his flawless good looks, and so this unlovely swelling must be an affront.

The idea that Ali was never hit is a fiction, of course. He was not a slugger and he was fast enough to keep his head out of range some of the time, but he was hit repeatedly in every fight, like every fighter. Leafing through these pages, it would be easy to get the wrong idea. To see the busted-beak industry for what it is, you need to look at the men Ali beat, at Joe Bugner and Chuck Wepner.

At Henry Cooper.

The famous photo of Cooper after his Wembley Stadium fight against Ali (then Clay) in 1963 is the most shocking in the archive. It renders literal Budd Schulberg's comment that great fights are 'allegories authored in blood' (Cooper: the damage always looked worse than it was). Cooper was cut above the left eye in round 3 and his corner wanted to throw in the towel, but he carried on. By the time the fight was stopped in the fifth, the eye was swollen shut and the cut was open like a mouth. In the photo, he looks butchered, with thick gouts of blood from brow to chin and a thinner tracery on his neck and chest. He has blood in his ear, blood in his hair. It looks like the make-up department got carried away. It looks like the end of *Rocky*. Except that this is no Technicolor fantasy, but the murky, black-and-white world of the real on newsprint. It reminds me of the scenes I pored over in *True Detective* where the bullet-punctured corpses of mobsters lay sprawled among overturned tables, broken dinner plates and white linen, in spills of blood that seemed to my innocent eye impossibly dark and extravagant.

Branko

The Louisville Loudmouth. My brother should know better than to show me these pictures. It's exactly the showing-off that made me dislike Cassius Clay in my schooldays. Having a big mouth was not a virtue then. We've gotten used to it now, but too much yackety-yak used to be seen as a feminine failing. Men kept their traps shut. They didn't cry either, but now everyone's expected to do it. If you hold your tongue and put on a brave face, people think there's something wrong with you.

You know, I was thinking about what you said the last time, Joe says. 'Listen to the material.' I followed your advice and I came to an interesting conclusion. The weirdest thing about all this stuff is that it's so silent. It doesn't say a word.

I look at a photo of Ali and words come pouring out of the mouth, the loudmouth, in a long beeline.

Isn't it strange? Joe goes on. He was famous for the patter and the poetry and all we ever saw was dumb pictures. I don't think I ever heard his voice. Can you remember?

It irks me that I can't. I say: He must have been on the radio.

That's what I thought, the transistor was on all day. We'd have heard him on the news. I am the Greatest!

There would have been clips from the fights on the newsreels too, on *African Mirror* or whatever.

Do you think so? Wasn't that all Stirling Moss and Danny Kaye?

Maybe when he fought Henry Cooper.

Here we are again: paging and smoothing. It's two months since I visited him in Troyeville and I thought this was behind us. But he's back at my dining-room table, unannounced as usual, with his pile of old paper. Where does this new single-mindedness come from?

As he fidgets through his archive the smell of dust and damp comes off it. It smells old. It actually stinks of the past.

It's true that the pictures are silent, I say. They're also still. Maybe that's even stranger when you think about it. Boxing is nothing but action – and look how calm it all seems. This staging, without a breath of movement, makes it seem so significant. This is the moment that matters, this moment and no other. It's all poise, all pose with nothing in between, none of the clinching, panting and grunting. There's no soundtrack. The world used to come to us like this. Stopped in its tracks.

Even the bloody moon landing escaped us. It was live on television, the single most dramatic moment of the century, and all we got were grainy pictures on the front pages the next day. Do you remember how we longed for television?

The nationalists thought it would be bad for us.

And they were right, boet.

Fucking Nazis.

Then he stops paging and points at another photograph. Also a characteristic expression: the snarl. Judging by how sweaty and tousled Ali looks, it must have been taken after a fight or a sparring session.

The photo jostles a memory loose in my mind. You were always worried about Ali's colour, I say.

What do you mean?

You don't remember?

No.

It puzzled you that he didn't really look black.

You mean he didn't look like one of our Afs. Like Caiphus.

After all these years, he still thinks I'm a racist. Caiphus is the guy Dad used to bring home from the warehouse on a Saturday afternoon to work in the garden.

I'm serious, Joe. We used to puzzle over these pictures and try to figure out who Ali was. *What* he was. He was black, that was obvious, but he didn't fit the familiar definition.

He takes this in. Then he surprises me by saying: I can believe it. You know, he was the great hero of my schooldays, but I never told my friends. I couldn't admit to it. It must have felt wrong to me. Embarrassing somehow.

I gave you a hard time about Ali, I say. I'm sorry.

You weren't as bad as the old man.

Still. It's weird to think about it now. Foreman looked black to me, I remember, he looked like an African. But Ali looked like something else. Maybe it was the first time I ever had second thoughts about these categories.

Joe is poring over a cutting that shows Ali at three different ages. Look how dark he was as a kid, he says, and how fair he is in this one here. Like a different person. Did they do it deliberately?

Who?

The newsroom.

For a moment I thought you meant the authorities.

We examine the photographs like a couple of clerks in the Bantu Affairs Department.

Check the kuif, I say. He looks like Elvis.

Jissus, Branks.

Before he became a heavyweight, of course.

I can tell you that the hair took a lot of work. He had a guy on the payroll whose only duty was to comb it, so he'd look good for the camera.

No way. The conversation about Elvis the Pelvis and Evel Knievel comes back to me. I say: I reckon he's just stepped out of a roadster into the ring.

Now Joe can't help laughing. Viva Las Vegas!

But our talk has unsettled him. Soon enough he gathers up his papers and goes. Em's working overtime at the museum, he says, and he's got to pick up a pizza on the way home.

Night falls with a hush and the neighbourly scent of wood smoke.

The rumble of the traffic recedes, the birdcall of a car alarm sounds and falls silent, and then the dark comes up over the lawn and the pool like a wash of Indian ink.

I should get up, put on the lights, switch on the heater. But the twilight has dazed me and I can't move. The backs of my thighs soften against the cushions of the armchair. I'm becoming part of the furniture. Sometimes I sits and thinks, Dad used to say, and sometimes I just sits. A line he picked up in a movie, I always thought, he and Mom were great moviegoers when they were young. Then Joe came across it in an old *Punch* miscellany. The caption of a cartoon from the Belle fucking Époque!

It's annoying that Joe didn't ask me about my so-called writing. My contribution to *the book*. He was so excited to hear that I'd made a start – and now he loses interest. Just when I'm finding my voice, he wants to talk about silence.

There was a time when I went to the movies just to listen. Training my ear. I'd sit through the whole film with my eyes shut. An old foley man at Reverb told me it would sharpen my ear. Or was it my eye? It's not enough to hear, he said, you must *listen*. Sounds have shapes, they're long or thick or rounded, they have colours, textures and weights, they're solid or hollow, sharp or flat. And it's all true. But it was a trial sitting there in the dark, eyelids itching to open, head reeling with talk and sound effects, doing my best to picture the thing in my mind. I sat through *Raging Bull* like this – or is it just my brother's obsession that makes me think so? – and my bones ached for a week afterwards. It's something the kung fu directors discovered long ago: half the power of the blow is in the sound it makes. That's why the boxing fans want to sit ringside and up close: they want to *hear* the fight. The real fans, I mean, not the frauds like my brother who can't stand the sight of blood. If it wasn't for the calm world of the broadsheets – I should have told him so – he would never have 'fallen in love' with Muhammad Ali.

I get up to close the blinds. And when I switch on the pendant over the kitchen counter, there it is, like a fighter in the ring: the ALI I scrapbook. Sneaky bastard! He thinks he's putting one over on me again, but actually I'm pleased to take another look at it without his Mickey Mouse gloves directing the traffic. I hook a stool closer with my foot and flip through the book from beginning to end and back again. I can't be bothered to keep order in his cuttings and a couple slip out onto the counter. Although many of them have come loose, others, for reasons a specialist might be able to supply, are still stuck to the paper. I page onwards and cuttings fly. Perhaps I'm doing it deliberately, flinging the pages flat in the face of Jimmy Ellis, Buster Mathis, George Chuvalo and scrambling up his little system.

Lights in the driveway. It's Jordan in the Corsa. After a few minutes he comes in with his girlfriend, who goes by the name of Gaia, a mousey little thing, or she would be if it wasn't for the strange haircut, soft bristles on the scalp and then a long yellow tail like a badger. Not that I've ever seen one of those.

What is this thing? He recognizes it from the last time.

It's your Uncle Joe's Ali scrapbook. One of several.

Awesome, says Gaia, prodding one of the cuttings with a sharp fingernail as if to check whether it's alive. She's studying to be a physiotherapist.

Uncle Joe the fight fan, says Jordan. Are you shitting me?

He talks like this, as if he's in an Elmore Leonard story. I've stopped trying to correct it. I say: It was a long time ago, Jordy.

No shit. This looks like it came out of the Ark.

Escape from the Planet of the Apes, says Gaia. She's reading the back of a Joe Frazier cutting. It's the Saturday matinée at the Capital Theatre.

That was the place to be seen, I say. In my own ears I sound like a voice-over on *African Mirror*. One of the movie palaces. It must have seated a thousand people. When I was a teenager it was past its heyday but it still had a sort of moth-eaten glamour. There was an enormous screen and a velvet curtain, and plaster statues of the muses – maybe – in alcoves. Overhead a midnight sky full of twinkling stars.

Like Montecasino, says Jordan.

Something like that.

'Police raid party in Waterkloof.' Gaia has moved to the back of Chuck Wepner. The good stuff's on this side, she says. It's like the return of the repressed. The cops raided this place because there were rumours that blacks and whites were dancing together. Scandal! Doesn't say what happened. It's cut off in the middle. Look.

He wasn't interested in that side, I say. Suddenly I'm protective: he was just a kid.

But the reverse world has become compelling. I'm surprised it never held my attention before. We turn the pages and look at the backs of the cuttings. Most of it is sports news, of course, the soccer at the Callies, hockey at the Iscor Club, athletics. But Ali was often on the front page of the papers too and the second page has all kinds of things on it, including politics and advertising. A world comes back to me. It rises from the yellowed pages like a kind of soundtrack. Mineworkers die in an accident ... The tea room at Garlicks ... is alleged to have taken his thirteen-year-old daughter to a shebeen where he flirted openly with Indian girls ... The Publications Control Board ... Capital Motors ... involving the Chinese in proclaimed White group areas ... Lawnmower Services in Bloed Street ... Internal squabbling in the Rhodesian Front ... after stabbing to death his four-year-old playmate Podromis Heotellis ... found Bierman wearing only a 'see-through' nightgown and Enozi in a state of undress, standing beside the bed ... he took flashlight photographs of them and –

My phone rings. It's Rita. Are you okay?

She sounds anxious. I'm fine, Reet. What's up? Where are you?

I'm in the street outside, she says. I got the fright of my life. The whole place is in darkness! What the fuck's going on?

When she comes in a minute later, she's still got the panic button in her hand to signal how much of a fright she got.

Jesus Branks. I thought something had happened. Oh, hello Gaia.

Hello Mrs B. She should only know what Rita says about her look: like a tennis ball with a growth disorder.

We're just getting a history lesson, says Jordan.

It's freezing in here!

She stomps around switching on lights and drawing curtains, pushing the dark out into the garden, back to the wall.

After Jordan and Gaia go to his room, I reach for the scrapbook but Rita gets there first. And this?

It's a scrapbook about the Fight of the Century. Made by Joe.

Was he here?

About an hour ago.

So I have to tell her the whole story, how he pitched up with the scrapbooks, the archive I mean, asking for my help, and wanted me to collaborate on his book, and insisted that I read part of the manuscript. I meant to tell him to get lost but instead I offered to write some things down, and it's harder than it looks. I'm worried about him, he's drinking too much, he might be cracking up, what if his mind's going, you'd think I was his editor. He was here again today to talk about the pictures, and their silence, actually it's quite interesting, you know, you remember things you thought you'd forgotten. There was a time, I tell her, long before we met, when I went to the movies just to listen.

Reet is a good listener herself. She lifts and angles her chin and holds her head still, and listens through the whole spiel without interrupting. She should have been a therapist.

Then she asks: What are you going to do?

Think I'll just see where it goes.

You're too involved already. You should get out while you can.

It'll be fine.

He's using you again.

He wants me in his corner.

Nonsense. He's trying to pick your brain. He always takes advantage.

You shouldn't be so hard on him. I think he wants us to be closer. You know we've drifted apart in the last while.

The drama about the car thieves wasn't my fault.

I know, Reet. It's more than that anyway. Our lives are just too different.

We go on talking while we get the supper together.

How's your mom? I ask. She was summoned to Silver Oaks earlier. The second time this month.

In trouble again, Rita says. She's set up a poker school.

That's against the rules?

Apparently bridge is acceptable but poker is frowned upon. It has the wrong ethos. They play for drugs. And Mom's the dealer.

When we go through to the lounge and switch on the TV, the news is all about the miners' strike in Marikana. The name is familiar: we used to pass the turn-off to Marikana when we drove out to the Magaliesberg for the weekend, to Mountain Sanctuary Park or Tonquani Gorge. I didn't know there was a mine out there.

Before I take the scrapbook back to Joe's place, I phone to make sure that he and Em are out.

I need a soundtrack for the drive. Last time Chris Gordon's salty swells worked well enough, but when I stick *Master and Commander* in the player it sucks me down in an instant. I skip to the battle theme and head for Troyeville in a broadside of drum rolls and brass.

The neighbourhood looks dodgier than ever. Flaking walls and sagging fences on all sides, three bursting garbage bags on his doorstep, lilac leaves crushed to yellow dust in the gutters. Could it have run down so much in a couple of months? Perhaps he's right that I can't see the improvements. His next-door neighbour has started a B&B. At least, he's got a handpainted sign with a cellphone number wired to his gate. FULL ENGLISH BREKFAST, it says.

My plan was to roll the scrapbook up and stick it in the postbox, the loudmouth box he had installed for his book deliveries, but now that I'm here I have second thoughts. What if some passer-by lifts it? He'll never forgive me.

The charlady might be here. I get out and rattle my key in the diamond grille of the back gate. The yesterday, today and tomorrow is budding early, thrusting small bruised fists out of its woody twigs. It senses a change in the season that's still hidden from us. Violet comes out in eyeglasses with pink lenses. She's just had her cataracts done at the Gen. She says Joe will be home in ten minutes, I should come in and wait. She's got the key in her hand and she's reaching for the padlock, but I say no, I've got to be somewhere, and I push the book through the bars.

Joe

To convey the brute force of the heavyweight boxer, the scribes portray him as a machine. His fists are sledgehammers, his punches are pile-drivers, and where normal men have a heart, he has an engine. Joe Frazier is described as a motorized Marciano. After Superfight II, one writer states that Ali was never able to douse the fire completely in the Frazier engine room.

During Ali's first fight against Joe Bugner, the British boxer was cut for the first time in 49 outings. But Danny Holland, the man who used to repair Henry Cooper, did a magnificent job of patching up the wound. Cooper's battered bodywork was a good place to learn your trade.

If Frazier and Cooper are steam engines or lorries, Foreman is a piece of earthmoving equipment. Alan Hubbard, looking ahead to the

Rumble in the Jungle, says that Ali will be unable to avoid Foreman's thudding, bulldozer fists.

Boxers also reach for this metaphorical toolkit. Cooper's fist is like a well-used tool. The 'ammer, he calls it. It went in – bang – short and sweet and hard ... When he talks about his hook, it sounds less like a punch than a piece of tackle attached to his arm.

These tools are strangely debilitating. A boxer with his gloves laced on is as helpless as a baby. He can work on his opponent, but he can do nothing for himself. He cannot pull up his pants or comb his hair or put in his gumshield – although many boxers bat themselves in the mouth with a glove to make sure it's lodged. If a gloved-up boxer needs to piss, someone has to hold his dick for him.

Sometimes it's as if the tool has a life of its own. Describing the moment he hurt his right hand during the Norton fight, Ali says: It hit Norton on the head and something went pop.

Cooper has a similarly detached view of his eye. He talks about it as if it belongs to a stranger and is out to get him. I could feel the blood dripping down. It was coming from above the left eye ... the suspect eye ... the eye that always seemed to go at the most crucial point of a fight. Occasionally the perspective tilts and you become aware that it's not him talking but a boxing writer. In less than half a minute my face was a mask of red. It's hard to imagine any boxer seeing his own face from the inside in these terms. This is the view of a spectator at the ringside.

The mechanics of the blow should not obscure the fact that the boxer is nothing if not a feeling body. Cooper knows when his punches are connecting because he can feel the jarring right up his arm. Jerry Quarry describes this feeling with anatomical precision: I knew it was all over. I threw in my Sunday punch and felt it jar all the way from my second knuckle to my shoulder. This is the punch that knocked out Jack Bodell in 64 seconds.

Boxers know where to find their organs – and the organs of the other guy. They have a special love for the kidneys. Before the Fight of the Century, Quarry, still smarting from his defeat four months earlier, makes it clear that he's rooting for Smokin' Joe: Clay will get his kidneys busted! This is exactly what Frazier has in mind: Clay can keep that pretty head, I don't want it. What I'm going to do is try to pull them kidneys out. I'm going to be at where he lives – in the body.

Branko

There are cinemas in town like the 20th Century and the Pigalle, but we only go there if someone has a birthday party. Mainly we go to the bioscopes down the road in Voortrekkerhoogte. Sylvie likes the Garrison Hall on a Friday night when the oumanne from the army camps arrive in their step-outs with their berets moulded to their bristly heads. Joe and I prefer the 1 AD on Saturday mornings. That's 1 Ammunition Depot.

Dad drives us there. Besides Joe and me, there are always two or three boys from the neighbourhood. Dad likes to pull their legs. We can tell when he's talking bull, but they don't know him. If Tim Knowles or Herbie Mitchell asks what film we're going to see, he says, Buck Jones in *The Daring Dive for the Dying Stompie*.

You can't really call the 1 AD a bioscope. I suppose it started out as an ammo dump or quartermaster's stores, a prefab put up in a hurry during the Second World War. It's a corrugated-iron half-barrel like a big oil drum that's been cut through lengthways and painted khaki. There's a heavy black curtain over the door where a soldier leans through a hatch to take our five-cent pieces and then we run down to the front and sit on the fold-up seats clutching our rolls of sweets. It's stifling inside and the air is thick with cigarette smoke from the troepies who fill the rest of the hall. These okes haven't had a weekend pass for a month and the girls know to stay away. The place smells of sweat, dust, boot polish, fruit gums. When the dangling bulbs go out the kids in the front rows whoop and whistle. Tiny beams of light drop from the iron vault as if the place has been pierced by shrapnel. Then the projector clatters at the back and an image reels onto the screen.

At the Garrison you'll see a film with Bette Davis or Alain Delon in it, but here the films are left over from the war years and my big hero is Gene Autry, the singing cowboy. I also like the black-and-white serials in the supporting programme, even though I always miss an episode or two and they sometimes show them in the wrong order. The Martians in the sci-fi serials are slimy lizards and live in underground caverns of papier mâché. The robots are tin toys made in Hong Kong and even a ten-year-old can tell there's a midget inside. In the adventure serials the hero always hides behind a pile of wooden crates to spy on the smugglers, and their trucks are just like the Bedfords waiting outside to take the soldiers back to the barracks. You know the episode is about to end when the truck goes on a mountain pass after the brake cable has been sawn through with a Bowie knife. The hero pumps the brake pedal but the music puts its foot down and drags you on, faster, faster, until the truck veers off the road and disappears over the edge of a cliff.

To be continued.

10

Questions

"Now I gotta win my greatest fight ever — I gotta get a visa for South Africa!"

House Sitters Service
Provides responsible people to live in and look after your house, servants, animals, garden, pool, while you are away. Telephone 41-3903

– The Star, June 1974

Joe

The press repeatedly raised – and dashed – my hopes that Ali would visit South Africa. Just months after I started the archive, it was reported that Ali, or rather Clay, was coming to the country to present a series of lectures. New York agent Richard Fulton, like many after him, tried to keep politics out of the picture. Ali's talks would not deal with race, he said, but with finding meaning and purpose in your life. We do not want people in South Africa building up any feeling that Ali is coming to cause trouble. The unnamed reporter pointed out that the anti-apartheid organizations, like the American Committee on Africa, had not yet commented on the plan, although they had condemned Percy Sledge's 1970 concerts and a proposed visit by Aretha Franklin. Whether or not resistance from these quarters played a part, the lecture tour did not go ahead.

In mid-1972, speculation about a South African visit flared up more intensely. Three promoters were trying to set up a local fight: Reliable NE Promotions, Danie van Zyl and Dave Levin (working with agent Bill Miller in New York). Reliable seems to have been the frontrunner. Ali's lawyer Bob Arum met company representative M A Karolia and two financial advisers in New York to discuss a fight against an as-yet-unnamed opponent at Ellis Park, Johannesburg in September. Arum called on the South African consul general in New York to gauge the government's attitude. Apparently the promoters had already approached the government directly.

Arum conveyed Ali's position: he would fight anywhere if the hotel and other facilities were acceptable and the visit would be completely non-political. On the racial segregation of the spectators, Mr Arum indicated that he would reluctantly accept segregated seating. He warned, however, that if the proposed fight became embroiled in South African politics it would be called off.

Arum also reacted, with no apparent irony, to a report in which promoter Danie van Zyl said that both Frazier and Ali favoured apartheid and were eager to box in the Republic. Dismissing this as outrageous, Arum said that politicizing the fight in this way would prevent it from happening at all. As far as Muhammad Ali is concerned, South Africa is like any other place in the world. If the financial arrangements are satisfactory he will fight but he will not get involved in the political situation.

Ali had been speaking out on race and politics for a decade and any attempt to hold politics at a distance in this case was doomed to fail. South Africa was *not* like any other place in the world. Asked whether Muhammad Ali, as a Black Muslim, favoured racial separatism as distinct from the enforced apartheid of South Africa, Mr Arum said Ali himself would have to answer that kind of question.

Later it was reported that the proposed fight had been postponed indefinitely because of uncertainty about the attitude of the South African boxing authorities and Government. Essentially, the government's position was that it would not proceed with the visas until the South African Boxing Control Board approved the fight. And presumably the Board was under pressure not to approve the fight or felt it could not do so until it was clear that the boxers would receive visas.

This bureaucratic impasse gave the Ali camp a way out. Ali's booking agent Chris Dundee explained that South Africa could not be fitted into the schedule. Ali would be facing Floyd Patterson at Madison Square Garden in September, and would then go straight for Frazier, and so another fight was out of the question. Apartheid had nothing to do with their decision.

Late in 1972, there were reports that Ali would be fighting Al Jones in Johannesburg in November. Ali denied that African delegates to the United Nations had pressured him to stay away from South Africa, but conceded that they may have pressured his lawyer. Arum himself was quoted as saying that tremendous pressure was being put on Ali to cancel his plans.

Ali commented: As long as there is an arena in South Africa where the Blacks will have separate but equal seating I will be happy. Odd as it is to see the phrase 'separate but equal' attributed to Ali, it does not come from the apartheid handbook: As a Black Moslem I am in favour of separation. We want to have our separate schools, our separate social institutions, our own culture. We want our own country and our own flag. This is more than an appeal for religious autonomy. We want everyone to marry into their own group, whether they are Black, White, Chinese or Mexican. We love ourselves and we want our children to look like us.

Ali tells another reporter: White and Black can't get along ... There's gonna be separation – physical separation – of the two races. I don't know when, but it's gonna be soon. Allah says so. Black people must have their own land. The American must repay the Black man for his work and slavery, or else America is going to be destroyed ... White people aren't my enemies ... I'm with them every day. It ain't hate we're teaching, it's racial pride. Look at my daughter, Maryum. She looks like me. My wife over there, she looks like me. It's not right for a man to marry out of his race.

It's easy to see how Ali's comments were construed as support for 'separate development' and racial purity. They would have warmed the hearts of the nationalists in South Africa who were then pursuing the homeland policy and prosecuting people under the Immorality Act. Yet the same people could not have taken kindly to comments like this: I'm fighting for my freedom and carrying the hopes of my 30 million Black people here and that's what my mission is.

Branko

In his last years at high school Joe falls in with a character called Mikey van der Plank, a cocky little bugger I don't like much, but at least he's a bad influence on my brother. They go into town on a Friday afternoon and they tell Mom they're going to Stereo Heaven, where their pal Davenport has a weekend job and they can listen to records all day. Instead they go to Perry's snooker saloon on the dodgy side of Church Square, a dim, dingy hall up a staircase that smells of stale beer and cigarette smoke, with twenty tables under lights.

I had my Perry's phase too. Some of the top-class amateurs use the place to practise (there aren't any pros) and you can watch a frame or two if you keep still when the guys are potting. You lighties aren't even suppose to be here, the manager told me and Louis Ferreira the first time we tried our luck there. If you eighteen, my name is Mary. I'll lose my licence if the cops find you here. So here the rules. Don't make noise. Don't drag the rests over the cloth. Don't lie on the table. We don't wanna see your trick shots. And don't put your quart down on the edge of the table here. These tables was recovered last year. If you spill beer on our lovely cloth, you or your old man will pay. Got it?

Then Joe and Mikey start hanging out at the Keg and Tankard. Despite the name it's just a garden-variety bar at the end of an arcade in Schoeman Street. The Suid-Afrikaanse Landbou-Unie has its HQ in the building and the boozers find this amusing. They're always joking about the Agricultural Union and the drought and the crops in the fields. When the place first opens the manager dishes out free monkey nuts and encourages everyone to throw the shells on the floor to create some atmosphere. In the end you're ankle-deep in shells. Then the fire department gets to hear about it and declares it a fire hazard, so it's back to the Marley tiles.

Mikey has a philosophical side, Joe says, and it comes out when he's pissed. As they're reeling home from Sportpark station after a night at the Keg, Mikey will look up at the stars and say: Is there anyone out there? Where does it end? What are we doing here?

Sometimes the two of them go to an actual kroeg, one of the hotel bars with batwing doors onto the street, the Belgravia, where Grandpa Reilly liked to drink, and drink, or the Edward on Paul Kruger Street, or they nurse a quart at the Culemborg where the beer is more expensive. They think they look like grown men on their stools at the long bar, but actually it looks like some barfly brought the kids. Ask me.

Mikey has a sister and she's Joe's first girlfriend. She's just a kid, but then so is he. He takes her to see Hawk at the City Hall – her Mom drives them there – and they sit around on the lawns among the hippies trying to look cool. Walter Battiss is there. Joe knows who he is because he taught Uncle Eddie art at Pretoria Boys. He's the only real artist any of us has ever come across. He's carrying around a bucket of water with a mealie in it and Frieda – that's the girlfriend – dares Joe to go and ask him if he can buy it. He must say he's hungry. So Joe goes over and says, Mr Battiss, do you remember Eddie Reilly? You taught him in the 1950s. And Battiss says, Yes, I remember him well, a very talented boy, what's he doing these days, and they talk a bit. Then Joe goes back to Frieda and says, It's not for sale. He's going to eat it himself.

Joe's notes about Perry's and Battiss are in the blue file and some of it rings a bell. But at the time my brother's secrets were of no interest to me. I was in the army and he had to grow up on his own. When I look back he's a younger boy than the one who starts boozing and gripping his girlfriend (as he inelegantly puts it) in the back row at the Capital. For me, it's like he spent the whole of high school in Standard 7.

Joe

It was early spring and the weather had warmed, but we were still in our winter uniforms of grey flannels and blazer, and I was sweating as I walked home from school down Rabie Street. I walked on the tar close to the kerb, keeping to the shade of the pines that grew in a long row beside the road. Beneath the trees was a barbed-wire fence and beyond that a field.

My thoughts must have been elsewhere, because I was almost on top of the fallen woman before I saw her. She was an old woman wrapped in a blue blanket and she lay on her back beyond the fence, with one leg folded under her and the other caught between two strands of wire. The trapped foot was in a blue slipper with a brightly coloured pompom on its toe. A barb had punctured the brown skin of her calf and a trail of blood ran down over the curve of the muscle. Her head was turned to one side and she was staring at me.

I should have gone to help her, but I couldn't move. The deadweight of my schoolbag dragged on my shoulders and sweat ran down my sides. I was rooted to the spot, as bound to the earth as one of the pines, and yet my thoughts lifted out of the everyday and circled upwards. What was I thinking? That a trap had been laid for me and was about to be sprung. But why? She gazed at me unblinking, and I gazed back, numb with dread. If she had called out for help (I tell myself) the spell would have been broken, but her lips were pressed into a grim line. We were muffled in silence as if the sky had fallen over us like a hot blanket.

A bicycle went past and skidded to a stop. The bike had thick tyres and a wicker basket over the front wheel and the rider was a small black man wearing a grey dustcoat over his clothes. He kicked down the stand, hoisted the bike onto it and came closer, stepping lightly, with his fists balled, and for a moment I thought he was going to hit me, but he turned aside and squatted at the fence. While he spoke to the woman, I read the words 'Henry's Stationery' on the back of the dustcoat, and then I looked at the bicycle and saw a large roll of brown paper canted in the basket. Kneeling in the grass, he eased the wires apart and freed her leg.

Wat makeer jou?

I thought he was speaking to her. But he had straightened up to face me and his tone was disappointed rather than concerned. What's wrong with you?

He did not expect an answer. Catching up the tails of his coat with one hand, he prised the wire strands apart by stepping on one and raising another, and stooped swiftly through the fence. The woman groaned as he knelt beside her.

The blood flowed into my limbs and I fell back into my own body. I went on walking down Rabie Street almost as if nothing had happened. My face was burning and I kept glancing over my shoulder to see if I was being followed.

Every open field around there had a path cutting across it to shorten a walker's journey. She must have taken a short cut and lost her footing as she climbed through the fence. The heat had made her dizzy. She was unwell. The strands of this explanation twisted together sensibly. But the logic of my part in the story, or rather my failure to find a part in it, escaped me.

I passed the Webbers' house. There were four brothers and they had a band, the Webber Brothers Band, like the Allmans. Sometimes on my way home from school I heard music coming from the house, clamorous versions of 'Born to Be Wild' and 'Aqualung', but today the place was quiet.

In the shade of the flyover, where Jean Avenue passed under the Ben Schoeman freeway, I put down my bag to rest for a minute. Cars and trucks droned overhead and the pavement seemed to tremble. Then I walked on again.

I turned into Von Willich Avenue and crossed Durham and Cornell and Columbia. We'd lived in Cambridge Road for years before I found out the streets were named after universities.

Wat makeer jou?

It was a good question.

11

The Rumble
in the Jungle

New York. – The Watergate special prosecutor's office has moved to subpoena former President Richard Nixon as a prosecution witness in the Watergate cover-up trial, it was disclosed today.

– *Pretoria News*, September 1974

Branko

There are smallholdings on the eastern side of Von Willich Avenue, plots of a few acres with the houses set far back from the road. We can see the Drummonds' house from our front yard, a small stone castle sticking out above a field of fruit trees. Morris, who's a year ahead of me at school, spends his afternoons on the ramparts practising the bagpipes.

His own mother doesn't want him in the house, Mom says, and who can blame her. You'd think he's strangling a cat.

The Drummonds' orchard might once have earned a smallholder a living, but the trees haven't been pruned for years. In this wild place full of crackling veld grass and scurrying animals, we play at being frontiersmen.

When Sylvie's cat Smokey disappears, we reckon he's been run over or killed by a dog. Six months later, or perhaps it's longer, Joe and Tim Knowles and I are rooting around under the Drummonds' apricot trees when we spot what's left of Smokey high up in the fork of a branch. At the sight of him, the grinning skull and bared claws, my skin crawls. Tim is up the tree like a monkey and poking at the fur with a stick. It hardly even pongs, he says. We're used to coming across the seeping carcasses of cats and dogs on the roads and stirring up the maggots in their broken ribcages. All the juice has gone out of this one: he's just a furry grey bag of bones, moulded to the branch like a rotten fruit the flies have sucked dry.

We tell Dad about our find and he says Smokey must have gone up there to die. It's a cat's instinct. Leopards do the same thing when they're wounded or sick.

He sends Joe and me back to the orchard with a saw to retrieve the body. He could do it himself more easily, but he wants us to do it. We're learning a lesson.

We take the rip saw from the pegboard in the garage and a length of old tow rope with frayed ends and we go all the way around the block and up Columbia Road so that we don't go past the Knowleses. With hardly a word spoken, we've decided to leave Tim out of this mission.

I climb the tree as easily as going upstairs. You could build a tree house in a tree like this, except that it doesn't belong to us. The carcass frightens me less from close up. It might have been made in the Arts and Crafts class out of chicken bones and fun fur. I tie one end of the rope around the branch, saw through it and lower it down to Joe. The cat's remains don't weigh much, but we bear them home solemnly between the two of us for the sake of ceremony.

We dig a grave at the bottom of the yard, between the last row of fruit trees and the wall, one large enough to hold cat and branch, and bury him right side up the way we found him, with his chin resting on a knot and his paws dangling down. Sylvie doesn't want to see him, she'll die, but once the hole's been filled in and a brick laid on top like a tombstone, she comes down and cries, and says we've done a very good job.

Joe

The sportswriters of the 1970s waged a rearguard action against the rise of television by asserting the value of newspapers as a means of documenting and understanding the world. They were champions of the written word.

You can see them at work in the blow-by-blow accounts of big media events like the Fight of the Century. On the whole, their descriptions of the bout are formulaic: Frazier, moving in close, dug two hard rights to Ali's body ... Ali pumped over a left and right and then another left and right to the head ... Ali peppered two more jabs to the head. Yet even these repetitive runs emit small flashes of life: Ali prayed in his corner before the opening bell ... The referee told both to stop talking ... Frazier taunted his opponent and then took two jabs to the head. But Ali had a worried look on his face ... That fleeting look in round 5 presages how the fight will end and tells us we are not yet in the age of the visual image. Even in the most functional contexts, reporters are still 'painting pictures' in words.

Telecommunications had sped up. On the day after the Fight of the Century, *The Star* proudly told its readers that the radio pictures published in that day's edition were received directly from Madison Square Garden. The films were processed in specially built darkrooms under the ring and transmitted by radio to London, where they were piped to The Star's picture receiver in Sauer Street in a non-stop operation. Piped? Non-stop. Like a canister full of cash down a pneumatic tube in a department store. But the point was made. The proximity of the reproduction to the flesh-and-blood fighters – 'under the ring' – and the immediacy of the transmission magically closed the geographical distance and put everyone 'ringside'.

The fact is that transmission did not always happen this quickly. On

14 March 1971, nearly a week after the event, the *Sunday Express* ran two colour pictures of the Ali-Frazier fight on its front page and seven more inside. The paper called this another great colour scoop.

South Africa was not the best place from which to observe developments in the mass media. In the absence of television, sport was still news rather than spectacle. Elsewhere in the world satellite technology was bringing about a fundamental shift and this can be traced through the archive in a rising tide of information about the arrangements and logistics, the facts and figures on television audiences and purses, all the trappings of a nascent global entertainment industry.

The first Ali-Frazier fight was watched by 20 000 spectators at Madison Square Garden and millions of others on CCTV in specially designated arenas. There were reports of near riots at some of these 'theatre TV' venues when the transmission was interrupted. The purse was $5 million. By the time of the rematch three years later, the purse had grown to $6 million and the projected CCTV audience to hundreds of millions. Superfight II was expected to gross $16 million once the TV receipts were counted.

The Ali-Foreman fight shifted the ground. Significantly, the announcement that the fight would take place in Zaire was made (in March 1974) by Hank Schwartz, the president of Video Techniques Ltd, the CCTV company that had contracted both fighters. The loudmouth money was in the media. The purse was $10 million. The Zaire government had put up guarantees and the promoters Hemdale Leisure Corporation, headed by British businessman John Daly, had coughed up the front money. The fight was scheduled for 3 o'clock in the morning to meet a 10 p.m. time slot on the East Coast of the US. In the face of the predictable outcry, Schwartz expressed confidence in Zaire's technical capabilities: We will be able to beam the fight to anywhere in the world where there is a TV set or a venue for closed-circuit. It will be the largest sports project of all time. He was also well aware that it was bigger than sport. Muhammad Ali, he said, had become the biggest draw in the history of *entertainment*, bigger even than Sinatra and Elvis. The company predicted a television audience of one billion people. In August, when a press conference was held to launch the ticket sales, it was announced that Madison Square Garden would participate in the telecast, joining 450 locations in the US and 35 in the UK where the fight could be viewed. According to Daly, the telecast would contribute ninety per cent of projected revenues.

Earlier that year Daly had spoken prophetically about the increasingly global reach of the mass media: ... we could soon see the day when you can stage an event and the whole world will watch. And it can't be long before everyone has a pay television, where you put your money in the set and tune in to the latest film or football match. Or war, he might have added, or earthquake, or election campaign.

The scribes were not all thrilled with the way things were going. Alan Hubbard wrote several articles lamenting the fact that the pursuit of cash by a greedy league of boxers, promoters and governments had turned the traditions of boxing upside down. Gone were the days when the cigar-sucking moguls of Madison [Square] Garden, or Miami Beach called the shots; now it was the Swiss bankers, the gnomes of Zurich – and Cairo. Listing the names of the stops on Foreman's world championship itinerary – Kingston, Jamaica, Tokyo, Japan, Caracas, Venezuela – Hubbard seemed to blame globalization itself for boxing's ills. Ironically, the pressmen who deplored the commercialization and professionalization of sport were an integral part of the evolving media machinery that made it possible for sport to become a global business. In his disapproving criticism of the Zaire staging, Hubbard put his finger precisely on what was happening: Kinshasa's stadium will simply act as a giant TV studio.

None of this had much relevance for South African boxing fans, who had yet to see a TV set. Local entrepreneurs did their best to compensate. In the run-up to the Rumble in the Jungle, the Sterland Complex in Arcadia, Pretoria brought the Ali vs Frazier rematch to the screen. For your ringside seat, contact Cine 16 now. In mid-September, Cine 303 in President Street, Johannesburg screened Ali's fights against Quarry, Bonavena and Frazier twice a day. Kevin McLintock, the promotions manager of Hunter Cigarettes, which had acquired the South African rights to the film of the Rumble, announced that it would be screened in the main centres in South Africa within a week of the contest.

Better late than never.

Branko

The call comes from Em's phone but it isn't her on the other end.

You don't know me, a man says. My name's Riaz and I'm your brother's neighbour, from number 42, the house with the blue wall.

I think: I know that house – but I can't speak. Why's he calling?

Listen, he says. You'd better come now. Something's happened to your brother.

What's happened? I say. Let me talk to Em. Is she there?

She's here but she can't talk now. She asked me to phone you.

What is it? I say. You have to tell me.

He's been shot.

Oh Jesus. What happened? How is he?

It doesn't look good.

What do you mean?

Just come.

Is he dead?

He rings off.

I look at the clock on the kitchen counter. Six fifteen. Rita won't be back before seven and I can't call her either: she's in her yoga class with her phone switched off.

I dial Joe's home number and get the answering machine. Em, are you there? If you're there, please pick up. Nothing. Riaz? Nothing. Fuck this.

Jordan comes out of his room. His ears are uncannily sharp when there's something he wants to hear. What's up Dad?

I'm not sure.

The salad is already on the table. Just the three tomatoes still to add standing next to the bowl: I always cut those at the last minute so the lettuce won't go limp. Who gives a shit? Rita says. Stop being so controlling. I'm holding the dressing in my hand, the honey-mustard mix I got from Sylvie, which I was shaking up in a Grolsch lager bottle when the phone rang. My mind can't settle, it keeps skipping from one thing to another, the salad, the tomatoes, my brother, the dressing. I put the bottle down and wipe my hands on a dish cloth.

We're supposed to watch the rough cut of Jordan's movie tonight. I've already put him off twice.

I need to go out. Mom will be home soon. I'll try to call her from the car, but you know how she forgets to put her phone back on. If she hasn't heard from me by the time she gets here, tell her I'm at Uncle Joe's and she should phone me.

What's going on?

I don't know. He had some sort of accident.

I take the umbrella from the stand at the front door.

Can I come with you?

No Jordy, I need you to look after things here. There's chicken in the oven. It should come out in twenty minutes.

Then I run for the car.

When I turn the key a red tide of strings surges out of the dash and almost drowns me. It's Morricone's score for *The Mission*. Not on your life. I grab a movie-theme compilation from the console and jam it in the player.

The drive is all jump-cuts and cross-fades. The wipers keep clearing my mind, flinging one anxious thought aside so that a new one can fall in. The traffic is thick on Houghton Drive. More people take their cars to work when it rains, apparently. Especially on a Friday. There's the usual current of hysteria that rises with the first rain of the season, pedestrians with garbage bags over their heads darting between the cars, a taxi without lights turning into the oncoming stream. But the traffic thins as I go up Harrow Road. It's been Joe Slovo Drive for five years and the old name still comes into my head.

Once upon a time I came this way often, driving to Yeoville or

Kensington or going into town. Now I hardly cross Louis Botha from one year to the next. Joe was right: I'm suburban to my core. The Becker Street corner still makes me uneasy. A man used to beg here near the shul, a youngish man with curly hair and shabby clothes, and Rita said he must have been left behind from the eighties when there were still Jews in Yeoville. He'd be waiting on the kerb and then he'd shuffle up to the car when you stopped at the light and show you to wind down the window. Making that circular motion with his finger that usually means you're crazy. Always wanting money for medicine. Ja sure. And then one day he was in a dressing gown and slippers, with his head shaved and a plastic cup in his hand, like someone escaped from quarantine.

While I'm waiting for the robot I call Em's phone. I let it ring until it goes to voicemail and then I don't leave a message.

What would I say? Is this emergency legit? Just checking. I'm worried about Joe, scared to death actually, but my mind keeps straying to other anxieties. What if I'm being lured into a trap? I think I've heard Joe speak about this Riaz but I can't be sure. Maybe someone stole Em's phone and now they're using it to set up her contacts. For what? Riaz could be in on the scam. Or maybe he's got a gun to his head.

The last time I came this way was when I took the ALI I scrapbook back to Joe's place. My plan was to leave it in his letter box, but I thought better of it and handed it over to Violet. I haven't spoken to him since. His nose must be out of joint. When was that? A couple of months ago. The end of winter.

The slip road that takes you down to Saratoga Avenue has always felt like the cold heart of the city. They put some mosaics on the pillars of the flyover before the World Cup and it brightened the place up. But on a wet night like this, in the yellow glare of the spots on the concrete overhang, the place looks like a butchery. Water sheets down from the motorway above. As always, people are asleep on the traffic island under mounds of blankets and newspaper. Tonight they look like graves. While I'm considering this and keeping one eye on the mirrors for smash-and-grab artists, *Cinema Paradiso* winds to an end, the beautiful love theme that plays over the closing montage of movie kisses. *Fine.* Now the credits will roll upwards. It's always up. So that we can read down. That's the way it is.

Saratoga Avenue is a mess. The lights are out and every intersection's clotted with cars and taxis. Forcing my way into the jam, I get stuck in the downpour sluicing off the motorway and it's like I'm in a car wash. In a movie, a car wash is always bad news. It's a place where people hold furtive meetings, where they pass on secrets and get killed. Then the CD pops out of the slot and the mood of imminent danger eases.

The old man didn't like the radio playing while he was driving. Something about being able to hear the engine. When we were parked somewhere he'd let us turn it on. He and Mom would go shopping at the OK Bazaars in Valhalla, while we kids sat in the car in the parking area and listened to the Pip Freedman show. And when we drove to a cycle race on a Sunday morning, Mom would insist on music: it was the price of her company. Then she'd tune the radio to the A programme and it was always the King's College Choir or some churchy a capella group. Why couldn't they just sing the words? Joe would get their nonsense into his head and drive us all crazy for the next three days. Da ba da ba da.

There's a pool of water in the dip at Ellis Park next to the Rea Vaya bus stop, but it can't be too deep because cars are inching through. I hit one of the preset tuning buttons on the radio. On Classic FM someone's chatting to the head chef of the new Thai place in the Hilton. Joe hates these bus stations. Such a waste of money, he says, all you need is a sign on a pole. The important thing is that the buses come, that they come on time, that they go where they say they're going. That's what you should spend your money on. *Our* money! Who gives a toss about the bloody stations. I switch over to 702. Business talk with Bruce Whitfield. He's chatting to an expert on small business development about the seven — or is it eight — phases every business goes through. They're busy with number three. The expert says everyone can be an ontroppanaw. So I end up on Khaya. Machine-made music, that's what I need, something untouched by human hands. Doef doef doef.

That's still repeating on me when I turn into Nourse Street and pull over. There's the car at the dark end of the block, where the street runs dead against the park, Joe's Mazda at an odd angle under the streetlight with one wheel up on the kerb. That stupid jalopy he drove because no one in their right minds would want to steal it. The driver's door is open. A knot of people there on the pavement under umbrellas. Some of them standing, some of them kneeling. A big striped beach umbrella. That was Riaz. It's our speciality, he told me afterwards, pulling together in a crisis. It brings out the best in us. Everything calm and still, coming and going to the rhythm of the wipers. What did I expect? Flashing blue lights, luminous tape, cameras, lights, action? I switch off the radio. Later, when I go closer, in a booming silence, I'll see that Joe has been lifted from the car and laid on the pavement on his back. Someone has rolled up a jersey and put it under his head. There are crystals of glass in his hair from when the hijacker smashed the window. That was outside his own gate, the one with the ingenious flaps, before he drove off down here with a bullet in his chest. Someone else has covered him with a blanket. Em wanted to rush him to the Kensington Clinic, it's just around the corner, you can almost see the turrets from here, or carry him inside out of the rain, but Riaz said there might be evidence to gather, you shouldn't disturb the crime scene. The police are on their way. She should have insisted. How he would have hated this, lying out here in the street. Riaz won't budge: everything just as we found it. The only thing that will be moved is the blanket. By the time I go down there, it will have been pulled up to his chin. She won't let them cover his face. He's white as a sheet, as they say, and there's a dark shadow on the pavement which is blood, as I'll discover when I put the heel of my hand down in it, leaning over to kiss his forehead, something I haven't done since we were children, if ever. But now I'm sitting in the car looking down the long dirty street. The rain has eased but the gutters are running like mountain streams, like Tonquani Gorge in spring. The wipers are still flicking, slow time, to the dead march in my temples. Doef doef doef. The phone will ring any second now and it will be Rita to find out where I am.

Joe

In the whole of my archive there isn't a single line on the Rumble in the Jungle. I have scores of cuttings on the buildup to the fight and scores more on the fights Ali had the following year. But on the Ali-Foreman fight in Kinshasa on 30 October 1974: nothing.

It's a glaring absence, yet I don't recall when it first struck me.

The fight could not have passed without my noticing. I wrote matric at the end of 1974 and studying for those exams took up my time, but I was collecting reports on the buildup until the middle of October, just a fortnight before the fight itself. Dad must have gone on buying the papers and could have set them aside for me. Chances are that when the new year came and I was waiting to register as a university student, the papers from the first week of November were still stacked up in the kitchen by the back door.

Could a scrapbook devoted to the Rumble have gone astray? There may well have been enough cuttings to fill a drawing book called ALI IV. Or did I gather the cuttings together in a folder, meaning to paste them up later, and then lose the lot? Perhaps Mom ditched them by mistake. The fact is that none of the cuttings from the following year – those recording the matches with Wepner and Lyle and the returns against Bugner and Frazier – were pasted into books. They were all left loose in cardboard folders.

For whatever reason, my archive preserves nothing of what many consider to be the greatest heavyweight boxing match of all time. Certainly it was the high point of Ali's career, a transcendent half-hour in which athletic grace and power, tactical cunning and experience, and flamboyant showmanship came into harmony.

I could put down what happened, but no one really needs the blow-by-blow account. It's a lucky break for me. So much was written about the fight at the time, and so much more has been written since, that I'm relieved not to frame it for myself. My deficient archive authorizes me to pass over the Rumble like a shadow.

Then again, I could pretend the archive is complete. It wouldn't be hard to track down the relevant copies of the *Pretoria News* and the *Sunday Times*. I could read Norman Mailer, Budd Schulberg, George Plimpton, who were all ringside. Hunter S Thompson was in the vicinity too. But what good would it do? You can read them for yourself.

Branko

Pierre Fourie fights Victor 'The Animal' Galindez at Ellis Park in April 1975. It's the Argentine's first defence of his WBA light-heavyweight crown. Pier-*rie* (we give it two syllables) has had two shots at the world title against Bob Foster and lost both narrowly on points. If he beats Galindez he'll become only the third South African world champion after Vic Toweel and Arnold Taylor. Galindez has won more than half his 46 fights by a knockout. Fourie has just four KOs in 52 fights. The match is billed, unfairly to Galindez, as the classic boxer-vs-brawler encounter.

Dad's old work buddy Manie Steenkamp gets us tickets and comes along to the fight. It's a pity because that means Joe and I have to sit in the back of the bakkie like japies. Dad always swore he would never drive a Japanese car, but when the price of petrol starts to go up during the oil crisis, he spends his Christmas bonus on a Datsun bakkie. His love affair with Pontiacs, Chevrolets, Buicks, with the sound of the names and the engines, is over.

It's the first time Joe and I have been to a pro boxing match. We're at the top of the stand and can't see much of what's happening in the ring, but we can tell the boxers apart easily, because Fourie looks so pale under the lights, and their styles are so different. Fourie has a light-footed, dancing style and he uses it to keep out of trouble. Halfway through the fight he's clearly ahead on points. But Galindez is fitter and stronger and just keeps coming at him. In round 8 Galindez is cut above the right eye, but his corner works on it and it doesn't seem to affect him. By the last few rounds Fourie is exhausted, trying to trade punches with the bigger man, and clinching and holding for all he's worth. Galindez takes the fight on points. When the announcement is made there are so many people in the ring, we can't see the boxers. All we see is the cops hanging over the ropes.

We talk about the fight for weeks afterwards. The main thing is being able to say: I was there. And also: We was robbed – it's never 'were' – our guy should have won. Cops everywhere and they didn't lift a finger.

Joe's gone to university in Johannesburg but I'm still trying to figure out what to do with my life. I'm not inclined to study and I don't have the pass marks anyway. Everyone's talking about television. In a year's time the SABC is going to start broadcasting and we're waiting for the switch-on. Mom and Dad already have a TV set sitting dumbly in the corner of the lounge. There are jobs to be had, Dad says, you can get in on the ground floor. The corporation is recruiting and training technicians. You could be a cameraman, a sound man, a lighting man. Put your name down. I put my name down and get a job in a furniture store in Paul Kruger Street. It's an excuse to bugger around with their hi-fi systems.

I learnt to drink in the army and keeping my hand in seems like a good plan. Most nights I'm at the Rose and Crown or the Assembly Hotel with Gordie Bradshaw or Louis Ferreira. Once I see Clyde Skinner at the Edward, slumped over a brandy and Coke like an old barfly, and I bump into Ronnie Baker at the Oklahoman Motel in Silverton and he tells me he's married with a kid and the second's on the way. In the spring there's a beer festival at the Harlequins Sports Club, our Oktoberfest, with a big marquee on the hockey field and an oompah band, and Bradshaw creeps in under the canvas at the back of the bar and swipes a fifty-litre keg of beer. He rolls it across the field in the dark and down the embankment to the fence, where we pick it up later in his car. The next weekend we open the keg with a shifting spanner and throw a party. It's the biggest blowout in living memory. On the way home Ferreira crashes into a jacaranda tree and totals his Fiat. He's thrown through the windscreen but emerges with hardly a scratch. No one can understand how his big body went through such a small opening. Being drunk probably saved your life, the doctor says, and Ferreira takes this as a compliment. When I came to (he says later) surrounded by purple blossoms, I thought I'd died and gone to heaven.

One night Bradshaw and I are at the Assembly and I'm coming back from the bar with a couple of ginger squares for some girls we met on the dance floor, when I'm attacked by the manager and his sidekick. Eloff is built like a prop forward and his helper – some say it's his son – is a little runt with one leg shorter than the other who spends all his spare time lifting weights. They fall on me like a loose maul. If it was Bradshaw they wanted to bliksem I would understand, he's always looking for grief, but I've done nothing to upset them. Unless I checked someone's girlfriend skeef or bumped someone's elbow and spilt his beer. Or maybe my long hair offends them. Or maybe they just feel like moering someone. The boere of Snor City don't need an invitation.

The two of them haul me onto the pavement – no point getting blood on the carpets – and start beating the hell out of me. The band is taking a break and a crowd gathers to watch the show. The girls we were chatting up are standing at the back waiting for their cocktails. A couple of cops stroll out of the lobby to keep an eye on things. Eloff is insane with rage. He hits me on the top of my head with his elbow. He pulls a clump of my hair out and stuffs it in his mouth. The runt keeps kicking me in the knees with his orthopaedic boot. This is a good time for him. When I'm rolling around on the tar it looks like all the spectators are wearing corrective footwear, but it's just the fashion for platform shoes.

After a while, I see Bradshaw in the front row pumping his arms. I think he's showing me a boxing defence, but he's actually telling me to run away, which I do, leaving most of my shirt behind in the manager's paws. I run all the way down Visagie Street and hide behind a little ornamental hedge outside a block of flats while the boere go up and down shouting and cursing and looking under cars. At last they give up the search and I walk over to my flat in Sunnyside in my shirtsleeves. When I get into the lift, Chuck Wepner comes at me out of the mirror.

We should fetch Ferreira and go round there with a wheel spanner, Bradshaw says when he pitches up, we'll teach that rockspider a lesson.

But it's just talk.

12

Inheritance

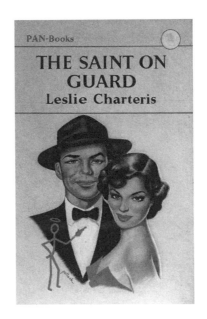

April 1st is OK TV day in the Transvaal when OK will present its TV line-up. Sparing no expense to bring you colour and monochrome receivers.

    – *Pretoria News*, March 1975

Branko

Joe's last will and testament leaves me with two timepieces: a chunky Seamaster wristwatch that belonged to Dad and the Ali archive. By the time I bring this inheritance home, my brother has been dead for eight months. The cuttings that say 'Writer dies in attempted hijacking' and 'City writer shot' are pinned to my noticeboard, but I don't believe the perpetrators will be caught. People get away with murder.

The archive consists of a cardboard box and a plastic crate. Of course, the Pres Les box is familiar. Easy Care Linens it says on the lid. I remember when Mom ordered these sets of sheets and pillowslips from a factory in the Cape. They were olive green and made of a synthetic material that dried in five minutes – a jiffy, we must have said – and did not need pressing, and they were so slippery you had to be careful not to slide out of your own bed when you turned over. 'Muhammad Ali' is printed on the side of the box in black Koki.

The crate is called Big Jim. It looks like a gigantic Tupperware lunch box and still has the Makro price tag on the lid. Its contents are a mystery. All I know is that it's the heavier of the two.

The reception is a family affair. Jordan slices Muhammad Ali open with a box cutter, folds back the flaps and lifts out the first scrapbook. This old crap again, he says. Sorry Dad, that's not what I mean.

Rita says: It's as if he had a premonition, coming around here all the time with his papers, trying to drag you into it.

How could he have known? He was just looking for someone to hold his hand.

He *knew* he'd never finish it, she insists. She believes in signs and hunches.

He thought he would live for ever. It's a common delusion among writers. Em had to package this stuff for me. It was in twenty different places.

It doesn't amount to much, does it? After a lifetime of effort.

Oh, there's plenty more but it's all gone to the Literary Museum. This is just the stuff he wanted me to have.

Rita pages through the scrapbook while Jordan and I rummage around in the box. As I thought: drawing books and folders.

What's in this one? She gives Big Jim a kick.

I'll bet it's some weird shit, says Jordan. Do you remember when that English poet died and they found a huge collection of porn in his house?

Erotica, I say. Your uncle would spin in his grave.

It could be teddy bears, Rita says, or snow globes.

You must be joking.

She sucks her cheeks in to show that she is.

We could sell those on eBay, Jordy says. My son the online ontroppanaw.

Enough, I say. He left this stuff to me and I'll open it when I'm ready. Now get out of here so I can do some work.

I really do intend to sit down at the Avid. But the archive is unavoidable.

There are six items in the Pres Les box: three scrapbooks and three collections of loose cuttings in cardboard folders. The books are marked

I, II and III, and the folders have schoolbook labels attached to them marked V, VI and VII. No sign of IV.

The books are held together by spit and Brylcreem, as Dad used to say. And love, the especially blind kind of love called hero worship. Here's a measure of it: sometimes Joe would find the same piece in two different newspapers, articles derived from the SAPA bureau and identical except for the headline or the size of a photograph, and he'd clip and paste *both* of them into the scrapbook. On the same page.

Hardly any of the cuttings have a source attached to them. The exceptions are those clipped from the top of a page that includes the newspaper's name and the date. No wonder he tried so hard to keep order in this shambles. If cuttings start falling out of the books I'll have the devil's job figuring out where they belong. No one will ever be able to quote from this stuff and say where it's from.

The reverse world comes back into view, a jumble of interrupted stories, jokes without punchlines, dismembered images. It was Jordan's girlfriend, ex-girlfriend Gaia who said this was the real thing … Introducing the radio cassette player. You'll see knobs and switches, buttons and gadgets such as you've never seen before … Mark Saxon and Sergei … Haig whisky. Don't be vague – insist on Whatchamacallit … painless metrication is within easy reach of all … Regent Conversation Ties. The mood sweeping the world … Modesty Blaise. The left side of Modesty Blaise, one enormous, fiercely lashed eye … These bits and pieces, which owe even more to chance than the 'archive' that produced them, reek of the past. I could cut them into a soundtrack, something you can almost hear and half understand. But I'm not making a film.

I pop the lid off the Big Jim crate and it exhales vegetable matter. More paper. Books, files, magazines. Here's José Torres's *Sting Like a Bee* and Mailer's *The Fight*. A tattered issue of *Sports Illustrated*. *The Fighters* by Chris Greyvenstein. *An Autobiography* by Henry Cooper. A faded photocopy of 'The Fight' by William Hazlitt. *The Fire Next Time*, *I Write What I Like*, *The Autobiography of Malcolm X*. Piles of Leslie Charteris. A dozen copies of *Boxing and Wrestling* and *The Ring* from the fifties. A VHS cassette of *On the Waterfront*. Also *a.k.a. Cassius Clay*. And Michael Mann's *Ali* with Will Smith in the title role. Joe thought there was something creepy about Smith's ears, said he'd had them surgically relocated, raised or lowered, I can't remember which. The disk is still sealed in cellophane.

Here are the files too. The blue one, which he showed me once, holds the manuscript. It's mainly accounts of Ali's fights and foibles, in no apparent order, and ruminations about the scrapbooks, with here and there a half-written piece about his own schooldays. Going to the rofstoei in the City Hall, getting punched in the mouth by Paul Skinner, losing all his marbles to Ferdi Kouters. Frankly, I thought he was further along. Then there's a file full of outlines and structures, notes towards this and reminders about that. Also half a dozen folders holding 'discards'. Where's the *book*? It's as if he thought the notes were the most important thing. If he'd put all this pencil lead and elbow grease into an actual manuscript, I'd have a sporting chance of making something of it. He should have taken his own advice and finished the thing while Ali was still alive. While *he* was still alive, the prick. If he wasn't dead already, I swear I'd wring his neck.

A page in the second file has my name on it. *For Branko* it says. For a moment I think it's a dedication, but then I see it's just for my attention, and it's another outline of the book. This one has alternating voices, his and mine, past and present. Straight out of the modernist writing manual, he says in a note, but that's not always a bad thing.

I tear the page up and throw it in the wastepaper basket. Posthumous control fucking freakery! Then I retrieve the pieces, stuff them in an envelope and put them in a drawer. You never know.

There's one more thing in the crate, an old State Express cigarette tin, triple sevens, cork-tipped. To judge by the weight it's empty, but when I flip the lid there's something inside. It looks like a stash of insect parts, the wings we boys used to knock off flying ants after a storm. No, it's strips of crackly yellow sticky tape, brittle and desiccated. All the strips that have come loose in the scrapbooks. What possessed him to keep them? It reminds me of the appendix he brought home in a bottle from the Little Company of Mary after his operation. And the bone-yellow conch the size of a child's fist given to him by Sonny Woodward that was supposed to be a whale's eardrum. Surely not. I empty the tin into the basket.

I told my brother I'd made a start on my side of the book and I wasn't exactly lying: I have twenty or thirty pages in a manuscript book. Now I've got his papers too. What a laughable double bill we make: his nickel-and-dime biography of Ali and my five cents' worth of memoir.

Jordan is right: it's a lot of old crap. But it needs to be unpacked anyway, I've already cleared space on my shelves. As I lift Big Jim onto the trestle table, I feel the full weight of my inheritance.

Joe

People stared out of the drawings, daring me to look away: voluptuous women, all lips, breasts, hips and thighs, pop-eyed urchins huddled around braziers, a man whose head was the shape of Africa. Their eyes followed me like Jesus on the cross in the cathedral.

The first art exhibition I ever saw was the one I chanced upon in the Barclay Square shopping centre with Rollie. It was a Saturday night. We'd eaten at the Sirloin Steakhouse and were heading downtown to see which folk singer was playing at the Keg and Tankard. Probably Ronnie Domp, he was a fixture. As we ranged through the centre, full of red meat and Lion lager and windgat notions, the exhibition distracted us. The drawings were pinned to boards or laid out on a table, and the artists sat to one side on fold-up chairs, three black men of our age. It must be a special arrangement, I thought. I had been at university just long enough to know that the absence of black people from places like this, places my cousin and I thought of as *ours*, was not the natural order of things.

We moved from the pinboards to the table and browsed through the images set out there. Prices on little paper squares were pinned to the tablecloth beside the artworks. I thought they might be etchings but I wasn't sure. The artist came over and stood on the other side of the table, watching us as we watched his work.

What do you think? he said at last.

I think it's a load of rubbish, Rollie said.

You can't say that, I said.

No he can, said the artist, if he doesn't like it, he must say so.

Sure, but there's ways of saying things.

The artist grinned at me. He obviously can't stand up for himself, I thought, in this situation.

Check at all the work that went into this one, I persisted. At least he's trying to do something.

He better try harder, Rollie said.

This one's pretty good, I said, although I was no longer convinced.

Hmm. The artist picked it up and turned it towards the light. I had some problems with this one.

It's fucken terrible, Rollie said, finding that the horse's mouth was speaking up for him. What's this thing here? A hand. Are you serious? I can do a better job than that and I can't draw to save my life.

Now I thought this would upset the artist, but he pushed his beret to the back of his head and burst out laughing. His colleagues came over to see what was happening.

He doesn't like this one, the artist said to them. He says it's fucken terrible.

They all laughed as if Rollie had said something wonderful.

I felt my gorge rise, the acid swill of two terms of History of Art and two more of tutoring black matrics for Race Relations. Fuck them. Sloping away.

Branko

Among other things, nearly all of them made of paper, my brother leaves me his collection of books featuring The Saint, forty rat-eaten paperbacks whose pages have the texture of old banknotes and give off the same odd mix of dust and damp as his archive. Simon Templar – the initials explain the nickname – was Leslie Charteris's great fictional invention.

One of the first things you learn as an editor is to order the material before you start working on it. Laying down timelines and logging shots is a bind, but without it you can't find your way.

I sort the books by date of first publication, from *Enter the Saint* published in 1930 to *The Saint on TV* in 1967. This last one is not actually by Charteris: it's Fleming Lee's adaptation of two stories from the TV series starring Roger Moore. Charteris stopped writing The Saint books in 1963, although he edited and revised some that were written afterwards by other people and published under his name, including this one. In his foreword to Lee's book, Charteris calls it 'an interesting and perhaps unprecedented experiment in teamwork ... I have done the back-seat driving and added a few typical flourishes of my own.'

The Saint books were popular for more than forty years and some of them ran to twenty impressions and half a dozen new editions. I reorder Joe's collection by the date in which they actually appeared so that I can see the different imprints and series designs. The best covers were painted by J Pollack for the Pan editions of the early fifties and show Templar in a collar and tie and a fedora. His eyebrow is cocked and his lip quirked. He looks ironic and debonair, and cheerfully, uncomplicatedly masculine. According to the back cover note he is a 'man of superb recklessness / strange heroisms / and impossible ideals'.

When Joe bought these books, they already looked out of style. Yet their lurid jackets concealed how old-fashioned they really were: most of them had been written before the Second World War. It surprises me now.

Charteris was prolific. In the first decade of his career he sometimes published two books a year. In 1934 there were three! A biographical note on the Pan editions says he was educated at Rossall School and Cambridge and worked as a sailor, rubber planter, tin miner, wood distiller, prospector and tramp before his invention of The Saint made him famous. The notion that a writer should be a jack of all trades was popular back then. The rest of the books say nothing about the author at all. Not one of them carries his photograph.

Was Joe curious about him? And if he was, where would he have gone to find out more? The reference section at the public library probably. Personal information was harder to find then and so it mattered less. Perhaps he was satisfied to know Simon Templar and to hell with Leslie Charteris.

I google him, of course. And now I see why they kept him in the shadows. Charteris was born in Singapore to a Chinese father, Dr SC Yin, and an English mother, Lydia Florence Bowyer. He went to school in England, where he was bullied for 'being different'. After immigrating to the US in 1932, he was for years prevented from getting permanent residence by the Chinese Exclusion Act, finally becoming a naturalized citizen in 1946.

But I'm distracting myself with research, if I can call it that, when the facts are easy enough to access. I know why Joe gave me these books: he wanted me to read them. He wasn't to know I've tried already – I still have the books here somewhere – and it helped very little. What did I learn? That Simon Templar had an alter ego called Sebastian Toombs.

That he yearned to write poetry. That he was a subversive of a kind, a left-leaning Robin Hood, the scourge of the powerful and champion of the poor, who loved to humiliate the magnates and arms dealers and give the big shots their comeuppance.

What did I miss? The obvious. It wasn't Templar my brother wanted to be. It was Charteris.

As I pick through the Big Jim crate I find myself thinking, despite myself, like his literary executor. What's happened to the juvenilia, the exercise books full of bad poetry that he hid in the not-so-secret compartment, the notebooks and diaries, the files full of correspondence? He once told me he kept copies of his own letters to make life easier for the literary scholars of the future. Did he give all this stuff to Grahamstown? Em says she sent a load of boxes there on his instructions. Or did he take a leaf out of Mom's book and use it to kindle a bonfire?

Finally I do what I should have done before I started our experiment in teamwork: I reread Joe's books. 'Reread' is disingenuous. When he started publishing, I read the first few to see if I was in them, and the next few because people said they were good, but I'm opening the later ones for the first time. It isn't compulsory, I used to say, just because he's my brother. I pile up the books from my shelves, snoop around on his publishers' websites, and order the missing titles off Kalahari. He's no Charteris, thank God. The complete works fit on my bedside table.

Jordan carries off a couple he hasn't seen before. I've always steered him away from his uncle's books. You're not ready, I would say. You'll enjoy them more when you're a year or two older. To the point where he lost interest. But now he wants to read them all. His new girlfriend is reading them too. Even Rita reads the first half of the one her book club recommended.

The well-known attributes are there, the eye for detail – too much of it, if you ask me – the magical flourishes, the social concern. There's a bit of me in some of his characters, which is only to be expected, as is the fact that he passes a lot of bad attitudes off on me. But there's nothing about boxing. Then again, he always insisted that he wasn't interested in boxing but in *Ali*. And anyway the book's not *about* Ali. Whatever you think it is, it's something else. He's working me over with the literary rope-a-dope.

13

Limits

In February last year when she was kidnapped from her apartment, Miss Hearst had seemed a normal, rather apolitical university student. According to Stephen Weed, her then fiancé, she had exclaimed "oh no, not me" when a White woman and two Black men started taking her away.

But soon, in recordings on tape cassettes forwarded to various people, she began supporting the SLA and denigrating her parents and American society in general.

— *Pretoria News*, May 1975

Joe

At university I discovered a view of America at odds with my own. In this view, the United States was not the bastion of freedom in the West but a meddling bully-boy state that undermined democratic governments and propped up corrupt and oppressive regimes in Central America and Africa, including our own. I liked this use of 'regime' and began to use it freely, but I wasn't persuaded by every aspect of the radical argument. Was popular culture really no more than propaganda? I couldn't see the music and films I loved as the stock-in-trade of cultural imperialism. Shortly after I heard the term for the first time, I understood that I was a philistine. Although I'd moved on from Charteris, I was still hanging out with the lightweights. When one of my teachers, a Montale specialist, saw me reading Kerouac, he sneered: 'That's not writing, that's typing.' I had no idea he was quoting Truman Capote.

After the Rumble, my fascination with Ali began to wane. He had reached the pinnacle of his career; the long, painful descent still lay ahead. All through my first year at varsity I went on collecting cuttings about him without bothering to paste them into books. In retrospect, this was good for the archive, as none of the cuttings was ruined by sticky-tape glue. These tatty hoards of newsprint stuffed into cardboard folders are the index of a fading enthusiasm.

In 1975, Ali defended his title four times, against Chuck Wepner in March; Ron Lyle in May; Joe Bugner in June, their second meeting; and Joe Frazier in October, their third, the so-called Thriller in Manila.

Chuck Wepner was a scrapper from Bayonne, New Jersey, a veteran of one hundred amateur and pro fights who still worked in a liquor store. Alan Hubbard called him the man from the back of Bayonne and joked that his face had launched a thousand snips of the surgeon's scissors.

Richard Walker made this vivid sketch of the Bayonne Bleeder, as Wepner was known in the boxing world: Wepner comes from the grim, unglamorous side of American boxing. He has spilt buckets of blood, most of it his own, in a decade of picking up 500 dollar purses in dirty steeltowns. He has never been able to afford to give up a daily job, and his wife, Phyllis, works too ... Wepner looks like one of these old pictures of 19th century prizefighters – a hunk of ham with whiskers, pulverized face stitched up like an old sock. It took 120 stitches to put him together again after one fight with Sonny Liston, back in 1970.

If it's true that Wepner needed this many stitches after a single bout, then the career estimate made by Hubbard in the *Pretoria News* was conservative: Wepner only gets angry when you refer to the 200 stitches he has had in his face. 'So I bleed a little – what was all that stuff around Rocky Marciano? Tomato ketchup?'

The scribes had made the connection with a more famous bleeder: Henry Cooper. A month before Ali met Wepner, *The Star* carried a piece by Alan Hoby on the first Ali vs Cooper fight headlined 'The night that 'Enry's 'Ammer crashed in'. Hoby was no fan of Ali. He made much of the claim that Angelo Dundee had deliberately torn one of Ali's gloves during this fight to give him time to recover from a knock-down. The article was accompanied by photographs of Cooper's bloodied head.

The Wepner folder, which I think of as ALI V although it's not a scrapbook, contains a dozen cuttings on the buildup to the fight and half that number on the fight itself. Foreman was always going to be a hard act to follow, but Wepner was a no-hoper who had barely made it onto the contenders' list. According to Ali's manager Herbert Muhammad, Wepner's race played a big part in the decision to give him a fight. Ali has beaten all the other White heavyweights, he said.

This was not Ali's finest moment. He did nothing to hide the fact that he was overweight, inviting reporters to count the rolls of fat on his stomach. In the photographs Wepner himself looks like a chubby ducktail. Billed as one of the biggest underdogs in heavyweight boxing history, he looks pleased as Punch to be in the same frame as The Greatest, whom he professed to admire as a boxer and a man, clowning around for the press and smiling genially. He introduced some theatrical flimflam of his own into proceedings by donning a pair of 'magic boots' inscribed with curse signs pointing at Ali. There is even a mock-blow photo in which Wepner lands a straight left on Ali's jaw.

This good humour evaporated in the ring, where Ali gave Wepner a terrible hiding. The referee let this savage, almost sadistic torture go on until the fifteenth round before stopping the fight. Afterwards Ali justified his viciousness on the grounds that Wepner had been allowed to foul him. The post-match photo of Wepner is nearly as shocking as the one of Henry Cooper. He is bruised everywhere – eyes, nose, cheeks, ears. He can hardly see out of his eyes. His eyelids and brows bulge out and over like two overripe, split plums.

Branko

On the anniversary of Joe's death, Em sends me an SMS: I miss him. I reply: Me too. I should say more, I want to, but I can't find the words. Ageing is full of surprises and one of them is that the birthdays make way for the deathdays. I've started adding them to my calendar with a little cross to show that it's the anniversary of a passing.

Now that my brother is dead, I must do the remembering for both of us. The responsibility sharpens my recall. Scenes from our childhood flicker to life and I write them down as they come. That's something he taught me: thinking about writing is not the same as actually doing it. I'm on to my second manuscript book.

My side of the book is under control. The problem is *his* side. I keep going through the blue file, trying to order his drafts, but the plan eludes me. How can I knock these fragments into shape when I know so little about Ali? I have the scrapbooks, but he's sucked the juice out of those already. And even if he hadn't, their limitations are too obvious to overlook. His archive is hopelessly inadequate and incomplete. If Dad had read the *Rand Daily Mail* rather than the *Pretoria News* the whole thing would be different.

There's the Internet. When he first started pestering me to collaborate with him, I spent a night or two online, clicking through the warmly lit pavilions of the Muhammad Ali Center in Louisville and the Boxing Hall of Fame in Canastota – they have the ring in which the Fight of the Century took place – and then wandering deeper and deeper into the backstreets where the fight fans hang out. There are boxing sites as dingy as old clubs where one-eyed sloggers trade opinions like blows. I'll go back there only if I have to.

I should read a good biography. Google presents the options. The one that catches my eye is *Superman vs. Muhammad Ali*, but that can't be a good place to start. Amazon suggests *Muhammad Ali: His Life and Times* by Thomas Hauser. Apparently customers who bought this item also bought *King of the World* by David Remnick and *The Fight* by Norman Mailer. This reminds me that Joe's copies of Mailer and Torres are on my shelf.

José Torres's *Sting Like a Bee* cost Joe R1.25 in 1974. Torres was a boxer himself and he knows what happens in the dressing room and the ring. Reading him, I finally get Ali's boxing style, how he dropped his hands and moved his feet, how he traded power for speed and timing, and put his faith in the element of surprise. It's not the hardest punch that hurts you, Torres tells us, it's the one you don't see coming. Torres loves Ali. He thinks of him as a mystery he has to unravel, an enigma he has to understand, but it's impossible. He cannot explain the magic. And he loves that too.

Torres switches on a light in my brother's gloomy archive and reveals how often he misreads things. Take Jerry Perenchio. Joe calls him a 'theatrical agent' – that's what it says in the cuttings – but he's a major showbiz player who represented celebrities like Liz Taylor, Jane Fonda and The Beatles. His idea of selling off the boxers' gear was no spur-of-the-moment pitch to make a buck, it was part of a merchandising strategy that extended to the advertising and broadcasting rights, in which his stated intention (Torres says) was to 'cut up and sell every part of the carcass, just like whaling'.

Norman Mailer wrote a preface for Torres's book, having taken a 'fatherly hand' in its writing. Torres was living nearby at the time, and Mailer read his drafts for him and 'functioned as a sort of editor'. In his preface, he sings the praises of the parts he edited and finds fault with those he didn't. These deficient passages, he says, have 'that air of the quaint (at a comfortably low literary level) which people expect when they read a feature story on a sports page'.

The book also has an epilogue by Budd Schulberg. He says writers and fighters have a special affinity, they understand one another and easily find common ground. Both have to stand or fall on their own, conquer their fears and absorb punishment, and draw on inner resources and personal experience to create something 'not only entertaining but meaningful and winning in the deepest sense'. At their best, he goes on, both mediums, writing and boxing, 'demand the same concentration, self-discipline and the aspiration of art'.

Presumably Joe shares this view. Somewhere he calls Ali an 'artist'. But is writing really like boxing? The text doesn't hit you back. The critics hit you, Schulberg says, with their 'left jabs' and 'hard right hands'. Another bit of macho nonsense: the judges can score you unfairly and make you lose, but they can't get in the ring and pummel you. Perhaps it's the reader who's in the other corner? But then the book stands between the two adversaries like a punchbag. It cannot defend itself.

Joe's copy of *The Fight* is a new edition published in the nineties. He disliked Mailer with a passion. What a jock, he used to say, always banging his dick on the table. I'm ready to dislike Mailer too, but his account of the Rumble in the Jungle disarms me. Get past the manly bluster, the occasional line that's purple around the eyes, and he's pretty good, if you ask me. He makes you feel like you're there, ringside. Or in the ring with him, throwing a punch or taking it on the chin. He has an interest in boxing, which goes a long way. And the prose is, well, punchy.

Joe

Early in 1975, Ali announced that a White group of newspapers had invited him to South Africa for a series of exhibition bouts, with the proceeds going to black schools. The papers were *The Star* and *The World*, which was then under the editorship of legendary newsman Percy Qoboza, and the money was to be administered by the paper's educational charity TEACH. In earlier years, Ali and his management had defended planned trips on the grounds that they had nothing to do with politics. Now they argued that the visit would benefit local people. Ali said he would be launching various schemes, from school buses to restaurants where Black people could eat in the sophisticated atmosphere that the Whites do. He'd called up the Jackson Five and they were willing to give free shows to help needy Blacks.

As it happened, the students around me were debating the nature and purpose of charitable work. One of the rites of passage for first years was the university rag, a street procession that raised money for charity. Radical students had begun to argue that liberal initiatives to uplift and support the poor did more harm than good. There was no point in trying to improve the conditions under which 'needy Blacks' lived in South Africa. The political system could not be reformed: it had to be overthrown.

I followed the arguments for Ali's proposed visit with mixed feelings. As always the plans came to nothing. The same paper that carried the reports of Ali's TKO victory over Wepner revealed that he had cancelled his trip. A similar visit by George Foreman, announced as a fait accompli just a few days earlier, soon fell through as well. The political pressure to boycott South Africa was growing.

Branko

'Blow by blow' suggests that everything is captured, but the words obviously don't do justice to the performance. The written account is the bare knuckles of the thing, it summarizes the routine exchanges – a short opening flurry, the fighters traded punches – and magnifies the big moments, the scoring blows and knock-downs. The scribe might mention the crowd, if they're unhappy, or the referee, if he steps in to stop proceedings, but generally he ignores everything that isn't a punch. The point is to abstract the fight and lift it clear of the visual and aural clutter. In the process, details that might have seemed crucial to another observer are edited out.

It's not just the blow-by-blow accounts that fail me: it's all the reports. There are things I've read about and would like to see for myself: the moment Ali stood over a fallen Liston. The old Irish timekeeper at the Blue Lewis fight with his mainspring wound down. The looks on the faces of Ali's corner after the Norton defeat. Frazier knocking Ali down in the last round of the Fight of the Century. Hubbard describes Ali as a ship running aground on Frazier's fists. My brother thought this was wonderful – but isn't it ridiculous? It does nothing but obscure what actually happened.

The Fight is on YouTube. My plan is to fast-forward to the last round for the knock-down, but the action starts and I can't stop watching. I'm in my element. Halfway through, a warning sounds in my head: I cannot go checking one archive against another. It will never be done. When the bell goes for the eighth and the seconds clamber through the ropes with their buckets and towels, I close the video and go to bed.

The very next day, like an addict falling off the wagon, I fall into the Net. I can't help myself. Nearly every one of Muhammad Ali's fights can be found online. Also half the fights of his opponents. And half the fights of theirs. I spiral out into the superabundance. Boxing was never my sport, but the fights look better in the past tense, the distance has given them charm, if not glamour. I drift from one ringside to another like a junior reporter with a press card in his hatband. If a contest bores me, as they often do, I click out halfway through and find the fight that went before or after. YouTube offers suggestions. Here's Norton vs Reno. Sometimes I arrive by broken paths at the obscure fights and they interest me most of all. I become a fan – for the moment – of the boxers who got short-changed in Joe's archive like Rudi Lubbers and Jürgen Blin. And then of those whose names he wouldn't even have recognized like Karl Mildenberger and Willi Besmanoff.

Days go by. Everything I click on floats me further away from the convention centres and casinos. While I'm fetching a beer from the fridge Terence Stamp starts to talk about Marlon Brando and so I watch that, and then the $99 violin test, and then a lesson that promises: How To Sing Better in 5 Minutes. I'm drawn in by the cluttered sidebars, the insistent pop-ups, the pictures, the tips, the lists. Especially the lists. The 10 Sportsmen You Didn't Know Were Born With A Cleft Palate. The 5 Best Ways To Lose That Stubborn Fat On Your Midriff. The 10 Coolest Hairstyles In The Premier League. The 22 Best Shots Of Celebrities

Getting Out Of Limousines Without Their Underwear. One moment I'm looking at photographs of Henry Cooper and the next I'm reading the lyrics of 'Lily the Pink'. Every line of every song ever recorded is somewhere on the Net: no one need ever again guess what the words of a pop song are. Here I am on the official site of the Procol Harum Fan Club. All five of the original members are still alive. It's a miracle. The band was named after a Burmese cat. What's a Burmese cat? I'm searching for an answer and then I'm looking at Rare Photos Taken Right Before Tragedy Struck. 15 Pranks That Backfired With Fatal Consequences. 103 Famous People You Might Not Know Are Dead. 6 Celebrities Who Have Extremely Troubled Siblings. Only six? What You Didn't Know About Brad Pitt's Brother. 24 Historical Photos They Didn't Show You At School. The Saddest And Most Shocking Celebrity Deaths Of All Time. Everything runs together. There's no frame. I can't tell where one thing stops and another starts. It all bleeds. It's a bloodfest.

I lock the door of the edit room. If Rita tries to open it she'll think I'm watching porn in here, but that would be less embarrassing than watching this crap.

I waste an entire evening on goal celebrations. The victory dances of soccer teams are watched more often than the goals that produced them. Questions spill out of me like ticker tape. When did it start? When did this strutting and crowing become acceptable? Perhaps it was prompted by rising salaries. Who invented the knee slide? When I played football as a kid something like that would have given you a grass burn to remember. The slide looks quaint now, almost modest compared to the chorus lines involving the whole team. Do they practise these moves on the training pitch along with the other set pieces? What do the experts regard as the greatest goal celebration? Are there soccer teams who don't do them? What is the most serious injury ever sustained by a player under a heap of his teammates? Has any player ever suffered a career-ending injury? Has anyone died?

Has anyone died?

This brings me back to Ali. He's the heart of the problem. It's not just that there's too much information about him, it's that his story is too big. It's freighted with a history I can't carry, no more than my brother could, despite a lifetime of training.

Joe

ALI VI covers two fights: Ron Lyle in Las Vegas and Joe Bugner in Kuala Lumpur.

Ron Lyle was a no-hoper, as you can tell from the dearth of press coverage. He'd learnt to box in prison and was out on bail at the time of the fight, facing two counts of felony menacing and one of second-degree assault brought against him by his wife Nadine. In his four-year professional career he had never gone fifteen rounds. Ali conceded that making a million dollars fighting a nobody like Lyle was a rip-off – but I can't stop fighting while I'm making all this money ... I want to take as much money from the rich as I can. Styling himself the Black Robin Hood, he spoke about buying three shopping centres in Ghetto areas. The Muslims will come in and clean up ... help make the place livable again. It was reminiscent of the scuppered South Africa visit: I just got through buying two school buses for a dirt-poor Muslim school.

The philanthropy extended to the media coverage. The Lyle fight was shown on home TV in the US. According to Ali, he'd agreed to work for low wages – the $1 million purse – so that the fans who couldn't afford $25 for a CCTV seat would get to see the fight in their own homes. In any event, the fight was dull. Scott Hagen wrote a disgruntled, sarcastic account of it as a lacklustre conversation piece. When Ali went into his customery [sic] shuffle, Lyle stood back like a spectator admiring his opponent's fancy footwork. It was comic.

There was nothing funny about the way the fight ended. After lying back on the ropes and falling behind on the cards of two of the three judges, in round 11 Ali launched a vicious barrage of punches that soon had the challenger in trouble. The referee stopped it.

Branko

Jordan is bringing his new girlfriend home for supper. Her name is Nomaxabiso.

Don't even try, he says. You can call her Nomz like everyone else. And don't ask her what it means.

He keeps telling me what I can and can't say. People like me (I'm sure he means *us*) must learn to listen. The idea is going around at the college. White people, white men especially, have been filling the airspace for too long. They need to shut up and listen to the other side. It doesn't matter if you disagree, he tells me, or you think someone's talking nonsense, you're in no position to judge anyway, the only appropriate response is to keep your trap shut. Silence. The historical moment demands it.

The week before the planned supper Michael Brown is shot dead by a white policeman in Ferguson.

Jordan makes me promise I won't say anything at the dinner table.

But I'm as outraged as the next person, I say. Police brutality affects all of us.

How does it affect you?

This kind of thing has always upsct me.

It's not about you and your feelings. That's the whole point.

But I'm interested to know what Nomz thinks. She's studying politics, after all. Surely you want me to take an interest.

I want you to shut the fuck up – the fudge – sorry Dad.

Don't talk to me like that.

I'm starting to worry about Joe's book. He should have finished it himself, long ago, when white people were still interesting.

Everyone is talking about race and reading Baldwin. Joe was on to him early: he left me a copy of *The Fire Next Time* in the Big Jim crate. I spend a day on it. Fascinating stuff. There's a passage about Elijah Muhammad marked in pencil – Joe never liked to write in books – with a cross-reference to Ali's proposed visits to South Africa. It could come in useful. Baldwin says that the separatism espoused by the Nation of Islam plays into a racist agenda. The white supremacists of the American Nazi Party like the idea. On an orange Post-it I find a note in my brother's hand that says Baldwin is a hard-boiled dreamer: the world is mangled by greed and dishonesty, of course he sees that, but still he refuses to give up on our common humanity. 'Love takes off the masks that we fear we cannot live without and know we cannot live within.'

What are you reading? Rita asks when she comes to bed.

I show her. The book falls open at another Post-it.

'White people cannot, in the generality, be taken as models of how to live.'

She looks at me over the top of her glasses. She only ever wears them after she's taken out her contacts at night, to set the alarm, and they make her look deeply serious.

I take the book back from her and read this line marked by an orange flag: 'How can one, however, dream of power in any other terms than in the symbols of power?' That's a question worth asking, I say. Perhaps we can talk about it with Jordy and Nomz on Friday.

Don't you dare.

But I'd like to know what they think. It's a question their generation will have to answer.

You like to provoke. Just like your brother.

We leave it there and go to sleep.

Baldwin has pricked my curiosity. What else came out of Big Jim? I spend the morning going over the shelf. A dozen books on sport, media, hip hop, slavery. I sit down with Francis Njubi Nesbitt's *Race for Sanctions: African Americans against Apartheid*. The index takes me to Ali and his proposed visit to South Africa in 1972. This is exactly what I need: it tells me what the cuttings don't say on the subject. Nesbitt writes about the intense, organized pressure that was brought to bear to stop the Al Jones exhibition fights. I could work some of this into the chapter on separatism and Ali's aborted visits to South Africa. Reporters for papers like *The Star* and the *Sunday Times* tended to underplay the opposition to sporting contact with South Africa: black activists were outraged.

I take some notes from Nesbitt and start tinkering with my brother's drafts. Covering my arse, you could say. There's not much room on the pages, nearly every margin is already crammed with bubbles and brackets, and I'm forced to add my notes on the blank pages opposite, where they suddenly look feeble. The fact is I don't know enough about anything. Not just boxing, but politics, music, technology. How much will I have to read to plug the obvious gaps?

It comes back to me now: Joe and I were discussing his book. I told him that everything he'd ever want to know about Ali was on the Net and he started arguing the case for his archive. Its merits are in inverse proportion to its limitations, he said, its saving grace is that it's full of holes.

And you were right, boet.

Before I can have second thoughts, I go back over the file and edit out all the little references I've woven in, including my well-chosen quotes from Baldwin and Biko and Torres. I'm telling a story: I don't have to demonstrate that I've read everything.

I'm relieved when Nomz gets the flu and can't make the supper. It's not that I want to avoid her, I just need to get a few things straight in my head. And on paper. I'm busy with my sixth manuscript book and my text is starting to look as chaotic as my brother's. It's time to go digital. And it's time to change the names of the people. Elementary, I know. Remembering things as they were is all very well if there aren't secrets to keep.

In the small hours, when I'm fretting over the book, the pathetic reality comes home to me. It was bad enough being stuck with my brother's problems. Now I'm stuck with his solutions.

Joe

After the sideshows of Wepner and Lyle, it was back to the big top for the Bugner return. Joe Bugner was Britain's first serious title hope since Cooper. Two years earlier, he had gone the distance with Ali. The return, scheduled for Kuala Lumpur at the end of June, would be Ali's fiftieth professional fight. Reports said he would be travelling with an entourage of one hundred people.

For the Malaysian Coordinating Committee, which reported directly to Prime Minister Tun Abdul Razak, this was a national event with the potential to put the country on the map. Promoter Ismail Kamat complained that when he tried to call Malaysia from New York, people sometimes didn't even know where or what this country was. And he added, Well, they soon will. The same had been said of Zaire before the Rumble. Much was made of the fact that Ali was the first Muslim world champion and it was reported that he had joined Abdul Razak in prayer at the national mosque. The Sultan of Perak had made Ali a Caliph of the Malaysian art of self-defence.

As they'd done before Wepner, Ali's camp joked about the racial contest with Bugner. Ali said: He's the perfect match for me. He's White, he'll draw a crowd and he can't fight. Ali would simply have to win, he said, to avoid the embarrassment of telling his daughters he'd been beaten by a blond, and to prevent Bugner from getting all the attention and the TV commercials. The Queen will be at the airport to meet him. He'll get a bigger reception than the Beatles. He'll be fighting for the honour of his country. England will be back on the map. At one press conference, Ali took the mickey out of British reporters by asking in a plummy accent: I say, chaps, would you like some tea?

Like Wepner, Bugner decided that two could play that game. Although he'd been born in Hungary (his family left after the Soviet invasion when he was six years old) he said he was thoroughly British and would fight the British way. Asked how he would deal with Ali's antics, he replied: I shall be firm but polite … The perfect gentleman. If there is one thing Ali can't stand it is politeness … He gets you mad and that way he's got you by the knick-knacks … But if he starts calling me a big boob, or anything like that, I shan't respond. I shall simply say, 'Don't be a silly chap. Please settle down.' That will really get under his skin. Either that or I shall ignore him. He can't stand that either.

Even by the standards set in Zaire the levels of hype were high, as suggested by the forty pages of cuttings on the buildup (the fight itself produced six). An official press conference was held in the Chempaka Room at the Kuala Lumpur Holiday Inn, on a dais with yellow and red flowers, and the president of the Malaysian Boxing Federation Tan Sri Abdul Aziz Yeop read out the rules. When he said the fighters could not use the ropes, Ali was astonished.

'I can't use the rope-a-dope?'

'You can use the ropes,' the Commissioner explained. 'But not take advantage of the ropes.'

'I won't hang him,' Ali said.

The gloves for the fight were displayed on a table.

'Red gloves,' Ali said. 'Now we can't see the blood. The gloves should be white.'

The weigh-in was an extravaganza featuring costumed Malay warriors and natives carrying immitation [sic] multi-coloured palms. Alan Hubbard, who had also reported on the Rumble, returned to the jungle imagery: Bugner is the traditionally equipped White hunter about to plunge into a tropical jungle in search of an awesome prey. He made a fuss about Bugner being in an alien environment – he is bound to find the atmosphere disturbingly foreign to him in every way – as if Ali would be right at home. Defeat for Ali would be unthinkable enough, without the additional humiliation of losing to a White man before an audience of Muslim brothers.

The fight was staged in an outdoor arena and the promoters hired a witchdoctor to ward off rain by chanting and rattling dry bones. Unfortunately he did his job too well and the water levels dropped, threatening the hydroelectric supply needed to power the generators for the TV transmission. Another witchdoctor was hired to bring back some rain – but not too much.

Just five years after Jerry Perenchio had the idea of auctioning off the boxers' gear, the merchandising department was in full flight, with tenders put out for the rights to produce and sell T-shirts, towels, travelling bags, ashtrays, key chains, caps and badges, which will feature pictures of Ali and Bugner and words and phrases referring to the fight.

Meanwhile the Kuala Lumpur Hilton where Ali was due to stay had created a Ringside Bar in the lobby to sell five special cocktails: the Knockout or KO, the Russian Tank, named for the defensive technique

Ali said he would be using, the Rope-a-Dope, the Uppercut and Ali's Punch.

Amidst all the joking, Ali complained, not for the first time, that he was tired. At a subdued news conference in the royal suite of the Hilton, he said: Horses get old, cars get old, the pyramids of Egypt are crumbling. His punishing schedule left no time for his family and his religion. The constant attention was also starting to pall. As much as he liked the fans and signing autographs, he wished he could take his family out sometimes without being bothered by anyone. When a reporter reminded him that he'd always revelled in the attention, he replied: I did, and I still would, if it was kept to a limit. It's terrible now, and it's getting worse.

From the beginning Ali had courted and goaded the press. Now he felt they were hounding him. In years to come, the pattern of chasing publicity and then running away from it would be repeated by people in the public eye often enough to become a cliché.

Despite the frenzy of promotion, on the day high ticket prices and live TV coverage kept the punters away from the stadium and only a third of the seats were filled. Ali won an unimaginative fight on points. Afterwards, he paid the young challenger a backhanded compliment: once he retired, Ali said, Bugner might even win the title. You've got the right complexion and the right connections. The jingle was tired too.

14

The Thriller
in Manila

The standing prohibition on gatherings in streets surrounding the Johannesburg City Hall, but not in the building itself, has been extended for another two years, according to a Government Gazette notice.

– *Pretoria News*, September 1975

Branko

I'm tidying the edit room on a Sunday afternoon – displacement activity, Rita calls it, I should be working – when I come across a disk marked 'Overkill'. It's the movie Jordan made for his finals two years ago. We were supposed to watch a rough cut on the night Joe was murdered.

Rita is reading under the gazebo.

Have you watched this? It's Jordy's movie, the rough cut anyway. It just turned up in my stuff.

She puts her book down on the table and blows smoke up at the thatch. Which one is it?

'Overkill'. I think it's a fan version of *Pulp Fiction*.

No, that was in his first year, this is the one after. The one about us.

What do you mean?

Haven't you watched it? I think we watched it together.

No, I was otherwise occupied. But I'm going to watch it now.

I go back through the French doors into the lounge and stick it in the player. While I'm fiddling with the remote Reet comes in, flops down next to me and hands me a disk. The finished product, she says.

I switch the disks and hit play. The title comes up on a black screen in wobbly white letters that might have been arranged by a child. OVER-KILL. A film by Juwardi X. Subtitled: *A speculative documentary about death*.

Jesus, this is promising.

Let's just watch. We can talk afterwards.

Why didn't he put his name on it?

He was worried about the reaction. And he was right to worry. They showed it on some student festival and there was a big gedoente.

Why don't I know about this?

Give me that. She takes the remote and stops the film just as some blurry heads and hands begin to materialize on screen. You were caught up with other things, Branks. It's not surprising.

So what was the fuss about?

The subject matter and him being a white film-maker. People thought he didn't have the right. They thought it was exploitative.

Is it?

How do I know? She hits rewind and the film starts again. OVER-KILL. A film by Juwardi X. *A speculative documentary about death.*

It's hard to say what it's about. Mainly it seems to be home-movie footage from the family archive – he's been snooping around my hard drives, the little shit – intercut with the cheerier parts of *Butch Cassidy and the Sundance Kid.* There's cellphone footage of me and Rita going over the household budget intercut with the bicycle scene. Paul Newman in the saddle, Katharine Ross on the handlebars. Now he's showing off – look ma, no hands – while she watches from the barn. The soundtrack's been stripped out but 'Raindrops Keep Falling on My Head' plays in the back of my mind. I fell in love with Katharine Ross when I saw this as a teenager. I would get horny thinking of her while I gazed at Kathy van Deventer who sat in front of me in Guidance. Nothing seems to fit. And there's Jordan when he played a wizard in the school play and Katharine Ross as Etta Place in the schoolroom. I want to hear what she's telling the kids but it's drowned out by some hectic bass piece. Could be the Prisoners of Strange.

Now the pace changes and the screen becomes bloody. Surgical procedures. In graphic detail, as they say.

I think it's *Botched*, Rita says, that's the one about people who've fucked up their bodies with cosmetic surgery.

Is it about me? The surgeon as editor. Or rather the editor as surgeon.

It's about body image, she says.

A close-up of a scalpel cutting through belly fat that's been marked up like a dress pattern with dotted lines and arrows.

Or maybe it's *My Extreme Excess Skin*, she says. Isn't it sad that some people just can't accept themselves for who they are.

A nurse in a green overall hefts a huge fillet of skin and fat into a plastic tub and waits for the needle on the scale to settle.

And here's my brother Joe talking at a launch in a book shop. I haven't seen a moving image of him since he died and it's like a punch in the face. A linger-on left.

Who's that he's talking to?

Beats me. Is it Jackie Wetzler?

I wish I could hear what he's saying.

Music surges over this footage also. Agonized sax, John Zorn perhaps. Jordan's been plundering my music files too. I must tell him that sometimes the sound you expect is exactly the sound you need.

A couple of shots of Ali and Foreman. What the fuck! I say. That's my stuff. He's rumbling in my jungle.

It's not about boxing, Rita says, it's about state violence and the violence of capital, and also the violence of the image and the violence done to the black body. That's how he explained it.

We watch in silence.

It's pretty good, she says.

Sure.

She turns the volume down. What do you think, Branks? Really.

Well, it's the work of a young film-maker, you can see that. It's a bit obvious and strung out. And it meanders. He doesn't have much of a sense of story, but then the story isn't everything, never mind what the manuals say. Main thing is he's got a good eye. And a good ear.

Got that from you.

It has an air of menace, which I like. There I am just pottering around the house in my slippers and he makes me look like a serial killer.

There's a commotion in the hallway and Jordan and Nomz spill in. I hit the pause button.

Hi Mr B. I wish she'd stop that. Hi Reet.

Thought you'd gone to a movie, Rita says.

Changed our minds, he says, went for a walk instead.

They slump down on the other sofa and I catch a whiff of smoke and peppermint. Nomz has been around here a lot over the last few months. She's practically living under our roof. He looks at the screen where a blurred image of Joe is suspended and I can tell he recognizes it. It could be the one they published on the front page of *The Star* the day after he died.

What are you guys watching?

Butch Cassidy and My Old Man.

No shit. You finally got around to it.

It's pretty good. I'm impressed.

Ja, but he's moved on, Nomz says. His new stuff's quite different.

Really. What are you working on Jord?

Well, I'm writing now. It's a feature. But I don't like to talk about it. That's what Uncle Joe taught me.

We all stare at Joe's face on the screen. He must have been turning away, fast enough to blur his features, and it looks as if he's just been shot.

Let's watch the rest of it. Rita's timing is perfect: she knows what to do in moments like this. She jabs the remote and the image comes back to life.

Now footage of a man in a car driving. It could be me, actually. The garage lent us a Corolla when the SUV was in the shop. But that was a white car: this one is grey. We're in the last act. The surgery has been put behind us. Newman and Redford are holed up in Bolivia surrounded by cops. Meanwhile, back in South Africa, the miners are on the koppie at Marikana. Is 'meanwhile' the right word? I've seen this footage of the massacre many times before, but it's different now that it's no longer news. The man in the car is still driving. Who is it? It might be my brother rather than me. Where did Jordan find it? Perhaps he filmed it himself, which means he must have gone driving around with Joe, and I don't remember that. As the nyalas rumble into the frame, dragging trailers packed with concertina wire, and the cops in body armour stalk over the veld with their rifles at the ready, the old dread chills me to the bone, and I'm back in the car on the night Joe died with water coming down on the roof in chunks like spadefuls of earth. Doef doef doef. The music punches through the afternoon light. The miners creep past some thorn bushes, crouching as if they're invisible, as if they've lost their way in the dark. There's the Man in the Green Blanket. We saw him on the news. The soldiers pour in and take up position on rooftops and ramparts, rifles pointed. Inside Butch is hatching one last escape plan. Butch: They speak English in Australia. Sundance: They do? Butch: That's right, smart guy, so we wouldn't be foreigners. In Marikana the police line moves backwards as if the film has been reversed. There's a shanty, some twisted fence posts, a thorn tree. Butch and Sundance break through the doorway, guns blazing, and freeze. Now it's the jack-hammer thud of automatic rifle fire. Nomz must have seen this too, but she gasps and presses her face into Jordan's shoulder. The image jerks back into life. Or rather death. The miners twist and fall. The hail of bullets sounds like stones down a chute. Cease fire! In films people often die in slow motion but these men are cut down quickly, they jerk and drop, and are lost in the dust kicked up by bullets and falling bodies. The fusillade goes on.

The credits roll over black. The last gunshots have turned into a dead march and the soft wet suck of a boot sole lifting out of mud in a narrow stope.

We are flung about on the sofas like accident victims. Rita leans over and switches on the table lamp. Lights a cigarette. We have an agreement that she won't smoke in the house but this is not the time to make a point.

Nomz takes a cigarette too. As she speaks the smoke comes out of her mouth in acrid syllables. You see, Mr B, this is what I'm trying to tell you. You say it doesn't matter what colour the body is and I say it's everything. We know what happens to Butch and Sundance, it's in the books, but they won't show it to us. It's like Princess Diana in the car crash in Paris. Those paparazzi got nowhere. But who cares about these men? They may as well be cattle. Do you see what I mean, Mr B?

I'm not sure I do. I can't tell if she's criticizing the film or coming to its defence. Rita said there was a fuss about it, people thought it was exploitative. Are these the scenes that upset them? Maybe there are things we can't talk about and the retelling only redoubles the insult. The gunsmoke from the cigarettes drifts across the screen. Who do I mean by 'we'? I look over her head into Juwardi's face and for a moment I think we're exchanging a meaningful glance, but then I see that his eyes are closed.

Joe

In the second half of 1975, the circus rolled on to the Philippines. Ali was scheduled to meet Joe Frazier for the third time in Quezon City, a fight he had dubbed the Thriller in Manila. Ali promised: It'll be a killer and a chiller and a thriller when I get the Gorilla in Manila. He also promised to unleash a new weapon: I'm going to use a unique acupunch. I've been studying karate.

The serious fans of the sport were sick of this nonsense. In the Johannesburg *Sunday Express*, Ray Woodley railed against the state of boxing in general and against Ali in particular. No one had the nerve to beat him, he said, to slay the golden glove of boxing, because it would ruin the financial fistic exchange ... Ali is keeping boxing going, but at the same time he is destroying a once noble art.

Woodley was annoyed that Joe Frazier had been invited to Johannesburg to watch the Fourie-Galindez return. He didn't see what Frazier could add to the fistic scene. Instead he wished they'd invited the incomparable Joe Louis. I know Joe has had a few medical setbacks, but this writer would like nothing better than entertaining Louis. He was my hero as a schoolboy. Neither of them came.

Although Ali was still generating columns by the yard – There, I filled your pad, he told reporters in Manila – the print media were no longer the heart of the enterprise. The socko of a lifetime, as Don King called it, was shaping up to be the largest single TV network show ever put together for a single sporting event, with a projected audience of over 700 million viewers. The satellite feed would go live to several Eastern Bloc countries and the USSR had taken a delayed broadcast. It was a long way from the two lines TASS gave the Fight of the Century four years earlier. China was still eluding Mr King.

Ali arrived in the Philippines with no fewer than 38 handlers, helpers and walk-around guys. While this was smaller than the party of one hundred who had accompanied him to Malaysia, the numbers irked him. You've no idea what it costs to keep the Muhammad Ali show on the road. I pay my manager, my trainers, my family and my friends. In Kuala Lumpur, when I fought Joe Bugner, there were 52 people all signing my name to their account. Some of them I ain't never seen before.

The scribes still liked to cast the rivalry between Ali and Frazier as a clash of lifestyles and values, but the animosity between them no longer needed to be magnified in this way. Ali clowned around as usual, threatening Frazier with a toy gun and calling him a gorilla. *I'm gonna make you uglier than you are.* By all accounts, Frazier was deeply hurt by these jibes.

Yet some of Ali's exchanges with the press reveal a new openness and vulnerability. He told Alan Hubbard how hard it was to keep training, like taking medicine, he said, and how he struggled to keep his weight down. *If I didn't train I'd be big as a balloon ... I'm a compulsive eater.* And he spoke about his fear of dying. And about fate. *Things have been going too good lately. Allah must make me pay for all this fame and power.*

He was paying already. His private life, if one can call it that, began to spill into the media. The main focus was on the spats between his wife Belinda and his girlfriend Veronica Porché, whom he would subsequently marry. Ali defended his philandering: Belinda was well off, she had two Rolls-Royces and a large mansion, and in any event, there was no such thing as bad publicity. Bravado aside, like many celebrities since, he still believed his engagement with the media was governed by rules of fairness and propriety that would keep certain subjects off limits. *This is going too far. They got on me for the draft. They got on me for my religion. They got on me for all sorts of things. But they shouldn't be able to get on me for having a girlfriend.*

The *Sunday Times* reported that the fight was now being discussed in the women's pages of the papers and millions of women were rooting for Frazier. *Male chauvinists are in full cry. Women libbers are outraged.*

Ray Woodley again accused Ali of *making a mockery of the once noble art of self defence.* He was especially upset by the shenanigans around *Cousin Veronica.* Woodley wrote plaintively: *I am one of those* old-fashioned fellows who still has fistic heroes like Joe Louis and Rocky Marciano, who did not need the sort of publicity Ali is generating for his fight with Frazier this week. Those champions of the past lived in monastic seclusion when they trained for their title defences.

On the subject of women, Ali did see eye to eye with President Ferdinand Marcos of the Philippines, who entertained him at the Presidential Palace. When Mrs Marcos came in, wearing a simply cut, hot-pink dress, Ali said: I respect you more than ever ... Looking at your wife, I know you are not a dumb man. You know how to pick them.

You are not far behind, Marcos responded, referring to Ali's companion, who was wearing a long, pale-yellow skirt with a veil modestly wrapped over her hair.

We're kinda nice looking ourselves, said Ali.

Then the two men discussed the role of women in marriage. A woman is what her husband makes her, Ali said with a glance at Mrs Marcos. A man is what he makes himself.

Perhaps his marital problems were on his mind, because he went on, If we got a divorce, you would still be the President, and I would still be the world champion.

Marcos pointed out that there was no divorce in his Roman Catholic country.

Ali did not feel compelled to mention that the woman in the veil was his girlfriend rather than his wife.

Later Joe Frazier arrived. Ali thoughtfully advised the President to keep an eye on his wife while Smokin' Joe was around.

Despite gloomy predictions to the contrary, the Thriller was a great fight, criticized by some as a bit of a brawl, but praised by others as one of Ali's best performances. Frazier's corner threw in the towel after the fourteenth.

This is Hubbard's livid description of Frazier in the closing stages of the fight: His face had become a swollen soufflé of pain and contusion, lanced repeatedly from the 10th round onwards by Ali's unmatchable left jab and a right which flashed across his features like an adder's lick.

Ali was scarcely in better shape. Dave Anderson attended the reception held by Marcos for the boxers after the fight. Writing in the *Pretoria News* under the headline 'Ali never looked like this before', he said Ali was swollen, bruised, walking stiffly, almost limping. The swelling would go down, Ali said, he wasn't feeling too bad. But his right hip hurt. He hit me with his left hook there. That stops you from dancin', stops you from moving. Frazier had gone to work on his kidneys and every other body part he could reach.

If there weren't many smooth moves in the ring, there were plenty at the reception. It was quite a party. The Temptations sang some recent hits like 'Tie a Yellow Ribbon' and some classics like 'Old Man River'. Mrs Marcos opened the dancing with Don King.

Before the Thriller, a few articles had questioned the ethics of taking a $3 million purse from the government of a country with a per-capita annual income of $240 (then about R168). But no one was bothered by the boxers' cosy relationship with Marcos. Nor had much been said about the jokey camaraderie with Mobutu in Zaire, where Ali stayed in the villa built for the dictator by the Chinese and lounged about on his yacht.

Over the years a pattern had been established in the press. In the same edition that carried the reports on any given fight, or in the paper published the following day, the speculation would start about Ali's next assignment. This was no exception. The final article on the Thriller – and in the archive – is by Alan Hubbard and its headline asks a question: 'Ali swansong in Haiti?'

The day after the fight, Don King was busy, meeting diplomats and dignitaries from around the world, all keen to present tenders from governments and financial consortiums for the next big fight (probably against Ken Norton). King was considering a bid from Baby Doc Duvalier in Haiti and had been invited to inspect the facilities in Port-au-Prince (presumably the sports venues and hotels rather than the cells where political opponents were tortured and starved to death). There was interest also from Indonesia, Munich, Singapore, Saudi Arabia and Teheran. As Hubbard put it, the globe-trotter in gloves would take the spectacle to wherever a prime minister seeks votes or a president international prestige. King liked the look of Haiti. I'll be interested to hear what they have to say.

And that was that. My love affair with Ali had run its course. I fell out of love with America too; perhaps it was the same thing. Distracted by new ideas about the world, exhausted by the sheer volume of hype, increasingly sceptical about the circus, I threw in the towel. It was a good time to close the bracket: from the Fight of the Century to the Thriller in Manila.

This last set of cuttings on the Thriller, gathered at some point into a cardboard folder and labelled ALI VII for the sake of consistency, shows the predictable imbalance, with five times as many articles on the buildup than on the fight itself. Scattered among them are the usual stories with a South African spin. In mid-1975, film producer John

Marshall was in Johannesburg to negotiate South African rights on a proposed Ali biopic with retail tycoon Tony Factor. Marshall, who had made documentaries on tennis player Stan Smith and on Arthur Ashe's visit to South Africa in 1973, was a lucky man according to one report. For years, movie moguls with an interest in Ali's life story had bumped their heads on a Black Muslim iron-curtain. It was not surprising that Marshall had leapt at the offer like a shipwrecked sailor being offered a four-course dinner. He wanted Al Pacino to play Angelo Dundee and had his eye on Diana Ross and Charlton Heston. The lead role? Ali is a natural to play himself.

There are also the usual speculations, predictably fruitless, that Ali was on his way to South Africa. In August, matchmaker Reg Haswell was trying to set up a title fight with South African champ Jimmy Richards. Haswell pointed out that the country was on the verge of launching a national television service with the facilities for broadcasting around the world. He also mentioned a signed contract to bring Ali to South Africa for three exhibition bouts, this tour to be handled by the black company Reliable Promotions. Ali was expected later in the year once everything has quietened [sic] down.

But everything did not quieten down. When the SABC was launched in 1976, one of the first big news stories it carried – and also suppressed – was the Soweto student uprising of 16 June, which disturbed the South African peace once and for all.

Branko

When we were small boys, still at primary school, we tried to build a tree house in the Knowleses' yard. We had some nails and a few planks to make a ladder and a floor, and we had a picture in our heads from Dennis the Menace of how the thing should be. Although we were barely strong enough to swing a hammer, we might have knocked a perch together. But the tree let us down. It was an old bluegum with a smooth trunk that took two of us holding hands to circle. The first branch was way above our heads. We finally got a few struts pinned to the trunk, but it was hopeless. We had the wrong tree! I feel like that now, trying to build a lookout for myself in the story Joe left me.

Ordering and typing up my brother's drafts gives me the impression that I'm doing something. Why did he insist on writing in pencil? In interviews he said it made things easier to erase. Perverse. Working through the scenes from his childhood and schooldays, the territory I'm supposed to make my own, it finally strikes me how seldom I appear. Blink and you'll miss me.

Watching 'Overkill' was good for me: it sent me back to the real world and the edit suite. I'm mixing a three-part doccie on hominins – not hominids, mind you, which is something else – and the pilot of a cop series for the Mzansi channel. In the evenings I go on typing.

Joe's publisher calls. She's back from Grahamstown and wants to know what's happened to the book.

Which book?

The Muhammad Ali book, she says. She knows all about it.

Oh that one, I say. I'm working on it.

You're working on it?

That's right. It's nearly finished.

The next day I send her an SMS: Btw the book is not actually about Ali.

Among the discards, I stumble on Joe's notes about the Butterfly and Bee Bed and Breakfast, which now occupies the training camp at Deer Lake where Ali lived in the seventies. The guest book is full of household names: the Jackson Five, Tom Jones, Andy Warhol, Norman Mailer. In the opening pages of *The Fight* Mailer mentions the sparring sessions at Deer Lake before the Rumble, when the gym was packed with tourists who'd paid a dollar to get in. Elvis came out there a few years before he died, according to Ali, to get some peace and quiet. It looks like Joe was planning a visit because he jotted down precise directions to the place from Philadelphia. I could follow in his footsteps if I wanted to write one of those travel books disguised as a biography. Why go to the trouble though when there's a mock-up of the training camp at the Muhammad Ali Center in Louisville? I should go there instead and do some research at the same time. They've got boxing machines. You can learn to hit a speed ball, feel the power of an Ali punch on the heavy bag, even shadow-box with the champ.

Who am I kidding? That's a job for a pro. An amateur like me must stick to the writing manual. I'm going with a multivocal text, or rather a bivocal one, if the term exists. I've kept Joe's parts in the past tense, because he's no longer with us; and I've done mine in the present, because I'm still here, at the time of writing, as they say. It's harder than you think. Sometimes I try to sound like him, I can't help it, I'll work in a metaphor or an excessive, unwarranted list. He was partial to those. And sometimes I snaffle his notes. You can probably tell. That stuff about language, the leaves and the roots, all that crap about marbles, or that line about Georgie Baker and the beetles coming out of Joe's mouth, I could never make up something like that.

Mainly I try to sound more like myself. It's important to sustain the narrative voice, says the manual, and the reader should be able to tell us apart most of the time. I wouldn't want to let my brother down, nor do I need to beat him at his own game. I haven't forgotten what Em said when she gave me his papers: he wanted you to have this stuff because he knew he could trust you. You always had his back.

It's nearly three years since Joe was murdered. Even when I put the book out of my mind, I can't stop thinking of Ali. There's always something in the news to remind me. Everyone's waiting for him to die, the obituaries are already written, and that will just be the start. As Rita once warned me, every second-rater who came within twenty paces of him will write a memoir about it. Meanwhile the news mills turn. Some people in England have launched a campaign to give him a knighthood. Sir Muhammad Ali. I say, chaps, would you like some tea?

One night I'm flipping through the channels and here's Laila Ali facing the judges on *Chopped*. Whose dish is on the chopping block? It's hers. She developed some good flavours, but this judge missed a bit of crunch, that one thought the chicken was overcooked, these are some of the reasons why they had to chop her. Her head falls. Disbelieving, she sighs into her tunic: Not the Champ!

I should chop myself. Throw the book in the recycling and go away empty-handed. It's been a good experience, the learning curve was steep, failure will only make me a better person. Fuck that. I should go weeping with relief. But my brother's outline, patched together like a crucial piece of evidence and pinned to the noticeboard beside my computer, reminds me how little choice I have in the matter. I've got to press on to the end.

Joe

In the fading years of Ali's career every fight was one too many. I'd put away the scissors and tape by then, but I remember when he was beaten by Leon Spinks, the gap-toothed no-hoper, in just his eighth professional fight. And when he won the return, becoming the first heavyweight boxer ever to hold the WBA title three times. I remember the fight against Larry Holmes, which took place in October 1980 after a layoff of two years. It's not unusual for boxers to cry when they're beaten; Holmes famously cried when he won this fight. More than a year later Ali fought Trevor Berbick in Nassau and lost again. It was the last fight of his career. I don't remember it, which is a good thing. But like everyone else, I remember when he lit the Olympic flame in Atlanta in 1996. By then the effects of his Parkinson's were visible. For me, as for many other fans, I suppose, the shaky middle-aged man was less substantial than the shadow of the young boxer floating around him.

In 1993 the papers reported that Ali was coming to South Africa, and he actually came. As history would have it, he arrived on the day Chris Hani was assassinated. Over the following fortnight, as the country teetered on the brink of civil war, he travelled to Durban and Cape Town, visiting mosques, meeting big shots, sports celebrities and fans. In Cape Town, he met with Archbishop Tutu and visited Robben Island, where he surprised reporters by lying down on the bed in Mandela's cell. Later he went for a sunset drive on Chapman's Peak. On 19 April, the day of Hani's funeral at the FNB Stadium, he was back in Joburg. He met with Mandela, their second meeting, the first having taken place at Mandela's request when he visited the United States after his release from prison. In the hopeful years after the advent of democracy, a long line of celebrities wanted to meet the world's greatest living statesman and be photographed with him. You could fill a gallery with their portraits.

Mandela had boxed to keep fit when he was young. One of the best-known portraits of him from the 1950s shows him in a sweatsuit and boots squaring up to lightweight Jerry Moloi on the roof of the South African Associated Newspapers building in downtown Johannesburg. Among the records of the meeting between Mandela and Ali in 1993 is a mock-blow portrait in which the Great Statesman lands a linger-on left on the Champ's jaw, while he winces under a shifty-looking moustache.

In my youth I would have gone to the airport or one of his public appearances to catch a glimpse of my hero. Now I was prompted only to take down the Pres Les box and page through the scrapbooks, where the world I grew up in had begun to look like history. Ancient history, people say, originating in the distant past, as if there's any other kind.

Branko

Chris Lessing was a Johannesburg advocate who collected boxing memorabilia. South Africa's 'Mr Boxing', as he liked to be known, owned one of the world's most valuable collections of fistiana. In 1972, he travelled to the US to meet some of the legends of the ring and collect items for his museum.

Lessing was mightily disillusioned with every boxer he met. Jack Dempsey was brimful of false bonhomie – 'How are you, pal?' and 'Nice to meet you, pal' platitudes. Then again, as the owner of a famous restaurant Dempsey was obliged to be nice to people, Lessing conceded.

If Dempsey was over-friendly, Gene Tunney was too remote. He had an office in New York but the nameplate on the door belonged to someone else and his telephone number was known only to a handful of friends. You couldn't just drop in to say hello.

Muhammad Ali was the biggest disappointment of all. Like countless scribes with a weakness for puns, Lessing discovered that the champ had feet of clay. Ali – or rather Clay – was a nasty bit of work, Lessing told Norman Canale. He is not a very tolerant kind of person. He's objectionable, childish and vain … He's washed up as a boxer. His speed and reflexes have left him, and he seems to treat boxing like professional wrestling – all face pulling and talking.

Lessing describes a scene he witnessed where Clay snubbed a well-dressed elderly White woman who wanted to shake his hand. Four strikes and you're out. It can't get worse, you think, but it does: he wears a bored, stiff expression when you are introduced to him. The comma in this sentence is faint (these were the days of mechanical typesetting) and it's possible that Ali's expression, as Lessing reported it, was 'bored stiff' rather than bored *and* stiff. Either way, he was not overly impressed with Mr Boxing.

How much there is of the scribes in Joe's archive and how little of him. In these hundreds of pages of newsprint, dutifully cut and collated, there is hardly a line in my brother's voice. To be precise, there is one. Before I seal the Pres Les box and pack it away at the back of a cupboard, I page through ALI II. Here it is. Canale's ill-tempered article has the headline: 'Clay is no great.' In the white space below, in boyish ball-point print that bears no resemblance to the familiar pencil scrawl, is my brother's affronted retort: Speak for yourself!

15

Death

'More lights for V'Burg'

VERWOERDBURG will spend
R60 000 on the second stage of
its street-lighting programme in
the coming year.

– *Pretoria News*, October 1975

Branko

It starts with a late-night flash on CNN that Muhammad Ali has been hospitalized in Phoenix, Arizona, with 'a respiratory issue'. The phrase comes back to me the next morning when the percolator starts to wheeze like an old man on a ventilator. The room smells of coffee; the winter sun slanting through the blinds lies in pale slices on the kitchen counter. As I take two mugs from the drying rack, I think: Ali is dead. I turn on the radio and it's true.

I carry my muesli to the lounge and switch on the TV. 'Boxing legend Muhammad Ali dead at 74.' Rita finds me there when she comes through for breakfast. She sits down beside me on the sofa and says, Oh shit. Bang goes the book. And I mean bang.

I can't speak. There's an echo in my chest as if a small organ has collapsed and left a void.

The news of Ali's death sweeps everything else aside, the weather, the financial indicators, the French Open, the Oscar Pistorius trial, the rescued circus lions, service-delivery protests, corruption scandals, the Zuma Must Fall campaign, the war in Syria, even the buildup to the US election. For the first day there is live reporting from outside the hospital and expert commentary over stock footage with subtitles. 'Ali converted to Islam in 1964 ... Ali was convicted in 1967 for refusing induction into the US military ... He mesmerized opponents with poetic jabs and lightning-quick footwork.' This gives way to interviews with old rivals and tributes by young admirers. George Foreman: 'A part of me is gone.' Mike Tyson: 'God came for his champion.' The politicians arrive. Jesse Jackson: 'A social transformer and an anti-war activist.' The focus shifts from the hospital in Phoenix to the Muhammad Ali Center in Louisville. Reporters are on the ground and in the air. Researchers trawl the archives to keep the newsfeeds fed. The twitter tape of celebrity comment speeds up just as the old news footage flickers into view. Don King: 'It's a sad day for life.' I catch glimpses of Ali in TV studios and on stages. Here he is in a big afro and some sort of kaftan. It's the Broadway musical *Buck White* which I've read about in Joe's words but never seen. Now he's talking to camera. The sound is turned down but you need no expertise in lip-reading to follow: 'I am the Greatest!' And now he shoots out a straight right and all four Beatles go down in a row with dopey expressions on their faces. The fans have their say. Men with white stubble on their cheeks laugh, weep, hold up photos of their grandchildren. Citizen journalists supply visuals of the mortuary van. Flowers are laid against walls and fences, candles are lit, balloons are tethered. In the small hours a toppled candle sets fire to a kindergarten condolence card in the shape of a boxing glove.

Jordan calls. What's going to happen to the book, Dad? Do you still plan to finish it? The sound of his voice makes my heart ache. He's been in London for eighteen months. He says there's a book of condolence at the O2 arena and he might go down there and sign it for Uncle Joe.

The call leaves me in a sweat of anxiety and remorse. The warnings have been sounding for years: the man is mortal. He hasn't been well for decades.

Rita is brutal. Ali has left the building. No one will be interested in your brother's stupid book now. You may as well put it through the shredder.

A 24-hour channel devoted to Ali pops up on DSTV. The Ali

Tribute Channel shows the fights, the signings and weigh-ins, the press conferences, the talk-show appearances, the documentaries and the biopics in relay, intercut with news as it breaks and commentary to order. The rich and famous troop in and out of frame. Here's Bill Clinton: 'Goodbye my friend, you were great.' Here's Hillary Clinton: 'The Greatest – unmatched not just in power and skill, but also in courage and conscience.' Bernie Sanders: 'What a hero, what a great man.' Donald Trump: 'A truly great champion and a wonderful guy. He will be missed by all!' Ferdinand Marcos – but he's been dead for years. It's 1975 and Ali's in Manila thanking the President and the First Lady for taking time out of their busy schedules to receive him.

George Foreman: 'You saw him on television: there was no one more beautiful. You saw him walking down the street: he was a beautiful thing to see.'

The passing hours confirm what I've always suspected: everyone knows what my brother knows. There's hardly anything new to be said about Ali and the chances of finding it diminish with every teary reminiscence. The book is shrinking in me. I turn off the TV. All I can do now is defend my ignorance.

Coward that I am, I hedge my bets. I hit the record button on the PVR for the entire channel. In the end, once the book is finished, I'll have six days of footage to go through.

The funeral is in Louisville on 10 June and I watch bits and pieces of it from the exercise bike, drifting from the procession to the tributes to the memorial service. Perhaps I'm in no position to judge, but there are signs of funeral fatigue. Just six weeks ago Prince died, three months before that David Bowie, and the big televisual death ceremonies have taken their toll. They were pop stars, though, while Ali was a boxer and that makes a difference. Among the young sportsmen saying how he inspired them, the politicians looking for a platform, the biographers and experts supplying sound bites, among all of them the poor relations, the old survivors of the fistic scene, scrappers and scribes alike, with their battered heads and badly cut suits, are a breath of stale air. Joe would have loved them.

On the stroke of midnight the pop-up channel pops down. The news about Ali drains away and the buildup to the US election surges back up the tubes like acid reflux.

The matron calls from Silver Oaks. The place is in an uproar. Rita's mother is offering to whack Donald Trump. Whack? Another Elmore Leonard fan. I've had a good life, she says, I might as well do something useful with what's left of it. Who'll suspect a little old lady with a walker? They catch me, what's the worst they can do? Put me to sleep? Please.

I can see Gracie assembling a rifle from the parts of her walker like the assassin in *The Day of the Jackal*.

Joe and I didn't live in one another's pockets, but we laughed about the same things. A few days ago there was an American comedian on TV talking about the three indigenous American art forms: hip hop, R&B and stand-up. I wish I could share that with him. Also the report that on the wall of his office Obama had the photograph of Ali standing over Liston. Get up and fight, you bum!

I miss my brother. I wonder if he'd still be an American now, if he'd quote Baudrillard at me the way he used to.

Remember when we were Americans? I asked him once. Nate Simms and his brother Harv.

Were? he said. You mean you're cured? I've still got mine. It comes and goes like a chronic infection.

In times of stress.

Exactly.

The commemorative inserts and photo features appear in the papers, the souvenir editions of the magazines are published. I package the mags and inserts in plastic covers and put them on the shelf. Something else to look at when I'm done. The full-length books will come soon, those that have been years in the making and those conceived when the news of his death broke. One may be the definitive biography. Another might start a craze. Or maybe not.

I go on writing, like a slugger who isn't smart enough to stay in his corner when he's beaten, who wants to go the distance. The problems with Joe's book are obvious. There's too much of him in it and not enough of me. It's as if I never grew up. In all my brother's musings, there's no mention of me as a grown man. Not a word about our so-called collaboration. My part is no better. What's become of Sylvie? She was the first person I called when Joe died and I've forgotten all about her. I should *make space* for her in the text. It was meant to be about our lives, not Joe's, and if it's turned out otherwise there's no one to blame but me. I can't see the past clearly any more. It's a dark, bewildering place. When I do battle with it, sometimes I'm Ali, floating and stinging. 'The hand can't hit what the eye can't see.' More often I'm Henry Cooper, looking out of one good eye while the other, the suspect one that always goes at the crucial moment, fills up with blood.

Jordan thinks it's cool that I'm trying to finish Joe's book. He says it's a special kind of bromance like Butch and Sundance. Rita isn't so kind.

She wants me to be done with it, to get back to my real work and bring home the bacon. She doesn't understand why it's taking so long. Are you waiting for someone else to die? she asks. Must George Foreman kick the bucket too?

I say: You only know who Foreman is because you bought one of his bloody grillers from Verimark.

Now that Ali is dead and buried, every channel is clogged with the American election. The endless buildup. It's been going on, month after month, like a series of *Survivor*, and it's reached the point where I couldn't care less who leaves the tribe.

Last night I'm watching TV and here's Trump in his mogul-size suit with the big red arrow of his necktie pointing to his dick, shooting people in the audience with little finger guns, his little five-shooters, his connections, you, yes *you*, it's going to be tremendous, people. And here he is with someone else. It's Don King covered in lapel badges and clutching an armful of flags, and he looks like a vendor outside a sports stadium, or the ambassador of an impoverished country, a place with one telephone that no one's ever heard of.

Sources of chapter-title illustrations

1. *Sunday Express*, 14 March 1971
2. IMDb.com
3. Republican Press, Durban
4. *Pretoria News*, 28 June 1972
5. *Pretoria News*, 18 May 1975
6. *Sunday Times*, 27 January 1974
7. Cassius Clay in 1964, *Associated Press*
8. (?) *Hoofstad*, May 1975
9. *The Star*, 2 April 1973
10. (?) *Pretoria News*, 1971
11. (?) *Pretoria News*, August 1974
12. Pan Books, London, 1952
13. *Sunday Express*, 14 March 1971
14. *Pretoria News*, 1 October 1975
15. *Time* Magazine, 8 March 1971

Acknowledgements

This novel draws on a collection of newspaper and magazine cuttings from 1971 to 1975. I am indebted to the sportswriters, local and syndicated, of the *Pretoria News*, *The Star*, *Sunday Times*, *Sunday Express* and other publications, and especially to the inimitable Alan Hubbard. Quotes taken from these cuttings are set in gray, and many of the sources are named in the text. I wasn't always able to identify sources but a list of the known details and best guesses can be accessed at www.ivanvladislavic.com

I am grateful to Jenefer Shute for her meticulous editing; and to Jill Schoolman, Zoe Guttenplan and the team at Archipelago for bringing so much flair to this edition. My thanks also to Isobel Dixon and Minky Schlesinger, who are always in my corner.

a r c h i p e l a g o   b o o k s
is a not-for-profit literary press devoted to
promoting cross-cultural exchange through innovative
classic and contemporary international literature
www.archipelagobooks.org